FALL OF A
PHILANDERER

Also by Carola Dunn

The Daisy Dalrymple Mysteries

Death at Wentwater Court
The Winter Garden Mystery
Requiem for a Mezzo
Murder on the Flying Scotsman
Damsel in Distress
Dead in the Water
Styx and Stones
Rattle His Bones
To Davy Jones Below
The Case of the Murdered Muckraker
Mistletoe and Murder
Die Laughing
A Mourning Wedding

FALL OF A PHILANDERER

CAROLA DUNN

St. Martin's Minotaur
New York

www.minotaurbooks.com

Library of Congress Cataloging-in-Publication Data

Dunn, Carola.
    Fall of a philanderer : a Daisy Dalrymple mystery / Carola Dunn.
      p. cm.
    ISBN 0-312-33589-X
    EAN 978-0-312-33589-2
    1. Dalrymple, Daisy (Fictitious character)—Fiction. 2. Hotelkeepers—Crimes
against—Fiction. 3. Women journalists—Fiction. 4. Seaside resorts—Fiction.
5. Police spouses—Fiction. 6. England—Fiction. I. Title.

PR6054.U537F35 2005
823'.914—dc22

                                2005046563

First Edition: September 2005

10 9 8 7 6 5 4 3 2 1

*Dedicated to the Royal National Lifeboat Institute,
whose gallant volunteers have been saving lives
on the coasts of Britain since 1824*

ACKNOWLEDGEMENTS

My thanks to Kathryn Furlow and David Rendell of the RNLI, and Bob Bulgin of the Port Isaac Lifeboat Station; Patrick Chaplin, darts historian; Tara Maginnis, Ph.D., costume historian; Doug Lyle, M.D., author of *Forensics for Dummies;* Allison Wareham of the Royal Naval Museum; Robert Bruce Thompson, technohistorian; Nancy Mayer, legal history consultant; and the many Siblings in Crime who shared their sailing expertise. Without their help, this book would be less accurate than it is. The author accepts the blame for remaining errors.

FALL OF A
PHILANDERER

1

T he glitter of the sun on the waters of the inlet made Daisy blink. Thank heaven the torrential rain had stopped. Perhaps the summer holidays of 1924 were not after all doomed to go down in history as a disaster of record-breaking precipitation. Belinda and Deva were well-behaved girls, but two days cooped up in a boarding-house parlour were enough to strain the best of best behaviour. One more game of Happy Families and Daisy would have run screaming into the downpour and thrown herself off a cliff.

Still, she thought, picking her way across the wet lawn, it would have been much worse if she hadn't brought Deva to keep her step-daughter company. The pair had dashed off to the beach after a bare minimum of lunch, leaving Daisy to drink her second cup of coffee in peace.

She reached the knee-high drystone wall surrounding the back garden. The still air was full of flower scents, mingled with a smidgeon of seaweed, fish and tar. Red valerian and creeping toad-flax sprouted from every crack and cranny of the wall; the top was a mosaic of gold and silver-green lichen. On the other side, the wall dropped nearly four feet to the grassy track leading from the village up onto the cliffs. Glancing towards the village, Daisy saw West-combe spreading up the hillside from the quay in a jumble of buildings washed in Mediterranean shades of pink, yellow, white and blue, topped with lichened slate roofs. Here and there a towering palm attested to the mild climate of this sheltered south coast nook.

A man was coming towards her along the path at a jaunty stride, full of vim and vigour. Pleased with himself and the world, Daisy thought.

She placed atop the wall the ancient cushion the landlady had lent her. Sitting down, she pivoted to face the beach, bare legs dangling. With the approaching walker in mind, she tucked her blue cotton skirt—hemlines were scarcely below the knee this year—under her thighs before she turned her attention back to the view.

Overhead, seagulls wheeled, crying, and a few bobbed on the ripples. A pair of sailing dinghies slid past, heading for the sea. On the far side of the sparkling water rose a steep wooded slope. Where the inlet narrowed opposite the town, a patch of sand and a wooden landing-stage marked the far end of the ferry crossing. The ferry was halfway across, its oars throwing up little flurries of white like bunches of lace on a blue frock.

Once a schooner-building port, Westcombe was becoming known as a holiday and yachting centre. Now that the rain had stopped, Daisy could see why.

On the other side of the track was a jumble of rocks, grey, black and rusty-red, and then the sandy beach where the girls were building a castle to rival Windsor. They were a study in contrasts, one plump and brown with black hair, in a yellow shirt and red shorts, the other a pale, skinny redhead in green and white. Daisy waved, but they were too intent on their earthworks to notice.

"Hullo!" The walker had reached her perch and stopped, raising his tweed cap to reveal thick sandy hair. "Hullo," he repeated with a grin which lent charm to an otherwise plain face and conveyed satisfaction with life, himself, and his view of Daisy. "Topping day."

She couldn't help responding with a smile. "Lovely. I'd almost given up hope."

"You're on holiday?"

Daisy's mother, the Dowager Lady Dalrymple, would have thrown a fit if she'd seen her daughter chatting with a man to whom she had not been properly introduced. But then, she would have thrown a fit if she'd seen her daughter sitting on a wall overlooking a public footpath. The stranger sounded like a gentleman and was unexceptionably dressed in a tweed jacket and flannels. Though he was tieless, his shirt open at the throat, that was surely excusable at a seaside resort.

"Yes," said Daisy, "and you?"

"I'm a resident. George Enderby, proprietor of the Schooner Inn, at your service." He bowed, and looked at her enquiringly.

Daisy wasn't so far removed from her upbringing as to grant the use of her name to an innkeeper, however gentlemanly, without further acquaintance. "You've chosen a very pretty place to live," she said. "I've been admiring the view."

"So have I." With a small smile, he kept his gaze on her face.

Though he didn't glance down, Daisy was suddenly aware of her display of legs. Feeling a blush rising, a Victorian affliction she despised, she willed it away, saying hastily, "One must be able to see for miles from up there." She gestured up the track. "I'm dying to explore."

"You shouldn't go alone. The cliffs are dangerous. I'd be happy to offer my escort."

Was he trying—in the vulgar parlance—to "get off" with her? "That's very kind of you, but I think I'll wait till my husband arrives next weekend."

The information that she was married did not appear to put him out in the least. "It would be a pity to miss the sunny weather," he said persuasively. "Another cloudburst may roll in by next weekend. Besides, I'm familiar with the ground. I can make sure you have a wonderful experience."

"It does seem a pity not to take advantage of the weather. I wonder if the girls would like to go."

Mr. George Enderby frowned. "The girls?"

"My daughter and her friend." Smiling, Daisy nodded towards the beach. "They're having great fun building sandcastles, but . . . Oh, who is that?"

An extraordinary figure was approaching Belinda and Deva. Around its knees flapped a reddish skirt. Below this, tattered breeches reached to mid-calf, leaving feet and ankles bare. The upper half of this apparition was clad in a sheepskin jerkin over a collarless man's shirt, the ragged tail of which fluttered behind. A straw boater with a drooping brim and a hole in the crown completed the picture.

The scarecrow trudged across the sand, pulling a ramshackle handcart, and stopped beside the girls.

"Sid!" exclaimed Enderby. Shouting angrily, he stormed off between the rocks down to the beach.

Daisy scrambled to her feet on top of the wall and watched anxiously, debating whether to jump down and follow. Surely Sid would be in an institution if he were dangerous. Was Enderby just taking out on the unfortunate creature his annoyance at being foiled in his pursuit of Daisy? There was something rather theatrical about the whole performance. Enderby was actually shaking his fist now, a gesture she had more often read about than seen except on stage. Perhaps he was putting on a show for her, hoping his defence of the children might coax her to a rendezvous despite husband and daughter.

The girls, who had merely raised their heads when Sid arrived, stood up and backed away as Enderby rushed towards them.

Sid swung round in alarm. He shrank back. Then, to Daisy's astonishment, he turned his back on his assailant, bent down, and peered at him between his legs.

Enderby stopped dead, apparently stymied by this unconventional manoeuvre. Hands on hips, he stared for a moment. Perhaps he realized he would look an absolute ass shouting and shaking his fist at a beachcomber's bottom, because he feinted a kick, then, with a disconsolate shrug, stalked away towards the hillside track.

Sid seemed to have come up with his own peculiar version of the soft answer that turneth away wrath.

Daisy missed the beginning of the next scene as she carefully lowered herself to the path. At three months pregnant, she was full of energy but inclined to move with caution. When she was again able to look towards the beach, Sid was holding out something to Belinda.

Whatever it was, Bel took it with a smile. Sid crouched and pointed at the highest tower of the castle. By then, Daisy was close enough to see that the object was a long, grey and white gull's feather. Bel stuck it in the top of the tower and Sid clapped his hands. Turning to his cart, he rummaged around in it.

The cart was a ramshackle construction of weathered lumber, knocked together with rusty nails, on a rickety perambulator chassis. As Daisy approached, she saw that it was decorated with scraps of ribbon, sea-worn coloured glass, shells, feathers and silver paper. The girls came nearer to admire it, and Belinda saw Daisy.

"Look, Mummy, hasn't he made it pretty?"

Sid looked round with a frightened face. Close to, he was, if anything, even less prepossessing than from a distance. His chin was stubbled, his hair shaggy, his eyebrows wild. The skirt Daisy had observed appeared to be a woman's red flannel petticoat hitched up under his armpits, perhaps to cover the deficiencies in his breeches, the visible parts of which were splitting at the seams. But he did not smell, the blue eyes beneath the unkempt eyebrows were timid and childlike, and his hat bore a wreath of daisies and pink thrift.

Daisy smiled at him. "Hullo, Sid."

"He can't talk, Mrs. Fletcher," said Deva importantly. "He just makes noises when he tries. Is he an idiot?"

The beachcomber shook his head, his mouth working.

"No," said Belinda. "Think how clever he was, Deva, to get rid of that shouting man so quickly."

The girls looked at each other and both bent down to stare at Daisy between their legs, giggling.

"That's enough of that, you two," Daisy said, afraid they would upset him. "You can both speak perfectly well. How nicely you have decorated your cart, Sid."

He stood back and regarded his handiwork with some pride, nodding vigorously. Then he delved again into the mixture of flotsam, jetsam, kelp, driftwood, and tarry lumps of cork he had collected. He came up with a greenish glass ball, nearly a foot in diameter. This he held out to Daisy.

"Oh, that's a fisherman's float, isn't it? What a wonderful find."

Sid pointed to himself, then to the ball, then to Daisy.

"He means it's a present, Mummy. That's what he did when he gave us the feather for a flag for our castle. Isn't it, Mr. Sid? Is it a present for my mummy?"

He nodded solemnly. Daisy took the ball, with some reluctance as she suspected he could probably sell it and he certainly looked in need of cash.

"Thank you, Sid. How very kind of you. We'll put it on the mantelpiece at home, Bel."

Sid shook his head. His expressive hands outlined a square in the air, delineated crosspieces, gestured at the sun. Widespread fingers became sunlight shining through his imaginary window onto the ball.

"Put it on the windowsill," Deva interpreted, "so that the sun shines through it."

The beachcomber's eager nod was accompanied by a grin that revealed several missing teeth. He turned back to the cart. Dismayed, Daisy envisioned a flood of gifts, each more inappropriate than the last, and Sid following them about for the rest of the holiday. Harmless as he seemed, she wouldn't be happy leaving the girls alone with him about. What had she got herself involved in now?

But he brought out a piece of fishing net and with a few quick knots fashioned a bag to carry the glass ball. Renewed thanks and admiration of his cleverness made him bashful. Ducking his head, he picked up the shafts of the cart and trudged away towards the far end of the beach.

Belinda looked after him, her freckled face worried. "He's very poor, isn't he, Mummy? Do you think he'd like a new hat? I've got all my pocket-money that I saved."

"I'll think about it, darling. We don't want to embarrass him. What a marvellous castle you've built. Are you still working on it, or shall we go for a walk?"

"You said we had to wait for you to come before we go in the water."

"Now you are here, Mrs. Fletcher, may we bathe?"

"Yes, do, and I'll come and paddle."

Bel and Deva whipped off their shorts and shirts and sunbonnets, and in their bathing suits dashed into the water, splashing and squealing. Leaving her sandals and the glass ball with their clothes and towels, Daisy followed. Here in the inlet, protected from the open sea, the waves were scarcely more than ripples. Each swirled a few feet up the beach, then withdrew with a soft *suss-suss-suss*. Venturing in up to her ankles, she realized why the girls were squealing: the chill was quite a shock at first.

Drawn by the sunshine, several other families had walked to the beach from the village by the time the girls had had enough and came out shivering, Belinda bluish with cold.

"In India, the sea is warm," said Deva as Daisy enveloped her in a towel.

"How do you know?" Belinda asked. "You were only little when you came to England."

"My ayah told me." Deva's Indian nursemaid was an oft-quoted authority.

"You'd better run up to the house and get dressed."

"Oh no, Mummy, there's a little boy looking at our castle. He might spoil it if we go. We'll just put on our things over our costumes."

In no time they were organizing a team of younger children to reinforce the construction with stones and rush about with buckets to fill the moat. Daisy returned to the garden wall to fetch her book and the cushion.

The landlady, Mrs. Anstruther, was in the garden cutting flowers. She was not at all what Daisy—who admittedly had little experience of the breed—would have expected of a seaside boarding-house landlady. She ought to be middle-aged and either plump and motherly or hatchet-faced and tyrannical. Instead, she was in her early thirties, just a few years older than Daisy, rather too thin even for the fashionable no-bosom, no-bottom look, with pleasing if not beautiful features and dark curly hair. Though hospitable, she was diffident almost to the point of aloofness.

"Oh, you startled me!" she exclaimed as Daisy's head appeared above the wall. "I'm just picking dahlias for the dining room." She said this with a tinge of defensiveness, as if Daisy might accuse her of neglecting the making of beds or the preparation of tea. No doubt she had suffered from faultfinders in the past.

"Food always tastes better with flowers on the table," said Daisy. "I was just going to take my book and your cushion down to the beach, but since you're out here, there's something I'd like to consult you about, if I may?"

"Of course." Mrs. Anstruther came towards the wall. "What can I do for you?"

"I'll come up." Even if it weren't for the virtual certainty of a crick in the neck, the questions Daisy wanted to ask were not the sort to be bandied about on a public footpath. She went along to the steps and ascended more conventionally than she had come down.

Mrs. Anstruther met her at the top of the steps, looking anxious. "Is something the matter, Mrs. Fletcher?"

"Not at all. I just want your advice. The girls and I have just made the acquaintance of a rather curious character, a beachcomber . . ."

"Oh, that'd be Sid." Her face cleared. "He's quite harmless. Simple, and a mute, as you'll have discovered, but he's a gentle soul. He wouldn't hurt a fly."

"Good, that was my impression. He gave me this glass ball."

"You must have made quite a hit with him! He can sell those at the newsagents' for a bob or two apiece. People buy them as souvenirs."

"Oh dear, I was afraid of that. And afraid he'd be offended if I offered to pay him."

"I couldn't say."

"No, well, we'll work out something. I'm glad to know I needn't worry about the girls meeting him when I'm not with them. I was a bit concerned because of the way Mr. Enderby rushed down . . . Are you all right?"

Mrs. Anstruther had turned pale, but she flushed as she answered, "Yes, thanks. Just for a moment I . . . It must have been because I was stooping in the sun."

"I should think you'd better wear a hat."

"Yes. Silly of me. You were saying . . . about Mr. Enderby?"

"I was sitting here on the wall talking to him, and when he saw Sid stopping by the girls, he rushed off, yelling at him. I must say, I was rather taken with Sid's response."

"He bent down and looked through his legs?" Mrs. Anstruther smiled faintly. "He doesn't do it often, but it always has the same disarming effect. I dare say he doesn't need to do it often, because people liable to berate him are so disconcerted the first time that they rarely try again."

"No doubt. It certainly sent Mr. Enderby packing, so I couldn't believe the girls were in any real danger. I wanted to ask you about Enderby, too. If he's a friend of yours, I hope you don't mind my saying that he seems to consider himself quite a Don Juan."

"He's no friend of mine." Mrs. Anstruther's light tone failed to conceal a hint of bitterness.

"I suppose it's all talk? All bluff and bluster?"

"You stay away from George Enderby. Don't let him cozen you.

That's my advice, for what it's worth. Now I'd better be getting on, Mrs. Fletcher, or your tea won't be ready for you. Would you like a deck-chair for the beach? There's some in the shed, there. The girl can carry one down for you."

"Thanks, I'll manage it myself. And thanks for the advice."

Returning to the beach with her book in her hand and a deck-chair under the other arm, Daisy told herself that any relationship—past or present—between Enderby and Mrs. Anstruther was none of her business. But curiosity was her besetting sin, and she couldn't help wondering whether Mrs. Anstruther was in fact a widow, as she had assumed. Or was there a Mr. Anstruther waiting in the wings whom she simply hadn't met?

At four o'clock, the holiday-makers on the beach started unpacking picnics or heading back to their lodgings for tea. Daisy called the girls.

"Just five minutes, Mummy. The big tower's starting to sag! We've got to shore it up."

"No, right now. I didn't think to ask for a picnic, so you have to wash off the sand and put on frocks. Come on." She flattened the green and red–striped deck-chair, as usual getting its wooden frame the wrong way round. "Bother, these look so simple but I always manage to get them tied in knots."

"We'll carry it for you."

"Let's pretend it's a palanquin," Deva suggested, as they each picked up one end.

"What's a palanquin?"

"My ayah says it's a sort of chair with poles for carrying a maharanee."

"What's a maharanee?"

"A sort of queen. Mrs. Fletcher, you can be the maharanee and we'll carry you."

"Gosh, no, I'm much too heavy. Besides, it would be bound to fold up with me inside, and pinch your fingers, too."

10

"We'll carry the towels and buckets and spades on it. And your book, Mummy."

"Not likely, it'd get all damp and sandy."

Somehow they made it through the rocks and up the steps without spilling off the buckets and spades more than a couple of times. When they reached the shed, Daisy said, "Thank you. Now I'll put it away while you run up and change. Go in the back way, we don't want to leave sand all over the front hall."

The girls scampered off. The deck-chair disposed of, Daisy followed them through the back door, standing open to the warm air. The passage led to the foot of the stairs, where it widened into the front hall. There Daisy saw Mrs. Anstruther standing by the hall table, a letter in her hand, a look of shock on her white face.

"What's wrong? Is there anything I can do?"

The landlady averted her face. "The post only just came," she said in a flat voice, picking up another letter from the table. "The van broke down on the way from Abbotsford. Here's one for you."

"Oh, good. Thank you. But are you all right? I'm afraid you've had bad news."

She shook her head, closing her eyes and swallowing. "No, not at all. My husband is coming home."

"You weren't expecting him to?"

"Oh, yes, but Peter's in the Navy, a warrant officer, a gunner. He's often gone for months and one can never be sure just when . . . His ship's in the Nore. He'll be here on Saturday. I'm just afraid . . ."

Daisy waited in silent sympathy.

"I'm afraid of what he'll do when he finds out about George Enderby!"

2

*N*ext morning, the beach hidden by high tide, the girls were very keen to take the ferry across the inlet. As Belinda pointed out, "We can go for a walk on the other side, Mummy, and tomorrow the water may be rough, and then it wouldn't be much fun."

"My ayah says I was seasick all the way from India, when we came to England," Deva said anxiously.

Daisy had crossed the Atlantic midst October storms with nary a qualm, but remembering Alec's misery she didn't want to subject Deva to even a few minutes on rough seas. They walked along the track to the village's quay and out onto the stone jetty where the ferry docked. It was just coming in, rowed by two stout fellows in blue jackets. The disembarking passengers had to climb a couple of narrow, slimy steps up the side of the jetty, with a rusty chain to hold onto on one side and nothing on the other.

"Careful," Daisy warned as their turn came to embark and the girls dashed forward. "Hang onto that chain. We don't want any ricked ankles."

"It's dirty," Deva objected.

"It's only rust," said Belinda. "It'll wash off. You didn't mind getting all covered with sand yesterday."

They all reached the boat safely. The girls went to kneel in the bows and leant over to dangle their hands in the water. Daisy paid the fares and sat down where she could grab an ankle if they leant too far, but a few minutes later they disembarked without incident on the floating dock at the far side.

When they returned to the landing-stage after a long ramble through woods and farmland, the tide had fallen considerably, leaving an expanse of sandy mud on either side of the inlet. They had just missed the ferry. The noontide sun shone down fiercely. The girls were hot and tired and hungry, and inclined to be squabblesome. Daisy sent them to opposite ends of the small beach to hunt for shells and pretty stones, resolving to fill her pockets with chocolate bars before they next went on a long walk.

Hot, tired and hungry herself, she sat down on a rough wooden bench to wait for the ferry's return.

A man came down the hill, a hiker on a walking tour to judge by his knapsack, Norfolk jacket, ex-Army khaki trousers, sturdy boots and stout staff. He sat on a rock and filled a pipe. The smoke drifted over to Daisy's nostrils, reminding her of Alec and making her wish he could join them before next Saturday.

Next to arrive was a farm cart pulled by a pair of draught-horses with shaggy fetlocks. The elderly driver and the boy with him started to unload heavy, knobbly sacks and pile them near the landing-stage. Daisy watched with dismay, hoping the sacks were not to cross on the ferry alongside—or under—the passengers.

A middle-aged woman carrying a large basket had descended the hill behind the cart. Her brown linen frock, polka-dotted with yellow, had long sleeves and white cuffs and collar. It reached nearly to her ankles to reveal a scant four inches of thick lisle stockings and brown laced shoes. Daisy thought she must be dying of heat, but the face beneath the outdated flat-crowned, broad-brimmed hat looked more indignant than exhausted.

She stopped by the old man and snapped, "I hope you're not intending to send those potatoes over in the ferry along wi' fare-paying passengers, John Ashton!"

13

"Nay, Mrs. Hammett," he said in a placatory tone, taking off his floppy felt hat and wiping his forehead. "The lad's going over to hire a boat to fetch the taters."

"I should hope so!"

Mrs. Hammett set her basket carefully on the ground and plunked herself on the far end of the bench just as Belinda ran up to Daisy. "Mummy, may I go and talk to the horses? Aren't they beautiful? Will you look after my shells? Be careful, one has a hermit crab in it."

Daisy eyed the shells nervously. She didn't like to display her ignorance. She had never been to the seaside before, having spent the summers of her childhood on her father's estate in Worcestershire. What was a hermit crab and did it bite? At least it must be quite small if it could hide among the shells.

She did know horses, however, and had been bitten once by a skittish gelding. "Ask the man if it's all right to talk to them. They look quite placid but you never can tell. And if he says yes, keep well away from their hooves. You'd be sorry if one of those accidentally stamped on your foot."

Mrs. Hammett looked on with a disapproving frown as Bel went over to speak to the farm labourer and then reached up to stroke the horses' noses. Daisy guessed she objected to girls wearing shorts, as did both her own mother and Alec's. Even Deva's mother, Sakari Prasad, had been doubtful when Daisy had suggested buying a couple of pairs for Deva for the holiday. But they were so practical and comfortable for the country, Daisy wished she were brave enough to wear them herself.

Or maybe the woman didn't like sharing the bench with a hermit crab, in which case Daisy could sympathize.

Deva came over with her hankie full of shells and stood in front of Daisy showing her little yellow snails and bits of mother-of-pearl. From the corner of her eye, Daisy saw that Mrs. Hammett had turned her frown on the Indian girl. Shorts again? Her dark skin?

14

Disapproval of the latter was all too common, but fortunately Deva didn't seem to notice.

"Are those Belinda's shells, Mrs. Fletcher?"

"Yes. She said she found a hermit crab."

Deva had been about to sit down but she changed her mind in a hurry. "Ugh! Is it alive?"

"I think so. Go and ask her."

"Those horses are awfully big."

"You needn't go near them. Fetch her, will you, please. Here comes the ferry."

Belinda scurried back to collect up her shells, and they boarded the ferry. Mrs. Hammett followed. Her basket appeared to be filled with hay but was obviously heavy. She handed it to the boatman before stepping down, and he set it down on the bilge planks with a thump, turning to give her a hand.

"Dolt!" she cried. "Don't you know a basket of eggs when you see one, Bill Watson? Haven't I been bringing a basket o' my brother's eggs across this ferry once a week for more years 'an I care to count? If any's cracked I'll want payment!"

"Nay, then, Mrs. Hammett, been't they well packed as allus?" Bill Watson's appeasing tone was just like John Ashton's.

She picked up the basket, placed it carefully on the seat, and sat beside it with a steadying hand on the rim. The hiker and the farm lad took places as far from her as possible. Several more people arrived just in time to catch the ferry, and then the rowers pushed off.

"Look, Mummy." On her outstretched palm Bel displayed a curlicued shell. "Watch. It'll come out in a minute."

"It's not likely to bite you, is it, darling?"

"Oh no, it'll just tickle when it walks. Granny would never let me have one but I've seen boys holding them. Watch!"

Deva peered around Daisy, on whose other side she had prudently placed herself. The hiker leant forward. Even Mrs. Hammett was looking, though she tried to pretend she wasn't.

15

Two minute claws poked out. Belinda twitched involuntarily and they pulled back, but a moment later they reappeared, followed by a pair of antennae that tested the air. Eyestalks came next, with black dots on the end for eyes. Daisy thought the poor thing looked rather alarmed, but it put out two legs on each side and started to scuttle across Bel's hand, dragging the shell behind it.

Again Bel twitched, and the tiny creature disappeared into its refuge.

"One of the *Paguridae*," said the hiker knowledgeably. "It won't live long away from the water, you know."

"Oh, I don't want it to die. Should I throw it in?"

"Well, it would prefer a rock pool, or even the beach."

"We'll take it to the rocks by the beach, won't we, Deva?"

"As long as I don't have to touch it," said Deva.

The young man grinned at Daisy, who smiled back. "Thanks for the warning," she said.

"I remember all too well my sister weeping for an hour over a dead hermit crab."

Mrs. Hammett stared at Daisy and muttered all too audibly, "Talking to strange men—I don't know what the world's coming to!"

The rest of the short trip was accomplished in uncomfortable silence.

The ebbing tide had exposed a whole flight of the slimy, seaweedy steps. Mrs. Hammett was the first to disembark. Standing on the lowest step, she half turned and reached back to take the basket of eggs from the boatman. One foot slipped slightly. In her effort to keep her balance, she missed the basket handle just as the boatman let go. Only Daisy's quick reaction saved the eggs.

With a wink, the boatman took the basket from Daisy and handed it back to Mrs. Hammett. Red-faced, her lips tight, she continued up the steps.

Belinda and Deva were equally red-faced, from suppressed giggles. The hiker's grin was broader than ever. "Go ahead," he said to Daisy. "I'll come behind and see that your girls don't fall."

16

At the top, Daisy found Mrs. Hammett waiting for her. "Thank you for saving my eggs," she said ungraciously. "They ought to keep those steps scrubbed. It's a disgrace. I shall complain."

"They are rather slippery. I'm glad you didn't fall." *If only because you would have fallen on me*, Daisy added to herself.

"A death-trap. Are you staying in the town?"

"Yes, we're on holiday."

Belinda came up the steps, followed by Deva. Seeing Daisy occupied, they moved aside to wait, whispering.

"I thought they didn't allow girls that age to be servants these days," said Mrs. Hammett, "but I suppose her being a native—"

"Deva is my daughter's school friend," Daisy said sharply. "Her father is an important official at India House."

"Oh, well, in that case—" She paused as the hiker reached the top, frowning when he flashed a smile at Daisy as he passed. "My dear, a word of warning."

Daisy suppressed a sigh, but short of being downright rude she couldn't think of a way to escape. "Excuse me for just a moment. Girls, run along and find a new home for the crab, then go and get ready for lunch. I'll see you at the house shortly."

The girls ran off. Mrs. Hammett started moving along the jetty after them and the other disembarking passengers. "A word of warning," she repeated. "A young woman on her own, without her husband to support her, simply can't be too careful. I dare say that young man you were talking to *may* be respectable enough." Her sniff conveyed a world of doubt. "But there's others as can't be trusted not to take an ell if you give 'em an inch."

"Oh?" Daisy's chilly tone was intended to make plain that she didn't feel her having saved the blasted woman's eggs gave said blasted woman a right to lecture. But she must be out of practice with the Dowager Viscountess's arctic pretension-depressing voice, for she might as well have saved the chill to cool her porridge.

"Just to give you a hint, for your own good. You stay away from that George Enderby, that's landlord o' the Schooner Inn. Married

Nancy Pinner, as ought to have knowed better, to get his hands on the hotel, and he can't keep his hands off any woman under forty. A real charmer he is, they say, though I can't see it meself, but he's going to get his comeuppance one o' these days, you mark my words. They ought to bring back the stocks."

And the ducking-stool for scolds, Daisy thought. Mrs. Hammett was the sort of person who made one think things one couldn't utter aloud.

"There, I've had my say. You'd best be off after your daughter, or they'll be late for lunch. Children don't obey their elders the way they did when I was young." She turned a look of suspicion on Daisy. "You look very young to have a daughter that age!"

"How kind of you to say so." Daisy beamed at her unwanted new acquaintance as if the woman had intended a compliment. "You're quite right, I must go and find the girls. Good day." With a slight bow, she escaped.

When she reached the guest-house, after stopping at the newsagent for chocolate, Bel and Deva were already coming up from the beach.

"Our castle's all washed away," said Deva mournfully.

"There's not a single sign of it. I wish we'd saved the feather Sid gave us. We can build an even better one this afternoon, though, Deva," Belinda assured her, "can't we, Mummy?"

"If you've recovered from our walk. Come on, now, we'll be late for lunch."

In the hall, they found the hiker. He was telling Mrs. Anstruther, "You were recommended to me as a particularly comfortable place to stay."

"Oh dear, I do have a room free, but I'm afraid I don't usually take young single gentlemen." She saw Daisy and the girls and her face cleared. "But as I have a family staying, I expect it will be all right. You don't mind children?"

"Not at all." He looked round and smiled. "We've already met, on the ferry. I'm a schoolmaster. I'll be out walking most of the time,

18

anyway. I hope you can give me a packed lunch and tea, Mrs. Anstruther?"

"Of course, sir, and there's plenty if you want to stop in for lunch now. Here, will you sign the guest-book, please?"

Daisy and the girls went up to their rooms to tidy themselves. A few minutes after they came down to the dining room, with its cheerful chintzes and its bay-window view of the inlet, the young man joined them. He was clad now in somewhat creased flannels, jacket and tie. He stood for a moment with his hands on the back of his chair, surveying the gate-legged table set for four, with a slice of melon at each place, a pitcher of lemonade and a basket of rolls in the middle.

"Jolly good show at a moment's notice. It looks as if I shan't starve."

"You're more likely to find your knapsack weighed down by your packed lunch and tea," said Daisy. "Do sit down. I'm Mrs. Fletcher and this is my daughter Belinda and her friend Deva Prasad."

"I'm Donald Baskin. How do you do, ladies. Are you staying here for long?"

"Two weeks," Belinda informed him. "My father's coming on Saturday. We put the hermit crab in a rocky pool. It had seaweed in it and snails, and sea amenomes and little fishes."

"Pomatoschistus microps, I expect; the common goby. Good, I'm sure your hermit crab will live a long and satisfactory life."

"Mr. Baskin," said Deva, her dark eyes round, "are you really going to walk all day, every day?"

"I am indeed, Miss Prasad. You see, I work in London and it's a great treat to me to walk in the beautiful countryside."

"Oh," she said doubtfully. "We went for a long walk this morning and my legs got very tired."

"Ah, but if you walk every day, you soon stop getting tired."

"Oh. Mrs. Fletcher, are we going to walk every single day, when it's not raining?"

"I expect so, Deva. I thought we'd go up the cliff tomorrow. Now let Mr. Baskin eat his lunch in peace."

"That's all right." He helped himself to a home-baked roll still warm from the oven, and Belinda passed him the butter. "And this is all right! I haven't had a chance to look about the town yet. The person who recommended Mrs. Anstruther's to me mentioned a hotel called the Schooner Inn. Do you know it, Mrs. Fletcher?"

"I've heard of it," Daisy said cautiously, "but until today it's been raining since we arrived, so we haven't done much exploring. The town's tiny, though, more of an overgrown village, so I'm sure you can't miss it."

"Ah. I thought I might pop in for a drink later. What have you girls been doing while it's been raining?"

"Playing games," said Deva. "Mrs. Anstruther has lots. Do you know how to play pachisi? It's an Indian game but it's called Ludo in England."

"Yes, I know it."

"What about Halma?" asked Belinda. "It's best to have an even number of people, so poor Mummy didn't play."

Mr. Baskin grinned at Daisy, obviously guessing she had not been heartbroken at her exclusion. "I'll be happy to challenge all comers at Halma this evening," he proclaimed. "If that will suit Mrs. Fletcher?"

Daisy agreed. After the morning's exertions and an afternoon on the beach, the girls shouldn't have enough energy to argue over every move, even if Baskin's presence didn't deter them. In the event, he played so brilliantly that he made Bel win one game and Deva the second, without either suspecting a thing. A clever man, Daisy thought, admiring his manoeuvres. She wondered if he would have given her the third game, had they played any longer. However, he went off for his drink.

"Isn't he a nice man, Mummy?"

Daisy would have agreed wholeheartedly had it not been for his question about the Schooner Inn. Not that she had the slightest objection to his popping into a pub for a pint or a g-and-t or whatever his favourite tipple might be. But she fancied his frank bonhomie had suffered a slight eclipse when he mentioned the place.

After Mrs. Hammett, however unlikable, had added her warning to Mrs. Anstruther's, on top of Daisy's uneasiness with the man himself, anyone in any way associated with George Enderby was to be mistrusted.

3

The sun shone again next day. Once again high tide covered the beach, and Daisy had less difficulty than she expected persuading the girls to walk in the cool of the morning. They took the track leading away from the town, up onto the high cliffs.

The track soon became a narrow path across wiry, sheep-cropped grass, or between thickets of blackthorn and heather, with occasional outcrops of rock. After the long climb, Bel and Deva enjoyed lying back in the springy heather, eating chocolate, while Daisy enjoyed the spectacular view, along with her share of the chocolate. She was eating for two, after all.

The sea was an unbelievable emerald hue, dotted with white sails. Besides the girls' chatter, the only sounds were an occasional distant *baa* and the ecstatic song of a lark, invisible in the cloudless blue above.

The girls soon recovered their energy and ran about exploring. Daisy sat on a fragrant patch of wild thyme and they brought her a miniature bouquet of autumn squills, harebells, and pink thrift to tuck in her buttonhole. Then Deva discovered what looked like a path down the cliff to a little cove.

"May we go down, Mrs. Fletcher?"

"Maybe there's caves, and pirate treasure," suggested Belinda.

Daisy surveyed the upper part of the path, the lower part being invisible from the top—if it existed. It started out relatively wide and smooth, but soon narrowed, the surface turning to uneven bedrock and shale. The outer side was open to a sheer drop of hundreds of feet to the deep green sea. Breakers frothed white at the foot of the rocky headlands on either side of the cove, where gulls and gannets circled and swooped.

The urge for exploration upon her, Daisy might have been willing to tackle the path if she hadn't been pregnant. As it was, she said, "We'll see. When your father gets here, we might do it. Just remember that if we go down, we have to climb up again."

By the time they returned to the guest-house, rather late for lunch, the tide was on the way out. The girls were itching to go to the reappearing sands, where what had been a lively, rushing stream after the rains had now calmed to dammable dimensions. They were also ravenous, in spite of the chocolate, and did full justice to salad, cold meat and baked potatoes in their jackets, not to mention the plum tart with Devonshire clotted cream.

Afterwards, they ran off to the beach while Daisy sat on over a cup of coffee. She ought to write some picture-postcards, but she had forgotten to buy any at the newsagent yesterday.

Mrs. Anstruther came in to clear the table, as Wednesday was her maid's day off.

"You look tired," said Daisy. "Sit down and have a cup of coffee with me. Give me an excuse not to move."

"Well, I will, then." Mrs. Anstruther took a cup and saucer from the sideboard and joined Daisy at the table. "To tell the truth, I didn't sleep too well last night."

"Worry?"

"I shouldn't've said what I did yesterday."

"About George Enderby? You weren't the only one to warn me against him."

23

"It's a small town." Stirring into her cup a spoonful of coloured coffee crystals, she stared despondently into the swirling liquid. "I suppose everyone knows about him and me."

"No names were mentioned. No women's names, I mean."

"No?" Mrs. Anstruther perked up momentarily, then her shoulders slumped again. "But someone's bound to know. Someone will decide Peter ought to know. If it was winter, I could go up to London to meet him. At least we'd have a couple of days together before he finds out. But with all three rooms let, I can't desert my guests."

For an alarming moment, Daisy found herself on the verge of offering to run the house for a couple of days in the absence of the landlady. She caught herself just in time. If it had been only her and the girls, she might have, but with Donald Baskin in residence and Alec arriving, it simply wouldn't do. Besides, Mrs. Anstruther did most of the cooking, and Daisy had never progressed much beyond scrambling eggs. Instead, she offered a wordless murmur of sympathy.

"It seems like a bad dream now. He's a cad. I can't believe I ever thought he was charming, ever trusted a word he said. It's no excuse, but I was lonely. Peter's often away for months on end. I expect your husband comes home from the office every day in time for dinner."

"Actually, his hours are irregular and he's often away for a few days. Never months, though."

"Is he a traveller? A commercial, I mean."

"No, a sort of civil servant." Daisy had seen all too often how people looked askance at the wife of a policeman. "The trouble is not so much how long he's away but that I never know in advance when he's going! My work helps me stay sane."

"Yes, that's why I take in paying guests, apart from the extra money. But that still leaves the winters. What do you do?"

"I write. Articles for magazines. Actually, I do a certain amount of travelling myself, though not often or for very long. So Alec has to put up with my absences, as well as vice versa."

"What about Belinda? Doesn't she mind?"

"If we both happen to be away at the same time, which doesn't

24

happen often, she usually goes to stay with a school friend. In fact, bringing Deva with us is intended to be a part return for Mrs. Prasad's kindness in taking care of Bel now and then. Of course, I get the best of the bargain, as the two of them keep each other occupied and leave me in peace!"

Mrs. Anstruther smiled. At least Daisy had managed to take her mind off her troubles for a few minutes.

She decided to quit while she was ahead. "Speaking of peace, I must use mine to write some picture-postcards. I'll just pop round to the newsagents."

"There's a better selection at the post office. I expect you'll need stamps, too."

"The post office it is, then."

"It's just past the . . ." Mrs. Anstruther stopped, then appeared to brace herself. "Just past the Schooner Inn."

"I don't suppose he'll jump out and ravish me in the street," Daisy said lightly.

"No, of course not." She shivered. "I'm beginning to turn him into a sort of bugbear. Do you know, I always do my shopping during licensing hours, when he's indoors being the jolly landlord."

"That sounds to me like plain common sense."

"Do you think so? I feel so cowardly! You're such a sensible person, Mrs. Fletcher."

"Why subject yourself to coming face to face with the rotter if you can avoid it?" Daisy finished her coffee and stood up. "I'd better get going or I won't finish writing those cards in time for the evening post."

She went out the back way and down to the beach, to tell the girls where she was going. They were busy damming the stream with the aid of a couple of small boys and their father. The mother, knitting, looked on indulgently from a deck-chair. She smiled at Daisy and said, "I'll keep an eye on them."

"Thanks. I shan't be long."

Walking along the track, Daisy met Sid with his cart and bade him good afternoon. In response, he waved his holey hat and grinned, then he raised a rusty mouth-organ to his lips and gave her a verse of "Widdecombe Fair" accompanied by a clumsy little dance. Daisy applauded. He bowed, and continued on his way.

Daisy wondered what she should do if she met George Enderby. He hadn't actually said anything overtly offensive to her. It had all been innuendo. Though his departure had been unmannerly, to cut him would lend too much importance to the brief episode. On the whole, she thought, a cool nod would do. She certainly wouldn't fall into conversation with him again.

Not that he'd want to talk to her, of course, now he knew she was encumbered with a pair of children.

From the quayside, the main street ran uphill to the left. The newsagent was on the corner, next to a chintz-curtained tea-shop. Turning the corner, Daisy saw that the narrow, cobbled street was quite busy. She noted the contrast between the holiday-makers, women in bright cottons and men in blazers, and the residents in their staider everyday wear.

Halfway up on the opposite side, the Schooner Inn's three storeys loomed over its two-storeyed neighbours. An uncompromisingly rectangular building of grey stone with dark blue paintwork, it had a somewhat forbidding aspect relieved by window-boxes overflowing with scarlet geraniums. Over the door hung a gold-lettered sign on which a two-masted ship with triangular sails cut through an improbably blue sea. The door and windows were all wide open on this warm summer afternoon.

Just beyond, Daisy saw the post office, its letter-box and telephone booth echoing the red of the geraniums. Crossing the street, she heard a buzz of voices from the hotel's tap room. It sounded as if George Enderby had married into a flourishing business.

The post office turned out to have a small lending library as well as postcards and other stationery. After choosing half a dozen postcards, Daisy spent some time browsing through the books. She selected a couple for herself and a couple she thought would appeal to the girls, paid the cost of a two-week subscription, and stepped out into the street.

The public bar next door was quiet now, lunchtime licensing hours over. Three men stood chatting on the front step, two visitors and an aged inhabitant.

A laden hand-barrow came up the hill. Daisy recognized the man pushing it as the porter who had taken the baggage from the quay to Mrs. Anstruther's when they arrived on the motor-ferry from Abbotsford, the nearest railway station. A couple and three children followed the barrow. It stopped in front of the Schooner Inn and the three men on the doorstep moved aside.

As Daisy started to cross the street, a raised female voice came through the window from the bar:

"No, you are not going for a bloody walk! It's Mrs. Penton's day off, as you'd know if you took any interest in running the place, and you can bloody well stay here and help clear up for once. Your farmer's daughter will just have to wait!"

The two visitors looked at each other with raised eyebrows and grinned; the ancient shook his head forebodingly; the newly arrived couple paused, taken aback, then the man shrugged and said, "We've booked rooms," and turned to the porter. At the same time, Daisy heard George Enderby's placatory voice within, but not what he said.

His wife's response was all too audible. "Oh yes, I know about her. You didn't really imagine I didn't, did you? And she's not the first, by a long way!"

On the other side of the street, a plump young woman with a shopping basket had stopped, turning an aghast face towards the hotel. Now she hurried on, her head bowed so that her expression was hidden by the brim of her hat. *Oh dear,* Daisy thought, *another victim.*

"Oh, I've given up caring about them," came Mrs. Enderby's strident voice again. "The poor fools were taken in just like I was. They soon find out how much your sweet talk is worth, don't they? As long as you pull your weight, I don't give a damn any more. But you've started to skive off and leave the work to the rest of us, and I'm not putting up with it. The Schooner's still in my name, remember. You do your bit or you can pack your bags! I—"

At that point, the nearest window slammed down. Several people who had been transfixed, all agog, stirred into shamefaced life, including Daisy. The dismayed couple from the ferry shepherded their children into the lobby, nervously sidling from the frying-pan into the fire. The porter carried their bags after them. The old man, cackling, hobbled away down an alley. The two men he'd been talking to exchanged another glance, their faces red with suppressed sniggers, and strolled towards the harbour.

Daisy crossed the street, realizing too late that Mrs. Hammett was standing on the opposite side.

"There, what did I tell you?" she said with all too obvious satisfaction. "Scandalous, I call it, washing their dirty linen in public. There ought to be a law against it. I've a mind to complain to the licensing authorities."

"I rather doubt they'd be interested," said Daisy, and hurried on, wishing she'd let the blasted woman fall, eggs and all.

After tea, Belinda and Deva were so exhausted from their busy day that they were more than happy to lie on a rug on the lawn reading the library books. Mrs. Anstruther suggested giving them an early supper and sending them early to bed.

"That's a wonderful idea!" Daisy was quite tired herself. "As long as it won't make too much work for you?"

"Not at all. I can put together a shepherd's pie in half a tick. Children usually like that. And there's the rest of the plum tart for afters."

"Perfect. I don't suppose you'd be able to sit down with me and Mr. Baskin for dinner, would you? Not that I think he's another George Enderby, but gossip does seem to fly in this place. It would be more comfortable, if you can manage it."

"I could," Mrs. Anstruther said hesitantly, "if he doesn't mind. And if you don't mind me getting up to clear and fetch between courses, Mrs. Fletcher."

"Not at all. I'll give you a hand. Just don't ask me to cook or you'll regret the results!"

Donald Baskin returned from his day-long ramble just in time to change into his flannels, now pressed, for dinner. "No room for a dinner jacket in my rucksack," he apologized. He professed himself delighted to have the landlady dine with them. "But what about the girls?" he asked.

"They're already fast asleep," Daisy told him. "You won't have them inflicted on you this evening."

"Oh, but I enjoy them. I'm a schoolmaster, as I think I told you. After hordes of little boys, it's very interesting to spend some time with two little girls."

Over cream of mushroom soup, followed by fresh-caught mackerel and then lamb cutlets with new potatoes and peas from the garden, they talked about Baskin's school and what he'd seen on his walks about the countryside. Mrs. Anstruther introduced the subject of Daisy's writing, which interested him. But over the summer pudding, he reverted to a topic the ladies would much rather have avoided.

"The Schooner seems like a friendly pub," he said. "It was full of both local people and visitors when I dropped in last night. Have the Enderbys owned it long?"

"Nancy's grandparents built it," said Mrs. Anstruther, "and her father left it to her when he died, her being the only child. To tell the truth, I think she found it a bit much to cope with on her own, before she married. It was getting a bit run-down."

"When was that? They've had enough time to do it up very nicely."

"A couple of years ago. No, three. He came on holiday that summer, and next thing we knew they were married. Quite a surprise, it was. She hadn't known him more than a week or two."

From the way Cecily Anstruther spoke, the look on her face, Daisy suspected George Enderby had not come to Westcombe on his own.

"He just turned up out of the blue?" Baskin asked. "Where did he come from?"

"Do you know, I've no idea. That's odd. He never talked about his past, except for a scar—a wound he got in the War."

"Where?" Baskin flushed. "I mean, where was he fighting? What unit was he with?"

"In Belgium when he was wounded. Wipers, he said—that's what the soldiers called Ypres, isn't it? He was in a tank, but I think they started as a cavalry unit. Would you like some more pudding?"

Where was the scar? Daisy wondered. She hadn't noticed one. Somewhere only a lover would see it, no doubt. Mrs. Anstruther obviously didn't want to talk about it, as Baskin realized at last. He accepted a second helping and told them funny stories about his War service in Mesopotamia, then took himself off to the Schooner for his pint.

Just what was his interest in George Enderby? It seemed to Daisy more than idle curiosity. The obvious deduction was that here was another deceived husband, in search of his erring wife's betrayer. But what did he hope to gain from finding him?

4

*T*hursday was another sunny day, but Friday brought a dank and dismal grey mist that left droplets beading everything it touched. Before dawn, Daisy's dreams were haunted by the mournful howl of a foghorn. At breakfast, the far side of the inlet was invisible from the dining room window. Donald Baskin decided to take the motor-ferry to Abbotsford and walk inland, hoping for better weather.

Belinda and Deva begged to go on the ferry too, just for the ride. They had been too tired and excited to appreciate it after the train ride from London, especially in the rain. The idea of sitting shivering in a noisy open boat did not attract Daisy, but nor did the alternatives of shivering on the beach, staying cooped up in the house, or tramping through the mists and doubtless falling over a cliff.

So she told Mrs. Anstruther they would have lunch in Abbotsford and off they went, dropping off the library books at the post office on the way to the quay.

The first part of the trip was as miserable as Daisy had foreseen, but as they wound their way up the branching inlet, the sun came out. They spent several pleasant hours in the market town. In a little dark shop in an eighteenth-century arcade, Belinda found a man's Panama hat with a pink and purple band, which she insisted on buy-

31

ing for Sid the beachcomber. It was very cheap because no one else wanted a pink and purple hat-band.

"But Sid will like it, won't he, Mummy?"

"I expect so, darling. He does seem keen on bright colours."

"Anyway," said Deva, "it's much better than his broken one. My ayah says beggars can't be choosers."

Halfway back to Westcombe, they could see ahead a solid-looking mass of fog lying in wait, crouching between the hillsides, "Like a big grey cat waiting to pounce," Belinda said.

But when they passed from sunshine into gloom, it felt more like a wet blanket. The girls had no desire to spend the rest of the afternoon on the beach, as they had planned in sunny Abbotsford. On arrival in Westcombe, they all went up to the post office library to choose some more books, walking with caution up the slippery cobbled slope.

When they came out, Belinda was pleased to see Sid coming down the hill with his cart. "Mummy, will you give him his hat?" she whispered.

"You bought it for him, with your own money. Don't you want to give it to him?"

Belinda shook her head.

Never having been in the least shy, Daisy didn't really understand what her stepdaughter felt. She didn't know what was the best way to help her, whether to make her buck up and act for herself or just let her be. She tried a compromise. "Why don't we all go over to him, then I'll tell him you have a present for him and you hand it to him?"

"All right."

Looking up, Daisy saw Mrs. Hammett on the other side of the street, in blue polka-dotted with white today. To her dismay, Mrs. Hammett spotted her, waved her umbrella, and started across. She stepped right in front of Sid. Trying to stop, he slipped on the slick cobbles. The heavy cart pushed him a couple of feet down the hill before he managed with a heroic effort to come to a halt, inches before he crashed into Mrs. Hammett.

Backing away, she whacked him with the umbrella and started berating him at the top of her voice. "You clumsy clown! You nearly sent me flying. You're a disgrace to the village, in your disgusting clothes with that load of smelly rubbish you pull around. You didn't ought to be allowed out on the streets. You ought to be in an institution, that's what!"

As she continued to rant, several people stopped to look and listen. Sid looked more and more frightened. Suddenly he turned his back on Mrs. Hammett, bent down, and peered at her between his legs.

"Look at him!" she screeched at the top of her voice, backing off a little further. "It's indecent. I'm a respectable woman. I won't be subjected to such disgusting treatment."

One of the local men who had gathered snickered and remarked, "He's just turning the other cheek, Mrs. Hammett."

"That's blasphemy, Jim Small. And obscenity, too!" She raised her umbrella as if to strike Sid across the buttocks, but another of the men took it from her and spoke soothingly. A third had caught the cart when Sid let it go, preventing a nasty accident. Quite a crowd had collected by now.

"Awright, awright, awright, what's a-going on here?" The local bobby turned up. "Awright, Sid, that's enough o' that. Straighten up, this instant. Stand up, I say."

Sid obeyed, more or less, cowering back against his cart.

"Awright, what happened?"

Several voices rose at once, but Mrs. Hammett's was the loudest by far. "This man nearly ran me down, Fred Puckle, and then he insulted me. I'll thank you to take him in charge. Disturbing of the peace, that's what it is. He ought to be put away."

As the hefty policeman's heavy hand landed on Sid's cringing shoulder, Belinda clutched Daisy's sleeve.

"Mummy, don't let them take him away. It wasn't his fault! Tell them. Tell them she stepped right in front of him and then she hit him."

33

"Darling, I will, but I'm not going to get dragged into a vulgar public brangle with that dreadful woman. I'll go to the police station and speak to the constable there."

Sid hung onto his cart. A couple of men jerked it out of his hands. "We'll get rid of this junk for you," one said with a snigger.

With a wordless wail, he reached back, as the burly bobby hauled him away by the arm. Mrs. Hammett followed them, still haranguing.

"Come on, Deva," said Belinda, and before Daisy could stop her she marched across the street. In a passable imitation of Daisy's imitation of the Dowager Viscountess's *grande dame* voice, she said, "We will take care of that. Bring it to Mrs. Anstruther's house at once. Sid," she called, "we're going to look after your stuff for you. Don't worry!"

Startled, the two men looked at each other. One shrugged. "Right you are, little missy," he said, humouring her, and he started wheeling the cart down the hill, followed by a very determined Belinda with Deva tagging along.

"Good for her!" A woman, a handsome, buxom, peroxided blonde, had come out of the Schooner to stand near Daisy and watch the goings-on. "Your kid?"

"Yes. I'd better go after her."

"Don't worry, Ned Baxter won't bring 'em no harm. The men like to tease the idiot, that's all. No harm in him either, come to that, poor soul. That Ellen Hammett's a troublemaker. Nothing but a farmer's daughter, when all's said and done, but she's been too big for her boots ever since she married James Hammett, poor chap."

"James Hammett?"

"Biggest fish wholesaler in these parts, he is, with lorries taking the catch from Abbotsford into Exeter to catch the London express. Not but what he ought to've known better, a smart business-man like him. Ellen'd've turned out a scold no matter who she married."

"She does seem to be a difficult person."

"That she is." The woman sighed. "But there, he's not the first to be taken in, nor won't be the last, and people who live in glass houses shouldn't throw stones."

This as good as confirmed Daisy's guess that the blonde was Mrs. George Enderby. "Handsome is as handsome does," she offered in a commiserating tone, being unable to think offhand of a more apposite proverb.

"A truer word was never said. Still, them as has made their bed must lie in it."

"No use crying over spilt milk."

"Nor spilt beer, neither. Well, I've work to be done. Don't you fret about the little girls. Ned Baxter'll see 'em safe and sound to Cecily's." With a friendly nod, Mrs. Enderby retired into the inn. If she was aware that Cecily Anstruther had been one of her husband's conquests, she seemed not to bear her any ill-will.

Slowly and reluctantly, Daisy proceeded up the hill towards the police station. Not that she was having second thoughts about interceding on Sid's behalf, but she didn't want to meet Mrs. Hammett while on her errand of mercy.

And there was Mrs. Hammett coming out of a whitewashed cottage with a blue gas-lamp over the door and turning down the hill. Daisy plunged into the nearest shop, which turned out to be an ironmonger's. Fortunately, as well as nails, screws, bolts, hinges, buckets and such, it had things like saucepans, patent egg-beaters and toasting forks. These were conveniently hanging in the window where she could keep an eye on Mrs. Hammett while pretending to examine them.

Luckily the ironmonger was busy with a customer. "I'll be with you in a moment, madam," he said, but Mrs. Hammett passed and Daisy escaped without having to buy a corkscrew she didn't need.

When she marched into the police station, Daisy found Constable Puckle seated at his high desk, chewing the end of a pencil and contemplating the big ledger in front of him with a puzzled frown.

"What can I do for you, madam?"

35

"I witnessed the . . . um . . . altercation in the street just now. I'm afraid Mrs. Hammett gave you quite the wrong impression of what happened. She stepped out into the street right in front of Sid, and it was only with a great effort that he avoided running her down. Then she hit him with her umbrella. He was frightened—that's why he did that trick of his. So, you see, if anyone ought to be arrested it's Mrs. Hammett."

"Sid can't be let to go around upsetting respectable people like that."

"He only does it when he's afraid," Daisy protested. "You can't let Mrs. Hammett go around hitting people with her umbrella."

"Aye, I've had a word wi' her about that. But it's no good talking to Sid, he's got to be given a shock so he understands he's not to be disturbing of the peace."

"That's utterly unfair! You can't arrest him for just trying to protect himself."

"Who says I arrested him?" Red in the face, Puckle was quite as indignant as Daisy by now. "Didn't I talk her out o' pressing charges? Breach o' the King's peace, likely he'd get thirty days seeing as he's got no money to pay a fine and the magistrate's a friend o' Mr. Hammett's. A night in the wash'se out the back won't do Sid any harm. More comfortable nor his shack, I reckon."

"Fred!" A stout woman bustled in. "What's that poor creetur doing in the wash'se? Sobbing fit to bust his heart, he is. You just hand over that key."

"Now you're not to let him go free, Martha," Puckle said feebly. "Creating an affray, he was, and Mrs. Hammett wanting to charge him."

"Well, I won't then," Mrs. Puckle conceded. "You've your job to do. But I'll take him some nice hot soup to cheer the poor soul up, for 'tis a nasty, chilly day for August. And then I'm off to the vicar to get some decent clothes to cover his back. There's plenty suitable in the jumble for the sale, and I won't have him leaving this house in rags." She held out her hand for the washhouse key.

36

Seeing Sid was going to be well looked after, Daisy slipped out before the constable could take out on her his ire at his wife's interference.

The mention of soup had reminded her that the fried plaice and chips in Abbotsford was a long time ago and Mrs. Anstruther would have tea on the table by now. Nonetheless, she descended the slippery slope with caution.

At last the sun was beginning to burn through the fog. There was blue sky overhead and the hills across the inlet were no longer invisible but veiled in mystery, like a Chinese painting. As Daisy reached the quay, a ferry was pulling in from Abbotsford, with the usual shouting and tossing of ropes. Donald Baskin stood at the rail, near the gangway, waving to her.

She stopped to wait for him. "You're back early today," she said as he caught her up and they walked on together.

"Yes." The sun-browned face was serious. "I wanted to talk to you, privately, and you mentioned that your husband will arrive tomorrow."

"He's coming down tomorrow, yes," Daisy said guardedly. "What is it?"

Baskin chewed on his lip for a moment, as if having second thoughts on the wisdom of what he meant to say. Then he made up his mind. "It's George Enderby. You may have noticed that I've asked one or two questions about him."

"I certainly have."

"Well, I've noticed that Mrs. Anstruther is reluctant to talk about him. Of course, it's only natural that she doesn't care to gossip about a neighbour." He paused.

Not at all natural, Daisy considered. In her experience, neighbours in general loved gossiping about their neighbours. Cecily Anstruther had a far more potent reason for avoiding the subject.

"Yes?"

"So I thought I'd better catch you alone. Being a visitor, you won't know as much as she does, but I hoped you might have heard something."

37

"About what, exactly?"

"Oh, well, you see, in the pub in the evening, they're both serving and they kid each other a lot and laugh and seem to get on like a house on fire and—well, I want to know if it's real or just show for the customers."

Daisy was puzzled. If, as she had assumed, Baskin was a betrayed husband after his wife's seducer's blood, why should he care about the relationship between the Enderbys? Perhaps he was afraid of upsetting Mrs. Enderby if he bloodied Enderby's nose, in which case, Daisy could relieve him of that apprehension. Nor would she suffer many qualms about doing so: George Enderby deserved a bloody nose.

Or was it possible that the hiking schoolmaster had fallen for the fair Nancy and wanted to know whether she might be available? Though he was rather too old for blind calf-love, a man could make a fool of himself at any age. In that case, to inform him of the state of things between husband and wife would be to encourage his pursuit. Daisy didn't consider herself a prude but, despite rationalizations about matching sauces for goose and gander, she couldn't consider it proper to promote any such scheme of Baskin's.

"Why do you want to know?" she asked.

He flushed. "I'm afraid I can't tell you. It's not my secret."

Unfaithful wife, Daisy decided. How much could she decently reveal to him? "The Enderbys may not be my neighbours," she said cautiously, "but I don't care to pass on gossip about them, all the same. I will just tell you this, because I heard it myself and several other people in the street were close enough to hear: The other afternoon they were quarrelling in the bar after it closed."

And if that earned George Enderby a pasting, thought Daisy, so be it. With luck, he'd be in no shape for Cecily Anstruther's husband to wreak vengeance upon him, which would lessen the likelihood of disruptions to Alec's first proper holiday since their honeymoon.

But Baskin did not look as if he contemplated mayhem. In fact, he looked relieved.

5

Saturday morning dawned misty, but with a promise of heat to come. Before breakfast, Belinda and Deva went out to the garden to make sure Sid's cart was still where Baxter had parked it, behind the shed.

Daisy had told them she thought the beachcomber would be freed today.

"We're going to stay nearby till he comes to fetch it," Belinda announced at the breakfast table, "so that I can give him his new hat."

"You don't need to do that, darling. You're bound to see him around sometime."

"But we have to stay at home today anyway, because of Daddy coming."

"He won't be here till after lunch. The train gets into Abbotsford just at lunchtime, so I'm sure he'll stop and eat there before he catches the ferry."

"He might come early, Mummy. You never can tell. We can't wait on the beach, because the tide's coming in. Anyway, we don't mind staying in the garden, do we, Deva? We'll go on reading *The Wind in the Willows* together. It's a ripping book."

"I like books with talking animals," Deva agreed. "My ayah knows lots of stories about Hanuman, the monkey god, and Ganesh, who has the head of an elephant, but Mole and Ratty are more fun."

Daisy was amused. This was the first time she had heard Deva prefer anything English to the Indian equivalent. "All right," she said, "wait to see Sid and give him his hat, and then we'll consider the rest of the morning."

Donald Baskin was intrigued. He hadn't come across Sid in his wanderings and asked all about him. Daisy let the children tell him.

"And it's not fair," Belinda said indignantly; "people pick on him just because he can't talk. It's not his fault! Besides, he can sort of talk with his hands, can't he, Mummy?"

"He certainly explained very cleverly that the glass ball he gave me should be kept on a windowsill to catch the sun."

"It sounds as if his intelligence is at least not far below normal," said Baskin. "I wonder whether something can be done for him. A friend of mine is active in teaching the deaf and dumb to express themselves in sign language and writing. Where does Sid live? In the town?"

"I don't know. Do you, girls?"

"No, but we'll ask him, won't we, Bel?"

"Yes. May we get down, Mummy? We don't want to miss him."

"Finish your milk, Deva, then you may both go." Daisy sighed as the girls rushed out of the door. "I'm quite new at this mothering business," she said. "It's sometimes rather wearing. Belinda's my step-daughter, you see, and this is our first summer holidays together."

"I thought you looked too young to have a daughter that age," Baskin said gallantly. "I'd say you're doing an admirable job, and I speak as an expert. I see all sorts of mothers in my work. May I trouble you for the marmalade?"

Passing the marmalade, Daisy decided another piece of toast with Mrs. Anstruther's heavenly raspberry jam would not come amiss. They munched in companionable silence. When they finished, Baskin opened the door for her and followed her out into the hall.

At that moment came a brisk tattoo on the front door. It was flung

40

open without ceremony and a stocky, bearded man appeared on the threshold, blinking at the dimness within after the bright sun outdoors. He wore a navy blue jacket, with gilt buttons and a narrow band of gold lace around each cuff, and navy trousers. In one hand he held a uniform cap with the crown, laurel wreath and foul anchor badge of the Royal Navy.

In response to the knocking Mrs. Anstruther hurried from the kitchen. "Peter!" she cried, and ran into his widespread arms.

Dropping his cap, he lifted her up and swung her around in a hug, his tanned face split by a wide, white beam between his neat moustache and the short, pointed beard à la King George. "Well, Cecily, m'dear, your sailor's home from sea. And in such a hurry to see his gal, he took the early mail train down and did without his breakfast."

Half laughing, half crying, Mrs. Anstruther said, "Put me down, you big lubber, and there'll be bacon and eggs on the table in a jiffy." As he obeyed, she caught sight of Daisy and Baskin. She smoothed her hair, blushing. "I beg your pardon, Mrs. Fletcher, I didn't see you. May I introduce my husband? My lodgers, Peter—Mrs. Fletcher and Mr. Baskin. Mrs. Fletcher has two little girls with her and Mr. Fletcher arrives today."

Polite greetings were exchanged and the Anstruthers went off to the kitchen, arm-in-arm. Baskin turned to Daisy with a grin.

"If I hang about, may I hope to see an equally enthusiastic meeting when Mr. Fletcher arrives?"

Smiling, Daisy said, "Don't delay your walk. I'm not sure when he'll get here."

Their landlady reappeared, pink-faced and flustered, with Baskin's packed lunch. Daisy went slowly upstairs. It was none of her business but she couldn't help wondering whether Cecily Anstruther was going to confess about her affair with Enderby or simply hope Peter would not find out.

At Belinda's insistence, Daisy and the girls met every Abbotsford ferry from mid-morning onward. As expected, Alec arrived after lunch. Daisy spotted him from afar, sitting in the stern, pipe in mouth. Her heart gave a little leap. If she hadn't been properly brought up and in a very public place, she would have been quite happy to run into his arms.

As it was, she left that for Bel, who barely let him step onto solid ground before launching herself at him with a squeal: "Daddy!"

"Darling!" said Daisy.

That was practically the only word she managed to fit in as they walked back to the guest-house, following a porter with Alec's bags on a trolley. Deva was somewhat in awe of Alec to start with, but with Bel chattering away about their castles and dams and walks, and more especially about Sid, Deva soon chimed in.

The porter led the way along the street, which was not much wider than the track by the beach and became an unpaved lane by the time it reached the house. Generally, Daisy and the girls avoided the lane, after an experience with a motor-car which had forced them to jump into the hedge and hold their breath to let it pass. However, the front door was no doubt more appropriate than the back garden for a new arrival with luggage.

Daisy opened the door and the porter carried the bags in. While Alec paid him, she rang the bell on the hall table.

Cecily Anstruther came out of the sitting room. Though obviously preoccupied, she welcomed Alec and had him sign her guestbook. "If there's anything you want, just let me know," she said. "I hope you'll enjoy your stay in Westcombe."

"Judging by my wife's postcards and my daughter's rhapsodies, I'm bound to," Alec said with a laugh.

"Oh, Daddy!"

"Off you go now, Bel, and let your father settle in in peace. The tide must be well on its way out by now. We'll come and find you on the beach, but—"

"Don't go in the water till you come," the girls chorused, and they ran upstairs to change.

Alec declined the assistance of the maid to get his bags upstairs.

42

But once in their corner bedroom, he ignored the view over the beach and the inlet, took off his jacket and tie, and with a sigh stretched out full length on the bed.

Daisy sat on the edge of the bed and took his hand. "Tired?"

"It's going to take me a while to get into the holiday spirit, love. We just finished up a nasty case, and I left the paper-work for poor Tom to cope with. He and his missus are going to Clacton-on-Sea for a couple of days next week. He sent his best regards, by the way."

"I just posted a card to him and Mrs. Tring." Daisy was very fond of Alec's detective sergeant. "Should I send one to Superindentent Crane?"

"Great Scott, no, Daisy! The less the super's reminded of your existence, the happier he is."

"It's most unfair. Anyone would think I actually went around searching for dead bodies!"

"I take it you haven't found any here. Let us be grateful for small mercies. Who is this Sid Belinda and Deva were going on about?"

"Not at all the sort of person anyone would wish to murder. He's a beachcomber, a simpleton but perfectly harmless." Daisy filled in the bits of Sid's story that Bel had left out. "There's the glass ball he gave me," she concluded, "on the windowsill."

Alec lazily turned his head. "Very pretty. And those long walks Bel mentioned and Deva bemoaned—you haven't been overtiring yourself, I hope, what with looking after those two and all?"

"I feel frightfully hale and hearty, darling. It must be the sea air. The girls have been very good, and the walks were my doing. Just wait till I get you up on the cliffs. You can see forever."

"Not this afternoon," Alec said firmly. "The farthest I intend to walk is to the best pub in town for a drink before dinner. I take it there's somewhere respectable enough for you to accompany me?"

Daisy hesitated. The Schooner was the obvious answer, yet she wasn't at all sure she wanted to patronize the place. Still, Alec would be bound to find out about it and wonder why she hadn't mentioned it, and she didn't want to spoil his holiday by explaining all the complications surrounding George Enderby. Surely the dratted man wouldn't approach her if she had her husband right by her side!

"There's the Schooner Inn," she said, trying to hide her reluctance. "It's the biggest hotel and it has a public bar."

"The Schooner let it be. Come and lie down for five minutes, love. I'm sure you ought to take an afternoon nap, in your condition."

Her condition didn't noticeably cool his ardour. A delightful hour passed before they joined the girls on the beach. If Enderby had a rendezvous on the cliffs that afternoon, Daisy saw him neither coming nor going.

6

*T*hough Daisy would not have broached the subject of the Schooner Inn with Mrs. Anstruther, Alec had no such inhibition. The inn had both public and lounge bars, she told them. Local women were rarely seen in either, and the public was the haunt of farm labourers and fishermen but the lounge was patronized by summer visitors both male and female. She offered to keep an eye on the girls if the Fletchers would like to go out after dinner, so they waited until Bel and Deva were in bed before they strolled into the village.

In the twilight, the inlet was busy with pleasure boats heading homeward on the incoming tide after a day's sailing and a few fishing smacks heading down to the sea for a night's work. When they crossed in the narrows, a good deal of shouting ensued, but it seemed mostly good-humoured, perhaps because of the glorious evening. The air was balmy, the fragrance of myrtle and nicotiana spiced with the pervasive tang of salt and seaweed. An owl hooted from the woods on the far side of the water.

"Idyllic," murmured Alec, his arm around Daisy's waist. "I'm not surprised the Germonds have come here every summer since the War."

"Yes, I'm so glad Melanie recommended it. Mrs. Anstruther is a dear, isn't she? I do hope everything will turn out all right for her."

"If she treats every guest as she treats us, I don't see why it shouldn't, though I suppose Westcombe doesn't get many winter visitors. But Anstruther's a warrant officer—I should think he makes enough to keep the household going." Alec had met Peter Anstruther at teatime and taken to him at once. "He doesn't seem the type not to send home part of his pay."

That wasn't at all what Daisy had meant, but she kept her resolve not to reveal the probability of marital discord in the near future. "He does seem a nice chap, doesn't he? You didn't seem so keen on Baskin, though." They had met at dinner.

"He's certainly a success with the girls." Alec's laugh was not quite as carefree as he'd probably intended. "Perhaps I'm jealous."

"You've no need to be," Daisy assured him, resting her head against his shoulder for a moment. The poor dear had these occasional fits of feeling he was too old for her. "Both Belinda and Deva think he must be slightly mad to spend all his holiday walking."

Alec laughed again, more cheerfully, but he said, "That young man impresses me as having some sort of ulterior agenda. I wonder what he's up to?"

"Maybe he smuggles brandy and silk stockings under cover of his hikes. Westcombe used to be quite a smuggling centre, I gather."

"Or drugs or diamonds," he said thoughtfully.

"Darling, you're on holiday," Daisy protested as they entered the Schooner and paused on the threshold of the lounge bar for a moment, surveying the scene.

"So I am, and I have absolutely no reason for suspecting Baskin."

"How lucky, as he seems to have got here before us. And there's Mr. Anstruther, too!"

The public and lounge bars of the Schooner occupied the same long room, divided by the semi-circular bar and a wooden partition, almost black from years of tobacco smoke. Equally dark panelling covered the lower part of the walls of the lounge; the upper part, hung with yellowing prints of sailing ships, was papered in blue stripes entwined with bright pink rosebuds, part of the "doing up" of

46

the inn, no doubt. A large gasolier in the centre and another over the bar illuminated all but the furthest corners. Above the empty fireplace, a ship in a bottle shared the mantelpiece with a stuffed octopus, glaring balefully from its glass case.

Anstruther and Baskin were both in the lounge. The hiking schoolmaster sat at a table chatting with a couple who looked like holiday-makers. Daisy saw his glance flicker several times towards the Enderbys, serving behind the bar, before he noticed her and Alec and waved a greeting. She waved back and Alec nodded.

The gunnery officer leant with his back against the bar, surrounded by several men who appeared to be some of the more prosperous local inhabitants, substantial shopkeepers and farmers, perhaps a lawyer or a doctor. He seemed entirely at ease, no doubt among friends he had grown up with. They were laughing and joking; snatches Daisy heard above the din of voices suggested Anstruther had just told some tall tale of his travels. But at least two of the faces she could see seemed to be concealing uneasiness behind their joviality. Did they know about Cecily Anstruther's affair? Would one of them betray her?

Seeing Alec and Daisy, Anstruther hailed them, "Mr. and Mrs. Fletcher, I'm buying, for my sins! What's yours?"

Alec took in the tankards in the hands of the group and said, "A pint of bitter, thanks," though Daisy knew he had intended to treat himself to a whisky. She settled for ginger-beer, having heard of the hazards of the West Country draught cider known as scrumpy.

Anstruther turned to the bar to give the order to Mrs. Enderby. A man on the public side saw him and called, "Hey, Pete, come and have a game of skittles."

"Nay," said someone else, his tone a challenge, "*Mester* Anstruther's an officer now, too high an' mighty to play wi' the likes o' we."

"I'll take you on for a pint, *Mister* Stebbins," Anstruther retorted cheerfully. He paid for the Fletchers' drinks and apologized to Daisy with a rueful grin. "Sorry to desert you, Mrs. Fletcher."

47

"I hope you beat him hollow," said Daisy.

She and Alec retired to a table, while Anstruther went through a door in the partition. Scarcely had it shut behind him when his lounge bar friends put their heads together and the pair in the know passed on their tidbit of scandal to the ignorant. Watching the relish of the enlighteners and the solemn head-shaking of the enlightened, Daisy was as certain of it as if she'd heard every word.

"What dreadful gossips men are," she exclaimed.

Alec stared at her. "I hardly think telling you the painters are due to start on our bedroom on Monday morning qualifies as gossip!"

"Oh no, sorry, darling, I'm afraid I wasn't listening. I hope I'll still like the colour when it's all done."

"Your choice, you'll have to live with it. I just hope they won't get paint on the floorboards or the furniture."

"Mrs. Dobson will keep an eye on them. It's very good of her to take responsibility for the painters and the dog while we're away—above and beyond the duties of a cook-housekeeper. I wish we'd brought Nana, though. She'd have loved the beach and the long walks."

"We'd better find a cottage to let next year, and take both Nana and Mrs. Dobson with us, and a nanny by then, too."

"I foresee endless confusion between Nana the dog and Nanny the nursery nurse."

"Perhaps we'd better find one of those starched-up women who prefer to be called Nurse."

"Not for my baby!" said Daisy. "A nice comfy woman with a big lap, one who won't be constantly at outs with Mrs. Dobson."

"And who likes dogs," Alec proposed with a laugh.

As they chatted of domestic matters, through the partition came the rumble of wooden balls on a wooden floor, the clatter of scattering skittles and occasional shouts of "Floorer!" and cheers. Then a bout of mingled applause and cheering was accompanied by an exuberant yell: "Ye ha'n't lost your eye, Pete, my boy!"

"Stands to reason," someone else said loudly as the clamour died down. "He's a gunner, arter all. Knows how to keep his eyes on the target."

"Pay up, Tom Stebbins! We all heard, a pint o' scrumpy was the bet."

"A'right, a'right, don't you be a-jostlin' me!" said Stebbins angrily. "But was you to ask me, he'd best stay home and keep his eyes on his wife."

Silence fell in the public bar, so that Daisy heard perfectly Anstruther's response, in a voice of quiet menace. "Just what do you mean by that, Tom Stebbins?"

"Nothin'." Stebbins sounded sullen now. "Only what everybody knows. There's been a cuckoo in your nest."

"You take that back, you lying bastard!" roared Anstruther, in a voice accustomed to making itself heard through artillery and storms at sea.

A general uproar ensued. The lounge was hushed now, listening to what was going on next door. Several men glanced towards the bar, but Enderby was not there—either he'd made himself scarce or he happened to have gone down to the cellars.

As the tumult in the public continued, Alec half-rose. Daisy put her hand on his arm.

"Darling, you're on holiday. Besides, you're a detective chief inspector, not a bobby on the beat. And it's not your territory."

With a rueful shake of the head, Alec sat down. The din subsided, and Enderby returned to the bar.

An instant later, tankards flew as Anstruther flung himself across the bar-top, face crimson with fury.

"You stinking son-of-a-bitch!" he snarled.

Enderby tried to duck, too late. Anstruther grabbed him by the tie and, still lying across the bar, started to strangle the gaping, gasping, goggle-eyed landlord.

Alec sprang to his feet, as did half the men in the lounge. But the public bar patrons were before them. A couple of hefty fellows grasped Anstruther by the arms and hauled him backwards. He dragged Enderby halfway across the bar before the necktie escaped from his fists.

As the two men forced Anstruther towards the door, Enderby lay panting, purple-faced, on the bar for a moment. With shaking hands he loosened the choking tie. He pushed himself backwards onto his feet and glanced at his wife, who had watched the attack with a stony expression, hands on her hips. He smoothed his hair, pulled his jacket straight, and gave his audience on both sides of the partition a would-be bright smile.

"Some people simply can't hold their booze, I'm afraid," he said. "I just tapped a new keg of cider. Who's first?"

Most of the patrons settled down, some sniggering, some disapproving, but Alec caught Baskin's eye across the room and Daisy observed their silent agreement. She gathered her handbag and started to rise.

Alec frowned. "I suppose you can't very well stay here."

"Certainly not."

"All right, come on."

The three went out into the street. It was chilly now, and dark once they moved away from the gaslight over the inn's door. Another, at the corner where the main street reached the quay, helped until they had passed it. Baskin produced an electric torch. Ahead they could hear Anstruther's slow—perhaps reluctant—but steady footsteps on the paved quay.

"His friends have scarpered," said Baskin. "Don't want to get involved between husband and wife, I reckon."

"Darling, do you really think Anstruther's going to beat Cecily?"

"Not if I can stop him," Alec said grimly. "When we reach the house, you're to go straight up to the girls' bedroom and stay there."

"Gosh no! She's going to need a woman at her side."

"Daisy—"

"It's no use Daisying me, darling. I'm staying."

Alec sighed but ceased to protest. They walked on in silence. The footsteps ahead were inaudible now, as Anstruther left the paving

50

and took the sandy track by the beach, but Daisy could make him out, a black figure against the paler sheen of the water. His shoulders slumped, he looked tired and discouraged. She felt a sudden pang of sympathy.

The Anstruthers' house rose on their right. Only one window was lit, on the ground floor. The kitchen, Daisy thought.

Anstruther trudged up the steps from the path, silhouetted by the window beyond him. At the top, he hesitated. Baskin hastily switched off the torch, in case their quarry turned round, but he just moved to his left and sat down on the wall, facing the house, barely visible in the scatter of light. He appeared to take something from his pocket and fiddle with it.

A gun? Daisy's breath caught in her throat.

7

*A*lec was fed up, to the back teeth. A delightful afternoon had not prepared him to be precipitated into a bar-room brawl followed by a domestic drama where his intervention might be necessary to avert tragedy. He was on holiday, dammit!

What was more, he suspected that Daisy had been aware of the possibility of the evening's events. He couldn't blame her for the events, nor even for finding herself in the middle of them, but he could blame her for not warning him. And he did. If they had not been caught in an extremely delicate position, he would have had it out with her here and now.

However, Anstruther appeared to be loading his service revolver. To approach him unnecessarily would be dangerously foolhardy. On the other hand, supposing the object in his hands were shown to be quite harmless, they could hardly waltz past him and into the house as if nothing had happened.

All in all, for the present they were stuck.

Either Baskin had come to the same conclusion, or he was following Alec's lead. In either case, Alec's opinion of the schoolmaster rose a notch.

Though Daisy was equally still and silent, Alec did not for an instant presume either that she had reached the same conclusion, by the same route, or that she was following his lead. No doubt she had her own reasons, which might or might not be vouchsafed to him sometime in the future. She might change her mind at any moment. He put a warning hand on her arm.

Smiling up at him—his eyes were adjusting to the near darkness—she sighed a tiny sigh, almost obliterated by the susurration of the waves on the nearby beach.

"I'm going to sit down, over there," she whispered, no louder than her sigh, and went to place herself wearily on a flattish rock nearby.

She was pregnant, he reproached himself; he ought not to have dragged her to the pub in the first place, far less have brought her back to face an angry armed man. But where else could she go?

Just as he returned his gaze to Anstruther, a match flared. The sailor was lighting his pipe.

Reflexively, Alec felt in his pocket for his own favourite briar and the tobacco pouch with his initials crookedly embroidered by Belinda. Baskin mirrored the gesture, then both withdrew their hands empty, with a rueful shake of the head at each other. Other than a shout, nothing was more likely to draw Anstruther's attention to them than the lighting of matches. If walking past him and into the house would be awkward, being found skulking in the shadows to spy on him would be horribly embarrassing.

They could go back and round to the front door by the lane. Yet the innocent lighting of a pipe did not mean he had no violent intentions towards his wife. They dared not leave.

A sound from the house brought Alec to full alert. Cecily Anstruther came out of the back door. A pale shawl draped about her shoulders, she glided across the lawn like a ghost. She stopped a few feet in front of her husband.

Alec and Baskin started forward.

Anstruther didn't move. He must have seen her, but he didn't stir. The only motion was a curl of smoke catching the light as it rose from his pipe. If he spoke it was too softly for the listeners to hear.

53

She joined him on the wall, sitting with perhaps a yard between them, head bowed. And she started to talk.

Alec made a deliberate effort not to catch what she was saying—that was none of his business. It was Anstruther's words he was interested in, words which might give warning of an assault in time to prevent it. But to intervene in time, he needed to be nearer. He continued forward, his tread stealthy, stooping so as not to appear above the wall. Baskin matched his actions.

So did Daisy.

Glaring at her, Alec waved her back. In the darkness it was easy for her to pretend not to see—or perhaps she really couldn't, but she must know he would disapprove. Not that his disapproval had ever made much difference to Daisy when she was set on her course.

He went on, wondering whether the same words from *HMS Pinafore* buzzed silently in her head as in his:

> Carefully on tiptoe stealing,
> Breathing gently as we may,
> Every step with caution feeling,
> We will gently steal away.

Except that she was not stealing "away," and he damned well wished she was.

When next Alec raised his head, Anstruther was on his feet, facing the garden wall but slightly turned away, towards his wife who, fortunately, was beyond him. His voice, though low, was impassioned, and clear enough for Alec to make out his words.

"It's my fault. You've been alone too much, with no family near to support you, no children to occupy you. I'll apply for a shore berth, Devonport or Portsmouth. I've been at sea over twenty years, that's enough. Cecily, you need never fear me." He held out his hands to her, and she threw herself on his chest, sobbing. As his arms closed about her, he repeated tenderly, "Never be afraid of me, Cecily." Then his voice rose, the tone turned menacing, and he spat out, "But as for that filthy lecher who took advantage of you, he'd bloody well better watch out!"

The sun shone through the open window onto Daisy's face, but she didn't want to get up. She was sure her bottom still bore the imprint of the cold stone step she had cowered on for what felt like hours, while the Anstruthers canoodled in the garden above. Of course she was glad they were reconciled, but they might have had the decency to take their billing and cooing indoors!

She had been too tired to face the slog back along the track and round by the lane to the front door, though if she had known how long the wait would be she might have changed her mind. Alec and Baskin had both stayed with her, all by silent consent too embarrassed to openly walk up the steps. When at last the Anstruthers went into the house, Alec swore his every joint creaked as he rose from his crouch.

Baskin still had a youthful spring in his step. But as he and Daisy and Alec crossed the lawn towards the back door, she had heard him mutter, "Well, that settles it! The man's a cad and a bounder and he's got to be stopped."

Last night, cold, cramped and cross, Daisy had considered it only right that George Enderby should get his just desserts, and the sooner the better. This morning, warm and comfortable in her bed, she was inclined to feel more charitable.

Or rather, since she was not at all inclined to make allowances for Enderby, she began to consider consequences.

Peter Anstruther's attack in the pub had not done Cecily's reputation any good, but at least his naval superiors were not likely to take a bar-room brawl too seriously. A premeditated assault, on the contrary, could lead to a court-martial as well as a prison sentence, besides confirming and spreading word of Cecily's downfall. The couple would be ruined.

Whatever Cecily's misdeeds, Daisy liked her. She liked Baskin, too, and he was pretty well bound to lose his job if he raised a hand to Enderby. Still, though she knew nothing of his family circumstances, she thought on the whole it would be a good thing if he put Enderby out of commission before Anstruther got around to it.

She wondered if she dared hint to him that he should stop procrastinating and get on with giving Georgie Porgie the thwacking he so richly deserved. But Alec would be furious if he discovered her meddling. The phrase "accessory before the fact" came to mind.

A glance at the clock on the mantelpiece told her she was too late, anyway. By the time she was up and dressed, Baskin would have finished his breakfast and gone off for his daily hike—unless he chose a shorter walk today, to the Schooner Inn and a confrontation.

Daisy was getting hungry. Alec had promised to bring her up some toast with homemade jam, but she was beginning to wish she hadn't surrendered to the temptation of her cosy bed. Scrambled eggs, she mused, her mouth watering, with a rasher of back bacon and one of those scrumptious sausages from the local butcher, nicely browned . . .

A knock on the door.

"Who's there?"

"It's Cecily Anstruther, Mrs. Fletcher."

"Come in."

The landlady entered, preceded by a laden tray balanced on one hand.

"You angel!" said Daisy. "You must have read my mind."

With a slight smile, Mrs. Anstruther set the tray on the bedside table while Daisy sat up and rearranged her pillows. "Mr. Fletcher said you were tired, not that you weren't hungry. I thought you ought to have something." The smile disappeared. "Besides, I wanted a chance to see you in private, to apologize."

"Apologize?"

"For the fracas in the Schooner last night."

"You weren't even there."

"It was my fault, though." Agitated hands twisted together. "I don't know what you must think of us!"

"As long as you and your husband have made your peace, that's all that really matters, isn't it?"

"Peter's an angel," she said fervently. "He's the one who's an angel. He says we'll sell the house—it was his father's—and move to Devonport, and he'll apply for a shore job. But I don't know what will happen if he . . . He's talking about having it out with George Enderby. I've begged him to let it be. I don't know what he's going to do. I don't know what to do."

"If he won't listen to you, he wouldn't listen to me. Would you like me to see if Alec will try to talk him out of it?"

"Oh no. Thank you, but better not. I'll just have to hope he thinks better of it. I'll leave you to your breakfast. Just leave the tray up here, the girl will fetch it when she makes the beds." She went out, looking almost as careworn as she had when she dreaded her husband finding out about Enderby.

Daisy lifted the cover off the plate and discovered exactly what she had wished for, still hot, as was the tea under its cosy. As she ate, she pondered the situation, but she could think of no solution short of having Constable Puckle lock Peter Anstruther up in his "wash'se" until the sailor's justifiable wrath cooled.

After lunch, the sun still shone but a cool breeze had sprung up. Daisy, quite restored after a peaceful morning in a deck-chair in the garden, decided the weather was perfect for a walk up the cliff to show Alec the view.

"Let's take a picnic tea," Alec proposed. "I brought a knapsack just in case."

"Oh yes," said Deva. "Let's go down that path I found, the one down the cliff to the secret cove, and eat our picnic there."

"The tide is still quite high," Belinda objected. "The cove's prob'ly under water."

"The tide is going out," Deva pointed out. "By the time we get there, there may be sand. We could go down the path anyway, to see, couldn't we, Mr. Fletcher?"

Alec cocked an eyebrow at Daisy, who explained. "I didn't want to try it without you, darling, but it might be fun to explore."

"Down a cliff? Don't forget we'd have to climb up again." He cast a meaningful glance at her midriff.

"We wouldn't have to race back up. I'd take it easy."

"Well, let's go up the track, anyway. I'll take a dekko at this famous path."

Mrs. Anstruther packed a picnic tea into Alec's knapsack and they set off up the hill. The girls were quite accustomed to long walks by now, and sped ahead.

At the top, the south-west wind was boisterous. Daisy had to hold down her skirt, and as soon as they reached the summit her hat blew off, though Alec somehow kept his cap on his head. The girls—Daisy had allowed them to go bare-headed—chased the hat and caught it when its erratic progress halted in a tangle of heather. Daisy decided to leave it near the path with a stone to hold it down.

"I hope the sheep won't eat it," said Deva with a giggle.

"I hope Sid won't come along and think it's been thrown away," Belinda worried. "But he'd give it back to you, Mummy, if we told him."

"I know he would, darling." Daisy enjoyed the feeling of the wind tossing her shingled curls, though she knew she would pay for hat-lessness with a new crop of freckles. She turned to Alec. "Well, what do you think?"

He eyed her with an admiring grin. "I always did like the informal look."

"I meant the view."

"That's beautiful, too."

They stood arm-in-arm, gazing out to sea. Even from their height, the Channel looked rough, the great rollers white-capped as far as they could see. Fishing boats bobbed in the middle distance, and farther out a majestic liner ploughed its way through the swells, but the wind seemed to have dissuaded the small yachts from leaving the inlet. Seagulls hung in the air, the "rolling level underneath them steady air," Daisy said with a vague memory of Gerard Manley Hopkins's poem, though that, she rather thought, was about a singular falcon, not plural gulls.

Walking on, Daisy and Alec stopped now and then to contemplate a particularly fine vista of the rocky coastline. At one high point they could see for miles inland, as far as what Alec claimed was Dartmoor in the hazy distance.

The girls had run ahead, with strict instructions to stay away from the edge. They came dashing back to announce that they had found Deva's path down the cliff.

Alec's stride lengthened. Pleased to see his enthusiasm, Daisy didn't try to keep up, saving her energy for a possible climb to come. When she joined Bel and Deva at the top of the path, Alec was already past the first switchback, his hand shading his eyes as he surveyed the rest of the way down.

"Mr. Fletcher said to stay here till he says it's all right to come."

"And then go carefully. No rushing," Belinda reminded her friend.

At that moment, Alec looked up and waved. Bel and Deva both immediately set foot on the path side by side. They looked at each other.

"I found it," said Deva.

Bel nodded reluctantly. "All right, you can go first. I'll help Mummy at the difficult bits."

"Gosh, thanks, darling," said Daisy, feeling a hundred years old. But perhaps it wasn't her age that prompted such solicitude. Officially Bel hadn't been told yet that there was a baby on the way, but she was a bright child quite capable of putting two and two together. Children today seemed to know far more of such matters than they had in Daisy's youth.

Deva continued downward at a prudent pace. Bel followed her, glancing back now and then to say anxiously, "Are you all right, Mummy?"

"So far, so good." The first part was easy, though rather steep, but soon the way turned rough and rocky. The return journey was going to be quite a toil. The almost sheer drop to Daisy's left was sometimes separated from the path by a rim of rock or a few tussocks of grass, sometimes by nothing at all. She averted her gaze, keeping it firmly fixed on the next couple of yards her feet had to cross. At least they were not buffeted by the wind. Some trick of conformation of cliff and headland sheltered them, and the sun felt warm.

They reached Alec. "I can't see sand at the bottom, if there is any," he reported, "but there are some flat rocks down there we can sit on for our picnic. They should be sheltered from the wind, and with the tide ebbing we needn't worry about being stranded. How are you doing, love? You don't think it will be too much for you going back up?"

With the girls' pleading looks upon her, and Alec's obvious lust for exploration, Daisy would have felt a monster if she had doubted aloud her ability to prance back up the cliff like a mountain goat. "I'll manage very well," she said, "as long as I'm not *rushed*."

As they went on down, they came to a place where the path narrowed alarmingly in bypassing a large boulder. On the sea side, a few clumps of pink-flowered thrift clung to the top of a steep slope of scree.

Alec turned his face to the rock and worked his way past crabwise.

"It's not difficult. There's all sorts of little knobs and cracks you can grip if you need to," he encouraged Deva. She and Belinda followed without a quiver and passed him.

Daisy, who had been certain her pregnancy barely showed, now felt as if she protruded at least a foot in front. She must not show the white feather, she admonished herself, especially in front of Belinda, whose grandmother would have forbidden this adventure on the grounds that only boys climb cliffs.

"Hm," said Alec, frowning, "maybe I'd better call the girls back. I'd forgotten the extra inches around your middle."

"Darling, how rude! I'm not too wide yet." She edged around the boulder, finding plenty of finger-holds but not really needing them. "See?"

He grinned at her. "Another month and we'd have had to leave you behind up there."

"Another month and I wouldn't have made it to the top in the first place."

"Not too much farther."

The path grew easier from there on, and the girls went on ahead. Soon they called back that they could see sand below, and then they disappeared among the tumble of rocks, all shapes and sizes, at the base of the cliff. Waves dashed against the headlands in fountains of spume, but their force seemed to be spent before they rolled into the sheltered cove.

Belinda briefly reappeared. "Mummy, there's the absolutely best rock pool ever, with amenomes and gobies and a *starfish!*" She had to shout to make herself heard against the muted roar of the sea. "Come and see. Come and see, Daddy."

"I'm going to find a good picnic place first," Alec called back. "This knapsack is getting heavier and heavier."

"That's the Thermos flask of tea," said Daisy. "Not to mention the lemon squash for the girls."

"I won't mention it. I just want to put it down." He picked his way across and between the rocks towards the small beach they had spotted from above.

Daisy scrambled over to join Bel and Deva. She found them arguing over whether a tiny transparent creature with blue and orange stripes could possibly be a shrimp.

"Shrimps are pink," Deva said dogmatically.

"Not until they're cooked, are they, Mummy?"

No more than Deva had Daisy ever seen an uncooked shrimp. "I have no idea," she admitted.

"If we catch one, can we take it home and cook it?"

That was an easy question. "No. Leave the poor things be. What a beautiful pool!"

"Three kinds of seaweed," said Deva, as proud as if she'd done the decorating herself. "This pink ferny one, and the green ribbons, and this green stuff like moss. Touch it, Mrs. Fletcher, it's soft and silky."

To Daisy's relief, before she had to decide whether to lower herself to her knees to touch something that looked to her unpleasantly squishy, Alec appeared around a huge rock and called to her.

"Daisy, would you come here a minute? Come and tell me what you think of the spot I've found." He was too far off for her to make out his expression, but his voice sounded strained.

The girls didn't notice. Daisy left them trying to catch in their bare hands the little finny fish that darted from nook to cranny among the pebbles and fronds of seaweed.

"What's wrong?" she asked as she joined Alec.

His face was set. "I saw a shoe sticking up above a rock, at an odd angle. I went closer and saw an ankle. The foot is still in the shoe. I must go and look, but I want you to keep the girls away, so that they don't follow me."

Feeling ill, Daisy sat down suddenly on a nearby rock. "Oh darling, not a . . . ! I suppose some poor soul fell overboard, or drowned while swimming, and was washed up by the waves."

"It's just possible someone stumbled among the rocks and knocked himself unconscious. I must go and look."

"Yes, of course. I'll stop them if they come this way."

Alec was not gone long. He returned tight-lipped and rather pale. Daisy tried not to wonder what could make an experienced CID detective turn pale. A sea-bloated body chewed by fish?

"Dead," he said. "I can't be sure but I think it's that chap from the inn, the landlord."

"Oh no!" Daisy exclaimed, aghast. "Not George Enderby!"

8

*F*lying high above the trenches in his observer plane, Alec had missed the worst horrors of the Great War. As a detective he had seen victims done to death in a variety of ways, but he couldn't remember ever having seen a body as battered as George Enderby's. Every visible inch of him was gashed and scraped, his shirt and fawn flannels ripped and blotched with blood. He lay twisted among the rocks near the foot of the cliff, partly on a patch of sand, one leg caught on a larger boulder so that his foot stuck up in the air. The contorted position suggested that most of his bones were broken.

So much Alec had taken in before returning to Daisy, thanking heaven neither she nor the girls had made the grisly discovery.

"I *think* it's him," he stressed, "I can't be sure. I must stay here. You'll have to get the girls away and report the body."

She looked at him in dismay. "Darling, can't you come too? You're on holiday, after all."

"This has nothing to do with being a copper. It's my duty as a citizen to stay, as you're available to report." He frowned, remembering that she was in no condition to make haste up the cliff path. "Unless you'd rather stay? The tide's going out, so there's no danger. And there's no need to go near the body, just to keep people away, and I rather doubt you'd be swamped with sightseers."

"No, I'll go," she said with a shudder. "It was . . . it *was* an accident, wasn't it?"

"That's what you'll report. It's none of my business, I'm happy to say. And you'd better not say it's Enderby in case I'm wrong. Don't give me away, will you."

"Of course not, darling. You're on holiday."

"And hope to stay that way. Now off you go, and don't try to hurry, love. Whoever he is, he's beyond help."

"What shall I tell the girls?"

"I'll leave that up to you."

Alec knew he sounded relieved at not having to face that problem, and he wasn't surprised when Daisy wrinkled her nose at him. He also knew she was pleased. When he first started seeing her regularly, he had more than once made a fool of himself by accusing her of not caring sufficiently for the welfare of his precious daughter. But Belinda adored her, and he could only plume himself on having married a woman who had turned out to be a wonderful, if unconventional, mother—not to mention an adorable, if unconventional, wife.

He kissed her and watched her pick her way back towards the girls, careful to take the easiest route and use her hands rather than trying to balance when she had to climb. It was going to be strange starting again with a baby after ten years of watching Bel grow up. A sudden sorrow for his lost Joan swept over him. Did Daisy still grieve for her dead fiancé, blown up by a German mine along with the ambulance he drove?

Putting such unproductive thoughts behind him, he started to wonder who would grieve for George Enderby's untimely end: not his wife, by the looks of things in the pub last night, nor the Anstruthers.

None of his business, he reminded himself. He could only hope he would not be called as a witness to anything beyond finding the body.

The girls and Daisy waved goodbye. Waving back, he watched their progress as they appeared and disappeared among the rocks, then started up the path. Daisy was moving slowly. Belinda and Deva pulled ahead, and Alec wanted to shout to them to slow down, but they wouldn't hear, and if they did, he might startle them into missing their footing.

Was that how Enderby had come to fall? Or had currents and waves brought him from the sea? He wasn't dressed for bathing, nor for boating, jacketless on such a blustery day and his footwear more suited for walking hills than decks. Unless his jacket had come off in the sea . . .

Alec found himself once more standing over the body. He couldn't help it, the detective instinct was too strong for him.

The boneless, twisted sprawl told him nothing. It could equally well have resulted from a long fall or from being tossed among the rocks by the pitiless waves, as could the superficial injuries. The clothes held Alec's attention.

Enderby's shirt had come loose from his trousers. It had great rents in it, revealing torn skin beneath. A closer look showed his braces dangling, two of the fastenings missing. The trousers, made of stouter cloth, had only one visible tear. More significant, the parts of the clothes uppermost as he lay, including the raised leg, were bone-dry, blotched with blood, as he had noticed before. The day was warm and windy but not hot enough to dry out sodden flannel trousers since the turn of the tide. Besides, the way they were draped on the motionless form was nothing like the way wet cloth would have clung as it dried. Blood had clotted around the injuries, including two on the top of the head where that distinctive sandy thatch was matted with dried blood.

Alec badly wanted to turn the body over. Even if it had been his case—supposing it turned out to be a case—he oughtn't to do so before a medical man had examined it and photographs had been taken.

Photographs! He'd quite forgotten the cheap Brownie camera he had bought on a whim at a station bookstall on his way down to Devon, to take family snapshots. He had stuffed it into his knapsack along with the picnic, intending to surprise Daisy. She was the photographer of the family, but the camera she used for photos to go with her articles was too big and complicated for informal holiday pictures. Alec always relied on police photographers at work, or Tom if they were away from London, but the girl at the bookstall had assured him that anyone could use the Brownie.

She had showed him right then and there how to put the film in. Then all one had to do was set the little lever to sunny or cloudy or indoors, point, and press the button. And not forget to wind the film on, he reminded himself, taking out the black box.

Set the lever to sunny, peer through the little window at the corpse, reduced in size and oddly distanced, less human almost. Press the button. Move and snap again, from four different angles altogether. And now for a few close-up views.

Kneeling on a flattish stretch of bedrock, Alec studied the body. The lowest four or five inches of the clothes had clearly been soaked and were still damp. The water mark was obvious. Below, bloodstains were faint discolorations, diluted and dispersed by the sea. He could see two nasty gashes in exposed skin that must have bled freely, for however short a period, before Enderby died; they had been washed clean.

The obvious inference was that he had fallen to his death, into shallow water. The local people ought to be able to work out when the tide had been five inches deep at this point on the coast.

Alec took another four photos, from a distance of about two feet, though he rather doubted the cheap little camera would produce pictures clear enough to make out all the marks he had noted.

Then, standing, he gazed up at the cliff face and took a shot of that. Daisy and the girls had disappeared from sight, though he thought they must still be climbing. Directly above him, the cliff shelved back in ridges, ledges and steep, rough slopes for some way before rising in a sheer black rock face for the top third. It was not so smoothly vertical as the wall of a building, but a man falling would not have the slightest hope of catching a protuberance to save himself. Some of the cliffs in the area were as much as four hundred feet high, Alec knew. Once Enderby had gone over the edge, his death was certain.

All the same, there was always a chance his murderer—supposing him to have been pushed—had come down to make sure. The surface of the path down the cliff was mostly too rocky to show footprints, the sandy patches too dry and hardpacked; besides, Alec and Daisy and the girls had all trodden it thoroughly enough to eliminate or confuse any subtle signs.

Here below, though, some indication might be visible. Stepping from rock to rock, Alec surveyed the patches of beach around the body. His own footprints stood out clearly on the damp sand smoothed by the ebbing tide. The only other marks were dimples and bubbles produced by subterranean marine creatures and those odd curved lines of darker sand often left by receding waves.

As he trod the low rocks, he realized he was crushing limpets and barnacles. He might be destroying evidence, or at least confusing the trail, if someone else had done likewise.

Glancing back the way he had come, he couldn't be sure which of two rocks he had stepped on. He looked more closely. Both seemed to have a few broken shells on top. Of course, rocks moved by the waves must do a certain amount of damage. An expert might distinguish footprints, but the chance of getting an expert here before sundown and high tide hid the evidence seemed remote.

All the same, Alec decided to move to higher ground to await the forces of the law. Scrambling up on top of a massive nearby boulder, he finished off the film with three shots of the rocks and sand surrounding Enderby's body. With luck, at least the pattern of rocks would be identifiable from the top of the cliff, giving a good idea of where he had fallen from.

Putting the camera in his knapsack, he took out the Thermos of tea and found a comfortable perch in the sun. From above, the contorted figure below was so obviously dead that no one need have approached any closer to be certain.

Was it actually Enderby? He hadn't taken much notice of the landlord of the Schooner last night until the man had been half strangled with his own tie. The body's face was unrecognizable. The thick thatch of sandy hair was the only distinguishing mark, a feature not so uncommon as to make it decisive in identification.

In fact, he had jumped to the conclusion that it was Enderby because when one has seen a man attacked by an avenging berserker one day, to find him dead the next cannot be regarded as entirely unexpected.

Daisy had not expected to enjoy the trek back up the cliff, but she found it even more trying than she had foreseen. Before they were a quarter of the way up, her legs felt like lead and she was "glowing" like a blast-furnace ("Horses sweat, gentlemen perspire, ladies glow," had been one of her nanny's favourite sayings). Maddeningly, the girls outpaced her without the least apparent effort.

When they reached the big boulder, they were a couple of hundred yards ahead of her. They stopped and looked back. Daisy prayed they were not going to make a fuss about passing it without Alec's encouragement.

Belinda came back down the path. "Are you all right, Mummy?" she asked anxiously. "You look awfully hot."

"I am. I wish I'd thought to have a drink before we left our picnic with Daddy, but if wishes were horses beggars would ride, as my nanny used to say."

"So did my granny." They exchanged a glance of complicity.

"It doesn't stop one wishing, does it? I could do with a horse right now, or perhaps a mule would manage this path better. Failing that, I'll just have to rely on Shanks' pony. Onward and upward!"

"I'll stay with you, in case you feel faint. You go first."

"I'm not ill, darling, merely pregnant. I just need not to be rushed."

"We'll go slowly. I'm sorry we were going so fast before." She hesitated. "You really are going to have a baby?"

"I really am. You guessed, didn't you?"

"Deva heard you talking to Mrs. Prasad and Mrs. Germond about it."

"Are you happy that you're going to have a brother or sister?"

"Oh, yes, but actually, I'm so much older it'll be more like being an aunt."

Daisy had no quick answer to this, and she needed her breath for climbing, so they continued in silence until they caught up with Deva. The boulder was negotiated without difficullty.

A few yards beyond, Deva, in the lead, pointed ahead and said over her shoulder, "There is a flat place where you can sit and rest, Mrs. Fletcher. My ayah says English ladies are very hardy, but this is an awfully high cliff."

"I hope there's room for you to sit, too, Deva, though you're getting pretty hardy yourself, after all the long walks we've dragged you on."

"I didn't think I'd like so much walking, but it's been fun. And the pool down there was full of interesting creatures. It's a pity Mr. Fletcher found a murdered man."

"I didn't say he was murdered!" With a sigh of relief, Daisy lowered herself to a patch of scrubby grass and the girls squeezed themselves in on each side. "I'm sure it was an accident."

Deva shook her head. "Mr. Fletcher is a detective, so he's bound to find people who have been murdered."

Daisy didn't feel up to refuting this tangled logic. "Well, that's as may be," she said, "but you are absolutely not to tell anyone it's a case of murder."

"If you do, Deva, they'll make Daddy find the murderer and he won't have any holiday."

"I shan't tell," Deva promised.

After a few minutes they went on. As they moved higher, they began to feel a cooling breeze, which helped Daisy no end. The part that had been the roughest on the way down turned out to be less a walk than a scrambling climb on the way up. At least it used different muscles from the upward plod, and the girls pushed and pulled Daisy over the biggest obstacles. Their solicitude was touching.

Staggering up the last, smooth stretch to the top, they all collapsed in the heather and lay breathing heavily for a while.

Then, "I'm dying of thirst," said Deva.

"Daddy will be wondering when we're going to send help," said Belinda.

Daisy sat up. "I'm quite restored. Let's go. It's all downhill from here."

That wasn't quite true, but the upward slopes were short and gentle compared to the rugged hike up the cliff. They found Daisy's hat, not too much the worse for lying on the ground with a stone to hold it down. Soon they were looking down on the inlet, then the beach and the guest-house came into view, and the village beyond.

When they reached the garden wall, Daisy said, "You two can go into the house or garden or down to the beach, but don't on any account breathe a word to a soul about what's happened."

"What if someone asks where you are?" Deva wanted to know.

"Just tell them Mr. Fletcher and I will be back soon."

"Oh no, Mummy," said Belinda. "We'll come with you. You're going to see that horrid policeman who put poor Sid in prison, aren't you? We're coming too."

Deva looked dismayed but resigned. Though Daisy wondered how Belinda proposed to protect her from the horrid policeman, she wondered silently. Like Deva, she recognized Bel's resolute tone. Once her usually diffident stepdaughter had made up her mind, she was as impossible to budge as a bull elephant.

They went on along the path. The whole way, Daisy felt eyes on her back, as if Cecily Anstruther and her husband guessed her errand and watched her every move. Daisy even glanced back once, but of course the track was empty behind them.

The town was empty too, on a Sunday afternoon with all the shops closed, too early for evensong at the square-towered parish church, much too early for the pubs to open. Their footsteps on the cobbles sounded loud as they trudged up the hill to the police station. The door stood open. The front room was empty.

"Sit down on that bench," Daisy told the girls. She tapped the bell on the high counter.

The *ping* had no immediate effect. Daisy was about to give the bell a sharp thump when Mrs. Puckle bustled through from the back. "You'll be wanting the constable?" she enquired.

"Yes, please."

"Puckle is just sitting down to his tea, madam. 'Twouldn't be urgent, would it?"

"I'm afraid it is," Daisy apologized.

"Ah well, 'twon't be the first time he's had to let his tea go cold, not by a long shot. I'll see he comes out to you right away, madam."

She went off. A murmur of voices was followed by a loud, protesting "But, Martha . . . !"

"Now, Fred, 'tis your job to see what the lady wants."

Constable Puckle came through, looking sulky as he shrugged into his uniform jacket. "Oh, it's you"—sulkiness changed to annoyance—"madam. I let Sid out yes'day morning."

"I know you did. This has nothing to do with him. My husband has found a body."

Momentarily startled, he then gave her a long, sceptical look. "A body."

"A dead person."

"A dead person. And where is this husband o' yourn? Why don't he report this dead person hisself, like a good citizen?"

"Because," said Daisy with all the patience she could muster, "like a good citizen he stayed with the body. In case anyone came by, to make sure they didn't touch him. It's at the bottom of the cliff in that little cove you have to climb down to—"

"So your husband stayed down in this tiny cove you have to climb down the cliff to get to, to keep chance passers-by away from this dead body he found . . . Sounds like a fairy-tale to me."

Scarlet with fury, Belinda marched up to the counter. "It's *not* a fairy-tale. My father knows what to do when you find a body, because he's a detective chief inspector at Scotland Yard. So there!"

Casting her an alarmed glance, Constable Puckle at last took out his notebook and found a pencil.

Daisy suppressed a sigh. Fat chance of keeping Alec out of the investigation now! Their holiday was doomed.

9

The first Alec knew of the arrival of relief troops was a hail from the sea.

"Ahoy there!"

"Ahoy!" he shouted back, hoping that was the correct nautical response. He stood up on his rocky seat. A lifeboat bobbed in the surf, the very sight of it making him slightly queasy. He waved.

"Ahoy! Chief Inspector Fletcher?"

"Oh hell!" he muttered. What had possessed Daisy to give him away? Reluctant but resigned, he waved acknowledgement.

The lifeboatmen shipped their oars. At that moment, Alec was hailed from behind. "Hulloo!"

Turning with caution he saw a stout constable, very red in the face, about two thirds of the way down the cliff path. Behind him came a shortish, slim young man in tennis whites. In place of a racquet, a black bag swung jauntily in his hand, proclaiming his profession.

At any moment, the beach was going to be covered with footprints. Alec cast a last quick glance around. The only marks he could see on the sea-smoothed sand were those of his own feet, but he wished he had his sergeant, Tom Tring, with him to make a proper survey of the area.

"No I don't!" he muttered to himself. He must remember he was on holiday.

He climbed down from his perch. Two of the lifeboatmen trudged towards him, ungainly in their bulky life-jackets. One carried a folding stretcher.

"Bloody hell," said the other, stopping with hands on hips, "he's a bit of a mess, an't he." He looked up at the towering cliff. "Long way to fall. You reckon he fell, Chief Inspector, or'd the tide bring him in?"

"That's for the local police to decide."

The man with the stretcher stared at the body. "Hey, an't that Enderby? Look at un's hair, Jimmy."

"Could be. An' if so 'tis, the question's not did he fall or did he drown, 'tis did he fall or were he pushed?"

A third man joined them. "Pushed? Hey, that's Enderby! If Enderby got pushed, I know who done it."

"Give over, Tom Stebbins!" said Jimmy. "I dunno why you got it in for Pete just acos he's done well for himself and you ha'n't."

"I say!" The voice was the same which had hallooed from the cliff path.

They all, including Alec, turned to see the young tennis player scrambling across the rocks towards them. Close to, he looked even younger than from a distance: an unlined face with a narrow fuzz of moustache, looking as if it was barely winning the struggle for existence, and ingenuous eyes now bright with excitement.

"Gosh, the poor chap's a bit of a mess, isn't he?" Staring, he unconsciously echoed Jimmy.

"Are you the police surgeon, Doctor?" Alec asked.

"Well, no, not exactly." He flushed to the roots of his dark, sleeked-back hair. "As a matter of fact, I'm not exactly quite qualified yet. Student at Guy's, don't you know. I'm staying with my uncle, who's the local GP. He's gone out to some farm at the back of beyond, so when the bobby said a doctor was needed, I said what-ho,

74

I'll come along and lend a hand. Oh, the name's Vernon, sir, Andrew Vernon."

"I see, Mr. Vernon," Alec said grimly. "And where, may I ask, is the bobby?"

Vernon swung round and pointed at the cliff. "Couldn't get down the path, I'm afraid. There's a bally great rock sticks out and he'd have gone over for sure if he'd tried to get past it. Stout sort of chap, don't you know."

The lifeboatmen nudged each other, pointed at the forlorn blue-clad figure up on the path, and snickered. "Aye, he's a stout chap, Fred Puckle is, surely," the man with the stretcher agreed, grinning.

For the moment at least, Alec was the only authority. He was going to have to make the decisions.

"I say, sir, you're the Scotland Yard 'tec, aren't you?" asked the youthful not-exactly-quite doctor.

"Detective Chief Inspector Fletcher of the Metropolitan Police, CID. Well, Mr. Vernon, it looks as if I'm the only police officer available and you're the only medical man. You'd better have a look at him, and we'll worry later about the legality of a student pronouncing death."

"Gosh, may I? Wait till the fellows hear about this!" But the moment he opened his black bag, Vernon put on the gravity proper to his future profession. He took out a small hand-mirror and a magnifying glass. "I'm afraid there's not much doubt about his decease, though. Should I try not to disturb the body?"

"Too late to worry about that." Another lifeboatman had arrived, a middle-aged, prosperous-looking man with COXSWAIN painted on his life-jacket. "We've got to take him aboard and get back to port. I don't like the look of the weather." He gestured out to sea, where a white bank of fog was creeping in, though not yet hiding the sun. The wind had dropped, but the waves crashed against the headlands with unabated vigour. "We need to be ready in case of a real emergency. Let's get that stretcher put together, Bill."

"Aye, sir."

While Bill, Jimmy and Tom Stebbins screwed together the poles and slung the canvas between, Vernon stooped to the mortal remains of George Enderby.

Held to the mashed mouth and nose, the mirror predictably failed to cloud over. Undeterred, Vernon felt for pulses and peered into mercifully unmashed eyes before he looked up to say, "Should I try the stethoscope, sir?"

"I don't believe that's necessary."

"No, he's about as dead as a corpse can be. I don't know much about rigor mortis, or cadaveric cooling, I'm afraid. Most of what we get in the hospital has died naturally and as often as not been pickled in formalin."

"The sun and the water may have changed the timing anyway. With luck we . . . *they* will be able to establish the time of death by other means."

Assuming Enderby had stayed behind his bar till the end of opening hours at three—no, two thirty on a Sunday, he had to have time to reach the top of the cliff. He must have left the pub on the dot and walked up at a good clip. Meeting someone?

Alec himself had been up there by half past three or soon after, and had seen no one else. Not that it was his problem, but as a witness he could narrow the time of the fall to a very short period.

He turned to the lifeboat coxswain. "I believe he fell into four or five inches of water. Can you tell me what time the tide would have been at that level?"

"Well, now." The coxswain eyed the level of barnacles, limpets and seaweed on the rocks, the edge of the wave presently creaming up the beach, the steel-cased chronometer he pulled from a pocket of his life-vest, and the position of the body. "Midway between neap and spring," he said, and his men nodded. "On-shore wind. Well, now, this is not a cove I'm very familiar with, so I won't commit myself, but I should say around three o'clock there would have been four or five inches right here."

The men nodded. "Aye, thereabouts," Jimmy agreed.

Their estimate matched Alec's. Barring definitive evidence to the contrary, Enderby had died at approximately three o'clock that afternoon. Which would not leave much time for an assailant—if any—to descend the cliff path, re-ascend, and be out of sight when Alec, Daisy and the girls arrived.

"Sir!" Crouching by the body, Vernon was examining the back of the neck with his magnifying glass. "Sir, there are splinters of wood in his skin here. Do you think it's important? Do you think someone hit him before he fell? Shall I leave them there or pull some out? I have tweezers in my bag. I could—"

"Hold your horses, lad!"

Alec scanned the surrounding area. A few small sticks, bleached by salt water, and the smashed remains of a packing case lay scattered among the rocks, none within a dozen feet of the body. A hundred feet to his left, a weathered log leant up against the cliff, jammed between two boulders. He looked up at the cliff. As his gaze rose higher and higher, he saw tufts of grass, thrift, even red valerian clinging to ledges, cracks and niches, but nothing remotely resembling a tree. Nothing Enderby could have hit on the way down that would have lodged splinters in his skin.

"Here." The coxswain, shaking his head, handed over binoculars. They failed to miraculously reveal a tree of any size, with or without broken branches, even right at the top of the cliff.

"Summun hit him," said Tom Stebbins with ghoulish satisfaction.

"Sir!" Vernon was almost dancing with excitement. "Shall I extract a couple of splinters? I can put them in a specimen bottle. There'd be some left in the skin for the autopsy. Sir, do you think I could attend the autopsy?"

"That's not for me to say," Alec pointed out firmly. "You'll have to ask the local authorities. Yes, you'd better pull a couple of splinters, just in case the body is damaged . . . further damaged on the way to port. I'll take responsibility."

Three splinters, ranging from a quarter-inch long to nearly invisible, were safely deposited in a small glass specimen bottle with a rubber-sealed stopper, which was then safely tucked away in the black bag. Alec went through the dead man's pockets, but anything that had been in them must have fallen out on the way down. Even through the binoculars, there had been no sign of a jacket on the cliff face. If the local police wanted to climb down the cliff to search along the way, that was up to them. Alec wasn't going to attempt it.

The lifeboatmen, with solemn mien, lifted the body and laid it on the stretcher. Covering it with a tarpaulin, they strapped it down and started down the beach towards their vessel.

"You'll be coming back with us?" the coxswain asked Alec.

Alec eyed the waves, which recalled to mind all too clearly his interior distress last time he went to sea. With relief, he remembered the village bobby who had failed to negotiate the cliff path. The blue figure still stood up there by the big boulder, feet the regulation distance apart, hands behind his back, staring into the distance, doing his best to look as if he were on guard duty.

"I must talk to the constable." Alec tried to sound regretful. "Puckle, is it?"

"Fred Puckle. You want to come with us, Vernon?"

"No, thanks, sir. Another day."

"I expect you'd better deliver the body to the police station," said Alec, "unless by then there's a Devon detective waiting for you on the quay to direct matters. Thanks for your help, Coxswain. I hope you're not called out again today."

"Believe me, so do I, Chief Inspector. I'd rather have a hurricane than a fog, and after lawyering all week, I must say I like to put my feet up on a Sunday afternoon." With a gesture halfway between a wave and a salute, the coxswain went after his men.

"A lawyer!" Alec stared after him. "I assumed he was a seaman."

"Oh no, sir, though he's a keen sailor. He has his own yacht. The lifeboatmen are all volunteers, mostly fishermen. When the maroon goes up, they come running from whatever they're doing. They've let me go out with them a couple of times. I generally spend a few weeks in the summer at my uncle's, don't you know. Mr. Wallace is a solicitor, the only one in Westcombe. If it's really murder, he'll be kept busy! Do you think it's murder, sir? It must be, mustn't it?"

As Vernon chattered, he and Alec made their way towards the foot of the cliff path. At this point, Alec stopped and gave the young man a stern look.

"I have not said so, and you are not to say so. To anyone at all. This is not my case; you are not a qualified medical practitioner, far less a police surgeon. I want your word that you won't speak to anyone of murder."

"Oh no, sir, I wouldn't. I can be the soul of discretion, I promise you." He followed Alec up the path. "I don't usually rattle on this way, it's just . . . Well, seeing a chap one knows lying there on the beach, it's a bit different from a pickled pauper on a slab of marble, isn't it?"

"I don't believe a name was mentioned after you joined us. Who do you think it was?"

"Why, George Enderby, the chappie at the Schooner. Not that I ever cared for him overmuch, but it's unsettling all the same, I don't mind telling you."

"Why didn't you care for him?"

"A bit of a cad, wasn't he? Fancied himself a lady-killer, and by all accounts a fair number of women fell for it."

Alec glanced back. Conditions for an interrogation were far from optimum, but he shouldn't be interrogating in the first place. "Were you in the Schooner last night?" he asked.

Vernon blushed. "No. As a matter of fact, I was at the Vicarage. Julia—Miss Bellamy is rather a friend of mine, don't you know." He changed the subject hurriedly. "I'm quite sure it was Enderby."

"What makes you so certain?"

"Oh, the hair, the eyes, the ears. One or t'other might be anyone, but all three together, in this place, add up to Enderby. I rather make a point of observing that sort of thing."

"Oh? A budding Sherlock Holmes?"

"No. When I was young I used to think he was the last word, but honestly, however clever he seems he's got to be a bit of a fool to be using cocaine, hasn't he? And as for learning to play the violin! And now Sir Arthur Conan Doyle's got mixed up in this spiritualist bosh. No, Dr. Thorndyke is much more the thing. Did you know R. Austin Freeman is actually a doctor himself? Of course, Dr. Thorndyke is a lawyer and criminologist as well, but it's something to work towards, isn't it? Besides, one can follow his logic, which I can't always with Holmes, and I like it that Thorndyke is as keen on defending the innocent against unjust accusations as hunting the guilty. Do you know *The Red Thumb-Mark*, sir?"

Alec admitted to having read the book, distressing to a policeman since it proved that fingerprints could be forged. He let Vernon continue his prattle, saving his own breath for climbing. With the youth hard on his heels, he didn't care to slow down. The lifeboat had disappeared around the eastern headland. He was almost beginning to wish he had risked seasickness and gone with it.

They reached and passed the boulder, and on the other side came face to face with Constable Puckle.

Standing rigidly at attention, he saluted. "Chief Inspector, sir, I thought as summun ought to stay on guard here to keep people away that didn't ought to go down."

"Good thinking, Officer. Besides, it was your decision. You're in charge until your superiors arrive."

"Me, sir? Oh no, sir! Them in Exeter was going to ring up Scotland Yard on the telephone and ask 'em to put you on the case. Seeing you're here already, sir."

"Dammit, man, I'm on holiday!" Alec had no illusions that Superintendent Crane would refuse his services. As soon as the super and the assistant commissioner heard that Daisy was involved, however peripherally—and since she had reported the incident, they were bound to hear—they would positively insist on his taking the case. They still laboured under the delusion that he was capable of reining her in. "Besides," he added, his tone irate, "what made them think this is a case worthy of the attentions of the CID?"

"Well, sir, murder, sir. The county constabluary often calls in the CID for murder, sir."

"But why should they think it was murder, not an accident?"

Puckle looked at him in surprise. "Acos of I told 'em you was here, sir. Stands to reason. If 'tweren't murder, why would a detective chief inspector from the Yard be on the spot, like?"

Turning a baleful glare on Vernon, who suppressed his snickers with an effort, Alec said irritably, "All right, let's get back to the police station and see what's going on." Until he was officially in charge, he really ought not to enlighten the village constable about the presumed identity of the dead man, nor his theory as to the cause of death. Puckle seemed too abashed even to wonder.

With the constable in the lead, the trek up the cliff slowed to a crawl. Unlike Tom Tring, also a large man, Fred Puckle's bulk was not mostly muscle. Alec found himself longing for his sergeant, but nonetheless determined not to send for him and spoil the Trings' holiday as well as his own and Daisy's.

Vernon's stream of confidences had stopped. After a few sighs of impatience, he was silent, even his rubber-soled tennis shoes making little sound on the path. Then a triumphant exclamation stopped Alec.

"Sir! Look here!"

Alec glanced back. Vernon was standing a few yards back, by a rocky outcrop at a point where the path doubled back on itself.

"What is it?"

"Do come and see."

Puckle had also come to a halt, puffing like a steam engine. "You go on ahead, Constable," said Alec. "We'll catch up with you. What is it?" he asked again, retracing his steps.

"Splinters, here on this rock. With the magnifying glass they look just like the ones from Enderby's neck. I bet with a microscope I could tell for sure. Dr. Thorndyke could, anyway."

"A pity we don't have him with us," Alec said dryly. "Well, you might as well take a sample. I suppose it's remotely possible the object used to hit Enderby was thrown over and happened to hit here on its way down." He looked down a steep slope of scree ending in a jumble of particularly jagged rocks between which the waves still surged, though the tide must be near its lowest ebb. "But if so, I doubt we'll ever recover it."

Vernon took an empty specimen bottle and a pair of tweezers from his black bag. "I never would have noticed if Puckle wasn't so slow. I ought to have examined the path closely all the way. Thorndyke would have. Only I didn't think of it till we slowed down," he said with regret.

"I'm sure you would have made an apt pupil if he were not a fictional character."

Unoffended, the medical student grinned. "Julia thinks I'm an absolute ass, but I do think I'd make a better pupil than Jervis. He's definitely not too swift in the uptake. It seems to be the fashion to give the top detectives rather thick assistants. Look at Dr. Watson. And do you know this new chappie, the Belgian detective? Same thing—he has the bumbling Colonel Hastings to crow over. There." Stoppering the bottle, he added optimistically, "You never know. It may be a vital clue!"

"Since it appears that I'm to be thrust willy-nilly into the case, I hope so. However, at present I'm no more than a witness. The Devonshire police would have every right to strongly resent my interference. I therefore do not feel justified in making a search of the area from which Enderby fell, though it would be a pity if any evidence were lost by delay."

"I'm with you, sir." Vernon's grin broadened. "You can count on me, and I'll claim it was my own idea."

Though he had half hoped for this response, Alec reconsidered. The youth was keen, but he was an amateur. If evidence was destroyed by his bungling, Alec would hold himself responsible whether or not anyone found out he had encouraged the boy.

Silently cursing his anomalous position, he said, "No, I think not, though I appreciate the offer."

He went on after Constable Puckle and caught up with him near the top. Glancing back, he expected to see the would-be medico-legal practitioner close behind, but Vernon had stopped some way down, apparently to examine the surface of the path.

With a smile and a shake of the head, Alec left him to it. He was in a hurry to get to the police station and find out whether he really was going to have to take over the investigation. Anything to be discovered on the cliff-top could wait. It wasn't as if the place was going to be overrun by trippers who might confuse the evidence, especially as that sinister bank of fog was advancing landward.

A solitary man stood at the top of the path, however, a dark figure against the sky. "What's going on, Constable?" It was Baskin, walking staff in hand. "Oh, it's you, Mr. Fletcher. I've been watching from up here. What's happened? I hope Mrs. Fletcher and the girls are all right?"

"Perfectly, thank you." Alec eyed his stick—six feet of polished, seasoned oak, an excellent weapon but with no sign of splintering. "You've been walking up here?"

"I was on my way home when I saw the lifeboat and stopped to watch the rescue. A holiday visitor, I presume? I doubt the local people are such fools as to sail close to shore or go bathing in a sea like this."

"Not such fools as to go sea-bathing at all," Puckle grunted.

"It's a local resident."

"Now who might that be, sir? Mrs. Fletcher didn't tell me."

"Mrs. Fletcher didn't know. I wasn't certain until the lifeboatmen and Mr. Vernon confirmed my guess, and as I'm sure you are aware, Constable, legal identity must be established by next-of-kin, if possible. However, I'll tell you: It appears to be George Enderby."

"Mr. Enderby bain't what I'd call a local man," muttered Puckle, shaking his head in dismay, "but there's them as won't be sorry."

Baskin's reaction was unexpected and much more interesting. After a moment of shock, he looked perplexed and frustrated. "Is he badly hurt?" he asked.

"Dead."

Relief lit Baskin's face.

As though a huge burden had fallen from his shoulders, Alec thought. A little delving into the connection between the landlord and the schoolmaster was called for. But not here and now—first to the police station to discover whether the delving was for him to do, or whether by some miracle it was none of his business.

10

*T*he sun had disappeared behind the hill, but the air was still warm and Daisy sat on in the garden, determined to catch Alec as he passed on his way to the police station. The girls, having solicitously settled her in a deck-chair with a book, had gone down to the beach for a while and were now indoors eating their supper.

Perhaps she dozed off. At any rate, she was startled when a voice nearby said, "Hullo, Mrs. Fletcher."

Donald Baskin was coming up the steps from the path, and beyond him Daisy saw Alec walking on towards the town with Constable Puckle and an unknown young man dressed for tennis.

"Alec, wait!" she called, and started to get up in a hurry. The deck-chair collapsed beneath her.

Baskin dropped his stick and rushed to help her. He had her on her feet and was righting the chair when Alec bounded up the steps.

"Daisy, are you hurt?"

"Not at all," she said crossly. She hadn't fallen far, but she was shaken and flustered.

"Sorry!" Baskin apologized. "I took you by surprise."

"It wasn't your fault, Mr. Baskin. It was yours, Alec. You were trying to sneak past without my seeing you!"

"You need your rest, love, after all that dashing up and down cliffs."

"I didn't dash, I took my time. And I'm perfectly rested, thank you. I'm coming with you."

"The girls . . ."

"Mrs. Anstruther is giving them supper. I'm sure she won't mind keeping an eye on them for half an hour. Would you mind giving her the message, Mr. Baskin?"

"Not at all. I'll be here, too."

"Thank you. And tell them I'll be back to tuck them into bed." Daisy took Alec's arm and tugged him towards the steps. "Oh, good, Puckle has gone ahead. Tell me all about it, now, before they drag you in to take charge and you go all official and secretive."

"Daisy, why on earth did you tell them I'm a copper?"

"I didn't, darling. Puckle was being rather dismissive—I'm afraid I set up his back the other day, over Sid—and Belinda flew to the rescue with the information that her daddy's a Scotland Yard chief inspector and therefore knows all about dead bodies. I could hardly deny it. Believe me, I'd much rather you took a proper holiday for once. What have you done with the body?"

"The lifeboat came and took it off. That young chap walking with Puckle is a medical student, the nearest thing on hand to a police surgeon. Enthusiastic, but he couldn't do much more than confirm that Enderby was dead, which was perfectly obvious."

"It *was* Enderby, then? You weren't sure."

"Yes, the lifeboatmen recognized him, as did Vernon, the doctor-to-be."

"Probably murder then," Daisy said with a sigh. "At least, plenty of people must have felt like murdering him. Oh blast, they're bound to rope you in, darling."

"Puckle seems to think the presence of a Scotland Yard detective on the scene is *prima facie* evidence of murder. I gathered his superiors in Exeter intended to ring up and ask for my help. It's not likely to be refused."

"Blast! I suppose Vernon couldn't tell you whether he fell or was drowned, or when?"

"There was evidence that he fell, probably around three o'clock."

"Not long before we got there! I don't want to hear the gory details. I just hope it wasn't Baskin or Anstruther who pushed him over. I like them both."

"Baskin?" Alec's sudden alertness told Daisy he was already mentally involved in the case, however outwardly reluctant. "What do you know about Baskin and Enderby?"

"Nothing specific, darling. Just that he seemed inexplicably curious about him. He wanted to know how long he'd lived in Westcombe, where he came from, where he spent the War, how he and Mrs. Enderby got on together."

Alec raised his eyebrows. "Odd! He asked you? How did he expect you to know?"

"No, mostly he asked Mrs. Anstruther. It was most embarrassing."

"Embarrassing? Why? Daisy, don't tell me you already knew about her affair with Enderby!"

"Actually, yes, I did."

"Great Scott, they weren't carrying on in the house, with Belinda and Deva here?"

"No, no. It was over already. She told me."

"How do you do it? You just gaze at people with those deceptively guileless blue eyes of yours, and they fall over themselves to make you a gift of all their secrets. I don't suppose Baskin told you why he wanted to know about Enderby?"

"I'm afraid not. The oddest thing was that when I told him I'd heard the Enderbys quarrelling, he looked relieved."

"Hmm. That is odd. He had the same reaction when he heard of Enderby's death. But at first, when he thought the man was alive but injured, I could have sworn he looked as if he didn't know what to do next, as if some long-held plan had been thwarted."

"That would fit, if he'd intended to have a go at Enderby himself and someone beat him to it. I suppose he was glad to hear the Enderbys were not on the best of terms because he didn't want Nancy Enderby to be upset by an attack on Georgie Porgie. But surely that means he didn't push him over?"

"Unless he's a damn good actor."

"He's a schoolmaster, not an actor," Daisy pointed out.

"So he says. But come to think of it, schoolmasters must act all the time, at least the good ones. They shouldn't let on when they take a dislike to a particular child, or a special liking, come to that, which is bound to happen sometimes."

"But if he was such a good actor, darling, he would have concealed his relief at Enderby's death."

"He doesn't know I'm a policeman. I don't suppose he has much opinion of Puckle's powers of perception."

"Well, if you want to get so convoluted, perhaps he put on a look of relief because he knew the police would find out he had good reason to hate Enderby and would wonder why he wasn't pleased by his death."

Alec laughed. "Who knows? At the very least, Baskin will bear investigation. For one thing, he was up on the cliffs this afternoon."

"I rather hope they *will* put you in charge, darling," Daisy said soberly. "It wouldn't surprise me if the local police don't look beyond Anstruther, after that row in the pub last night."

"I'll look, love, but however much you like him and his wife, you must admit that Peter Anstruther has to be the top name on my list."

"I suppose so. You can add a couple of others below him, though. Nancy Enderby, for one. She knew about his carryings-on and wasn't a bit happy about it. And his latest flame was a local farmer's daughter."

"Name?"

"No idea. You can bet someone in the village will know, though. I wonder if she was the woman I saw looking upset when the Enderbys were quarrelling? But I only had a glimpse and she wasn't in any way distinctive. I doubt I could pick her out if you lined up every female in the district." At this point they reached the corner of the main street. Daisy eyed the steep cobbled hill. "I won't come any farther," she decided.

"You're not to rush back and tell Anstruther he's under suspicion."

"I wouldn't!"

"I wouldn't put it past you. Do they know Enderby's been found dead?"

"*I* haven't told them, and I told the girls not to mention the 'accident.' But Baskin may be letting the cat out of the bag right this minute."

"I asked him to keep quiet about it. There's the lifeboatmen, though. No chance they'll all hold their tongues. It'll be all over town soon, if it's not already. It's a pity we're staying at the Anstruthers'."

"Do you want to see if we can get rooms at the Schooner? I'd feel like a rat deserting a sinking ship."

"No, it would probably cause even more talk. We'll stay put. I'll see you later, love."

"Much later, no doubt," Daisy said gloomily. "I'll ask Mrs. Anstruther to leave out a cold supper for you, though it's a bit much to be asking favours when you may arrest her husband any minute!"

Alec followed Puckle and Vernon up the hill. The boy had caught up with them long before they reached the village. His slight shake of the head Alec had interpreted as meaning that whatever had fixed his attention on the path had come to nothing as a clue for the powerful intellect and meticulous methods of the surrogate Dr. Thorndyke.

He had a nasty feeling he was going to have to contend with meddling from both Daisy and Vernon in this case. As far as the latter was concerned, it was entirely his own fault.

The police station was lit by two ancient and inadequate gas fixtures. By their wavery illumination, Alec saw Vernon seated at the high counter with a pad of paper, a wooden pen, and an inkwell. "I'm writing an official report of my findings, Chief Inspector," he said grandly.

"I trust your penmanship hasn't yet deteriorated to the level of most medical men."

"If it's illegible, it's the fault of this damn' pen! Beg your pardon, Mrs. Puckle," he added with a cheeky grin towards the constable's better half, who was poring over a telegram form with her husband. "One doesn't usually need a fountain pen when playing tennis, but I'll be d—bothered if I've written with one of these horrible things since I was seven or eight."

"I'm sure Thorndyke would cope admirably with whatever writing implement was put in his hands."

"By Jove, sir, I believe you're right!" He buckled down to his scratching with renewed enthusiasm.

Alec turned to the Puckles.

"This is the wife, sir. A wire come while I was gone. Show the chief inspector, Martha."

" 'Tis for you, sir, but it don't seem to make much sense. I writ it down just like the exchange said, sir."

ALL YOURS I DONT WANT TO KNOW CRANE, Alec read. He sighed. "It's confirmation that I'm to take over the case. Thank you, Mrs. Puckle."

"You'll want a bite to eat, sir, missing your supper at Mrs. Anstruther's, I'll be bound. I've a nice fish pie and some runner beans from the garden."

"That's very kind of you. A bit later, perhaps, when I've got things sorted out."

"It'll be waiting when you're ready, sir. Now, Fred, mind your manners and ask the gentleman to sit down." She trotted off through the door to the living quarters.

Speechless, the constable waved Alec to a seat by the front window and stood uncomfortably shifting from foot to foot. The ladder-back chair looked as if it had had a long, hard life in someone's kitchen before being demoted to constabulary use, but it felt solid enough when Alec sat on it. Hoping its partner on the other side of the small, square table was equally sturdy, he invited Puckle to be seated.

"When are we to expect reinforcements from Exeter?" he asked.

"Torquay they do be coming from, sir. 'Tis a mortal sight closer. How long—well that depends, sir. Being Sunday, likely they'd have to call someone in. The superintendent said as they'll be motoring down, there being none so many trains and ferries of a Sunday evening."

"At least we'll have transportation, then."

"Oh no, sir. The superintendent said the motor-car'll drop them in Abbotsford for the last ferry, and it do have to go back tonight, being needed elsewhere."

Alec sighed. "All right, let me have your notebook and a pencil and tell me what you know about Enderby's affairs."

Reluctantly, Puckle handed over his notebook. "I don't like to gossip, sir. It don't do in a small place like Westcombe."

"Your discretion is commendable, Constable, but misplaced. This is now officially a murder enquiry. Anything you tell me is not gossip but essential background information."

"Yessir. He first come to Westcombe three years since." Puckle glanced at the door his wife had gone through, then at the youth industriously scribbling at the big desk, and lowered his voice. "He weren't alone, like. Had a woman with him. Claimed they was brother and sister and took rooms next door to each other with a connecting door."

"You're sure she wasn't his sister?"

"What I heard was, the chamber-maid said one o' their two beds weren't slept in. Mrs. Hammett come in here and complained, said it shouldn't be allowed, though how she expected me to—"

His story was interrupted by the sound of boots on the cobbles outside. The lifeboatman Bill stuck his head around the door. "Ned and me's brung un up along, sir. What'll us do wi' un?" he enquired.

Alec looked at Puckle, who stood, pushing himself up with his hands on the table. "Take un to the side gate, Bill. I'll go round and unlock it. He'll have to go in the wash'se for now. I'll light a lantern."

He went through to the back and the face at the door disappeared.

"I'll have to go and break the news to Mrs. Enderby," Alec said to Vernon. "How well do you know her? Is she likely to need a medical attendant on hand?"

"Not when you tell her, I shouldn't think. You can't run a pub if you're a shrinking violet. But does she have to see him?"

"Briefly. By oil-lamp, I gather."

"He's . . . he's a bit of a mess, isn't he? My uncle must be home by now. Shall I ring him up?"

"If you would. My compliments and can he come at once. If not, I dare say you've learnt how to cope with fainting or hysterics?"

"Y . . . yes." The prospect obviously daunted him far more than examining the dead man had. "Sort of."

"We'll hope your uncle can come, or the police surgeon arrives before I get back. Cheer up. You've done remarkably well so far and I expect you can manage if you have to."

Alec went out into the dusk. Sunday was late opening, but the bars at the Schooner would have been open for some time by now. Half the lifeboatmen were probably in there drinking. More than likely they had already told Mrs. Enderby that her husband was dead, unless the lawyer-coxswain had warned them not to.

On the other hand, surely decency would demand closing the bars when she heard the news. The seamen might decide to hold their tongues to preserve drinking time.

Pure speculation! Alec recognized he was postponing his duty, a part of his job he loathed. He walked down the hill.

The windows of the public bar were lit by the soft glow of gaslight behind curtains. One was open and through it came a subdued murmur of voices. No rumble and clatter of skittles. Alec remembered seeing a sign: NO SKITTLES ON SUNDAYS. On the far side of the open front door, the windows of the dining room were also lit.

Of course, it was dinnertime for the hotel guests. Mrs. Enderby must be cursing her absent husband.

Or had she pushed him?

Alec entered. The narrow lobby was empty, the cubby-hole behind the registration desk unlit. He rang the bell on the desk, to no effect. As he stood there, wondering whether to knock on the middle door to his left, which must lead into the space behind the bar counter, Mrs. Enderby came out of the dining room, harassed and hurrying. A babble of voices and the chink of china and cutlery cut off as she shut the door behind her.

"Oh, did you ring, sir? Sorry, I'm short-handed and all the rooms are taken. You'll be lucky to find a place at this time of year but you could try—"

"I must ask you to spare me a moment, Mrs. Enderby. Police. Is there somewhere quiet we can go?"

She took in a sharp breath. For a moment she held absolutely still, then she exhaled and said, "If you're looking for him, I don't know where he is. If you've got him, you can keep him. What's he done now? Don't tell me his latest victim is below the age of consent?"

The door to the lounge bar opened and a man came out. He nodded to Alec, who recognized one of Peter Anstruther's pals from the previous evening. " 'Night, Mrs. Enderby. I'll send one of the lads first thing tomorrow to get that drain running properly."

"Thank you, Mr. Dale. Good night." As Dale stepped out into the street, she lifted the counter of the reception desk. "We'd better go through here, Officer." She led him through a door into a tiny but comfortable sitting room and lit a lamp, keeping the gas turned quite low. "Something to drink? Well, you won't mind if I do. Have a seat."

He watched as she poured herself a short gin from a bottle in a corner cabinet, filled the glass with tonic water, and took a swig. Apart from unnaturally blond hair, Nancy Enderby was good-looking, with brown eyes, naturally dark brows and lashes, and a

93

minimum of cosmetic assistance—carmine lips and a dab of powder on the nose. Her artificial silk frock was tight-fitting but the neckline suggested a compromise between the barmaid and the business-woman. She sank wearily into the nearest chair, and Alec sat down.

"My name is Fletcher. I'm afraid I have bad news."

Her unblinking stare disconcerted him. So did her words: "That depends on what you mean by bad, don't it?" When he hesitated how to respond, she went on. "It is something about George, I reckon? I obey the licensing laws, and if I didn't, Fred Puckle'd be round here like a shot wi' Ellen Hammett chivvying ahind him, not a plainclothes gentleman-copper as was drinking in the lounge last evening."

"Yes, it's your husband. He fell from a cliff. I'm sorry . . . he's dead."

She breathed a long, deep sigh. Alec thought her lips quivered momentarily, perhaps recalling the early days of courtship and marriage, then her mouth hardened and she said harshly, "Fell—or was pushed?"

"That's what I have to find out. I'll need to ask you about any enemies he may have had—"

"*May!*" she snorted.

"As well as whatever you can tell me about his movements today, and your own."

At that she gave a sour smile. "That's easy. I were right here, doing his share o' the work along o' my own."

"But first," Alec said gently, "as next-of-kin, you'll have to come along to the police station and make a positive identification of the deceased."

"If it's right now you mean, Mr. Fletcher, that's just what I can't do. I'm a working woman. I've got a good staff but they need overseeing. There's customers to be attended to." As she spoke she stood up, her mind apparently already returning to business.

Alec rose with her. "That's all right, Mrs. Enderby. Come round at closing time, and you might want to bring a friend with you."

Much better than right now, actually, he thought with relief. By half past ten, either Vernon's uncle or the police surgeon would have had a chance to prettify the battered remains of George Enderby's face.

11

As Daisy left Alec on the corner in the twilight and turned back along the quay, she was startled by a faint, despairing wail. Then she recognized the sound of a distant foghorn. The local one was silent, and stars were beginning to show in the darkening sky, but far ahead, at the mouth of the inlet, a bank of white fog lurked like—in Belinda's words—a cat waiting to pounce.

And like a cat, the law was waiting to pounce on Peter Anstruther. Things looked black for him, though at least Alec would make sure all possible suspects were given due consideration.

Daisy hadn't told him what she had heard when she and the girls returned to the house after reporting the "accident" to Constable Puckle. They had entered by the back door. The kitchen door was ajar, and from within came Anstruther's sombre voice.

"What's done is done, Cecily," he said. "It's no good crying over spilt milk."

Hurrying the girls past, Daisy had heard no more. She didn't know if he was referring to Cecily's fall from grace or Enderby's fall from the cliff, but she did know the police were bound to put the worst possible construction on his words.

She could only hope he had an unimpeachable alibi, one not provided by his wife.

Baskin, on the other hand, with his solitary tramping habits, was most unlikely to have an alibi. Alec said he had been up on the cliffs, not off across the inlet or wherever else his wanderings took him. If only she knew what had prompted his interest in the Enderbys! Would he reveal all to Alec, or would he try to keep the secret that wasn't his to tell? Whatever it was, the police would ferret it out sooner or later. But might he not find it easier, given a little encouragement, to confide in Daisy?

Climbing the steps to the garden, she chided herself. She mustn't give Alec any justification for accusing her of meddling. In fact, perhaps she ought rather to take the girls away. Sakari wouldn't be pleased to hear her daughter was staying in a house with two men suspected of murder.

There was no need to upset Sakari by telling her, though. After all, Daisy had every intention of keeping the girls in ignorance. And being a witness of sorts, she ought to stay within reach of the investigation.

Mind made up, she went into the house. The kitchen door was closed, so she knocked and peeked in. Cecily Anstruther was stirring something on the stove. Her husband, in his shirt-sleeves at the table, stood when he saw Daisy. They both smiled at her.

"Mmm, that smells good. Don't get up, Mr. Anstruther. I just wanted to make sure my message reached you."

"Sandwiches for Mr. Fletcher? Yes, that's all right. I'll leave them on the table in the dining room if he's very late."

"Thanks awfully." Daisy ignored the curiosity in both faces. "I hope the weather's not going to change again. There's a terrific mass of fog sitting out there on the sea."

"I shouldn't worry, Mrs. Fletcher," said Anstruther. He seemed quite calm and contented, not at all like a man who has just pushed another man off a cliff. Or perhaps it was the tranquil satisfaction of a job well done. He had not been around when Cecily was packing up the picnic tea, Daisy recalled. "The fog sometimes lies out there for days without ever coming up the inlet, though at this time of year it'll likely be gone by morning."

96

"I hope so." Daisy wondered whether to suggest that the Anstruthers dine with her and Baskin, but Baskin was more likely to talk freely if they were alone together. "Time I was getting those girls to bed."

Anstruther grinned. "Baskin's entertaining them, and having a grand time by the looks of it. Says he's never had much to do with female children, except for his sister. He claims their minds are fascinatingly different from the little boys he schoolmasters."

"I shouldn't wonder," said his wife, "and a very good thing, too. They're in the sitting room, Mrs. Fletcher."

Daisy found the three sitting on the floor of the pleasant room with its faded chintzes and gleaming wood. They were studying an Ordnance Survey map of the area. Belinda jumped up and ran to hug her.

"Mummy, Mr. Baskin saw Sid's house." As she spoke, Bel guided Daisy to an easy-chair, settled her in it, and fetched a footstool. "He showed us on the map. He talked to him and he says he's really quite clever."

"It's remarkable what he manages to convey without speech and, as far as I can gather, without any sort of education, scarcely even what you might call an upbringing. His house, too, though it's no more than a shack, seems very soundly constructed, entirely out of bits and pieces he finds on the beach. I found him working on a sort of lean-to shed at the side, to keep his cart in."

"Poor chap." Daisy was really more interested in the fact that Baskin seemed more relaxed and cheerful than he had since he started asking questions about Enderby. "What a pity most people don't take the trouble to communicate with him."

"I mentioned—didn't I?—that a friend of mine in London teaches the deaf and dumb. I believe Sid is quite bright enough to learn standard sign language, perhaps to read and write, as well."

"But do you think he could be happy away from his home, from the sea and people and places he knows?"

"He's afraid of that horrid policeman, Mummy."

"That's why we haven't seen him since he fetched his cart," Deva explained. "Mr. Baskin found out Sid won't come down to West-combe any longer. So he might as well go to London, don't you think?"

"He could always come back," said Baskin. "I'd be quite prepared to pay his fare if necessary. This is such a beautiful part of the country, I wouldn't blame him for missing it."

"Mrs. Fletcher, Mr. Baskin showed us on the map where he went today, up the little stream that comes down to the beach, the one we dammed? It sounds just like Ratty's river in *The Wind in the Willows*. Bel and I would like to explore it tomorrow. May we, please?"

"It's a bit of a scramble." Baskin eyed Daisy doubtfully. She wondered if the girls had told him she was pregnant. Surely they realized it wasn't something to be chattered about. "But of course you'll have Mr. Fletcher with you."

"I'm afraid my husband's going to be rather busy tomorrow. It'll have to wait, Deva."

"Well, if you wouldn't mind entrusting them to me . . . I'm a Boy Scout leader, you know, and would take good care of them."

"That's very kind of you, Mr. Baskin, but won't you want to be going on one of your long hikes?"

"As a matter of fact, I had been thinking of leaving this morning. I've done what I came . . . That is, I've covered most of the country hereabouts. But another day is neither here nor there. The stream is very pretty and full of creatures I didn't take the time to investigate."

Deva looked as if the mention of "creatures" was going to change her mind, but Bel said enthusiastically, "Oh, it would be such fun, Mummy."

"We'll ask your father," said Daisy. Curiouser and curiouser, she thought. Baskin had been going to leave today, having done what he came for. Alec would have put a stop to his departure, at least until he had questioned him thoroughly. But what had Baskin come for, if not to make sure Enderby was the man he was after, and what had he accomplished, if not Enderby's death? Yet he was ready and willing to put off his departure just to give the girls some fun.

Perhaps he realized the police would stop him leaving openly and therefore intended to sneak out tonight and do a moonlight flit. Or perhaps he really wanted to stick around and watch the course of the investigation. Criminals often did, Alec had told Daisy, and often it was what got them caught.

"Bedtime, girls," she said. "You may read in bed. I'll come up after dinner to turn out the lights. Don't forget to brush your teeth."

She went to the downstairs lavatory to wash her hands and tidy her hair. No need to change—Baskin had not brought a dinner-jacket and Alec had made quite plain that he absolutely refused to have anything to do with stiff collars while on holiday. Then she re-joined Baskin in the dining room.

The maid brought in the soup. Looking at her with a new eye, Daisy decided she would be absolutely hopeless at giving anyone an alibi or reporting overheard conversations.

A plump, fair, pink-faced farm-girl of sixteen or seventeen, Vera was an efficient, hardworking housemaid and passable parlour-maid. However, she worked like a well-oiled machine, her head in Holly-wood. She lived for her weekly day off. She spent Wednesday morn-ings and early afternoons at home on the farm, but late afternoons and evenings were dedicated to the picture-palace in Abbotsford, where she managed to fit in two shows before the last ferry back to Westcombe.

Though a question connected with her duties usually elicited an adequate response, trying to engage her in conversation was point-less. She would half-emerge from her dream, only to go into rap-tures over Rudolf Valentino or John Barrymore.

Daisy had long given up any attempt at friendly chat. Now she gave up hope of Vera as a witness.

The maid served them and departed. Daisy tasted the soup, fresh green pea with just the right amount of mint—delicious.

"Your husband's not home yet?" Baskin enquired. "The police are keeping him rather a long time."

"I dare say there are formalities to go through," Daisy said vaguely, trying to avoid awkward questions which might lead to a premature disclosure of Alec's profession. "Especially as Enderby wasn't exactly popular in certain quarters. You weren't terribly keen on him yourself, were you?"

"I?" Voice and face were guarded. "I never spoke to him except to order a pint. That business in the pub last night suggests he was a rotter, doesn't it? Unless, of course, Anstruther went off the deep end over nothing but rumour. He seems on very good terms with his wife now."

"He's a frightfully nice chap."

"Yes. Yes, he is a good fellow. I suppose they'll have an inquest."

"Alec will have to tell the coroner about finding the body." Botheration, she thought, she hadn't meant to display her familiarity with the legal requirements following unnatural death. "I've read a few detective stories," she explained.

"So have I." He grinned. "I'm constantly confiscating Sexton Blake from my boys. For myself, I'd rather see them reading those than nothing, but my headmaster has other ideas."

"Oh, your pupils, of course. You're a bit young to have children old enough to read Sexton Blake, but when you said 'my boys' I thought for a moment maybe you had sons."

"Not I. I'm not married and I live in the school. We have both day-boys and weekly boarders who go home at the weekends."

Daisy nearly asked whether he had nieces or nephews, as a way of finding out whether his sister was married. She decided regretfully that such probing into his family on short acquaintance would be unforgivably ill-bred, worthy of Mrs. Hammett.

Baskin took a last spoonful of soup and changed the subject. "What a wonderful cook Mrs. Anstruther is. These holiday boarding-houses usually feed one on tinned soup, fat mutton and cabbage boiled till it's grey, just like at school."

Vera came in with crisply breadcrumbed fillets of Dover sole and went out with the soup plates. Thoughtfully, Daisy squeezed lemon juice on her fish. So Baskin had no wife for Enderby to have seduced. The sister was a possibility, though. He had spoken of her several times without mentioning a husband. Assuming she was single, he might have come to Westcombe hoping to force Enderby to marry her.

How had he known Enderby was here?

Daisy recalled his saying Mrs. Anstruther's had been recommended to him. And the friend who gave the recommendation had mentioned the Schooner. Now just suppose the friend had known that Baskin had a bone to pick with one George Enderby, and coming across a man by that name had passed on the information. Then Baskin had come down to check whether it was the right man, and if so, to deal with him.

It wasn't the sort of thing either Baskin or his sister were likely to have talked about to anyone else, though, Daisy thought, eating absent-mindedly.

But the friend need not have known exactly what Baskin's quarrel with Enderby was. Or perhaps he had been courting Miss Baskin and knew the whole story. No, in that case he would have taken his own revenge instead of calling in her brother, wouldn't he?

How complicated it all was! Daisy realized crossly that her sole had disappeared without her tasting a morsel and she hadn't even come to any conclusion. She might just as well have wasted brainpower on the young woman she had seen in the street—the one who had looked so upset when Nancy Enderby was accusing George of multiple affairs—or the unidentified farmer's daughter who was apparently his latest love.

The friends and relatives of both women must be considered suspects. Beyond that fact, Daisy knew precisely nothing about either of them. However, she was acquainted with someone who probably knew all there was to know. Could she bring herself to call upon the abominable Mrs. Hammett?

12

When Alec returned from the inn to the police station, the small front room was so crammed with people he could only just open the door and squeeze in. At least three conversations were taking place, all in raised voices to be heard over each other. He stood there for a moment, leaning against the door, gathering his energy to make his presence known.

Young Vernon had retained his place at the high desk. Catching sight of Alec above the massed heads, he banged on it with his fist and cried, "Here's Detective Chief Inspector Fletcher of Scotland Yard!"

Silence fell. The burly backs in constabular blue that were blocking Alec's way parted like the Red Sea. As Alec stepped forward, a small, balding plainclothes man in black moved to meet him. At least, he wasn't really small, only seeming so in comparison with the outsize officers he had brought with him, but he stooped slightly, which added to the impression. He looked like an elderly, amiable vicar. For a moment Alec wondered if he was in fact the incumbent of the parish, come to pray over the remains of his unsatisfactory parishioner.

"Inspector Mallow, sir," he said with a benign smile, "Devonshire CID. I'm here to give you whatever assistance you require. Our police surgeon has come too, of course. This is Dr. Wedderburn, from Abbotsford." He indicated a man lounging at the table, who nodded. "And this gentleman is Dr. Vernon, the local GP, who has kindly come to give us the benefit of his expertise." He beamed at both doctors impartially.

Young Vernon's uncle was as short and slight as his nephew, but his bearing was military—Army Medical Corps, Alec thought. "You don't need me," he said gruffly, "since Wedderburn's here." The scowl he aimed at the police surgeon suggested a fierce disapproval. "Come along, Andrew, we'll be off."

"I have to stay, Uncle." Vernon sent a pleading glance Alec's way. "Mr. Fletcher might have questions about my report."

Alec succumbed to the plea. "We'd appreciate Mr. Vernon staying a little longer, sir. Thank you very much for turning out tonight. I may have to consult you later about the medical history of the deceased."

"Enderby was not a patient of mine, sir. As far as I know, he enjoyed the rudest of good health."

"Well, that's worth knowing. Thanks, Dr. Vernon."

"Good night." With a stiff little bow, the doctor stalked out.

Given his small stature, his departure barely eased the crowding. "First things first," said Alec. "We need room to breathe. Any suggestions, Puckle? We don't want to drive your wife out of house and home."

"Ah," said Puckle ruminatively. The monosyllable reminded Alec of Tom Tring, but an "Ah" from Tom meant his brain was buzzing along at a great rate and Alec doubted the same applied to Puckle.

"The parish hall, I should think," said Vernon, bouncing down from his high chair. "I'll go and ask the vicar."

"No, I want you to go out to the washhouse with Dr. Wedderburn."

Vernon turned rather pale but said steadily, "Right-oh, sir." He took the "wash'se" key from Puckle.

"Doctor, the wife of the deceased is coming at about half past ten to identify the body. I'd appreciate your having him as much as possible in a fit state to be looked at, even if you haven't finished your preliminary examination."

The police surgeon nodded silently and hauled himself to his feet. As he passed, Alec smelt whisky on his breath. Was that why Dr. Vernon so obviously disapproved of him? Perhaps it would have been wise to retain the GP's services. Frowning, he watched Wedderburn and young Vernon go out through the back of the house.

Next, he sent Puckle to ask the vicar's permission to use the parish hall and to rouse out the sexton to unlock it and light the lamps. Then he turned to the inspector.

"Thank you for your patience, Mr. Mallow."

"Not to worry, sir. You've cleared the decks, nicely, if I may say so." He lowered his voice. "I noticed as you wasn't too happy about the doctor, sir. He's all right. The Jerries shelled his Red Cross tent in the Salient, right in the middle of cutting off some poor chap's arm, and now he needs a bracer before he tackles anything in the way of a mangled body. Give him a rheumaticky old woman or a kiddy with the measles and he don't turn a hair, and that's what he mostly has to deal with, after all. We don't get too many mangled bodies down here."

"I see."

"Leastways, when we do, they've mostly been in the sea for a while, and after a good dousing they don't seem to bother Dr. Wedderburn." He beckoned forward a plainclothes man Alec hadn't noticed in the crush. "This is my sergeant, Horrocks, sir. My left-hand-man, I always say, being left-handed. And the super had me bring these two constables in case you might need 'em."

"I may. I don't know much about what's going on at this early stage, but let me put you and Sergeant Horrocks in the picture."

Alec waved the inspector to a chair. Horrocks, a young man who looked more like a farmer than a police detective, perched uncomfortably on the windowsill and took out his notebook. The uniformed constables retired to the nearest thing to a discreet distance possible in the small room, behind the high desk.

104

Even stripped of theories, Alec's story was comprehensive enough to earn Detective Inspector Mallow's admiration.

"Well, sir," he said, "it looks to me like you knew who done it before it even happened. All you've left for us is to put this Anstruther chap behind bars."

Suspecting mockery, Alec gave him a hard look but, at least by the murky light, his eyes were as guileless as Daisy's. As *misleadingly* guileless? No doubt he'd find out in the course of the investigation.

"Not so fast," he said. "It may come to that, but for all I know, Anstruther spent the afternoon pouring out his soul to the vicar. There are other people with reason enough to wish Enderby to the devil. His wife, for instance. Mrs. Enderby was present when Anstruther went for him in the pub, and I can vouch for it that she didn't look as if she was prepared to lift a finger to save him from strangling."

"Do you reckon she already knew, then, sir? About him straying, I mean."

"Perhaps not about Mrs. Anstruther specifically, but she certainly knew he had mistresses. The two of them had a row about it the other day, in the course of which she mentioned a farmer's daughter."

"Why, he was a regular rake!" DS Horrocks muttered. "I wouldn't blame anyone as done him in."

"Now, now, Horrocks," Mallow said soothingly, "it's your bounden duty to take up them as pushes people over cliffs, without fear nor favour."

"And so I will, sir." Pencil poised over his notebook, Horrocks demonstrated his zeal: "What's this farmer's name, sir?"

"I don't know," Alec said irritably. "I arrived in Westcombe just yesterday and I haven't had a moment to talk to people since I found the body. Here's another name for you, though—Donald Baskin. He's a visitor here and he's been making enquiries about the Enderbys."

"If you don't mind me saying so, sir," said Mallow, "you've already found out a wonderful lot, considering. It's a pleasure to see how Scotland Yard works."

Alec simply couldn't make out if the saintly-looking inspector was being sarcastic, or if, unlike most of his provincial brethren, he genuinely admired Scotland Yard and appreciated the chance to work with a Met detective. In any case, Alec was not going to accept credit where no credit was due. "My wife has been here for a week and happens to have come across a few snippets of information which may prove useful."

"Very handy, sir. Gives us somewhere to start."

"Yes. We must also take Enderby's past into account. Puckle informs me that he arrived in Westcombe only three years ago, with a woman claiming to be his sister. Gossip says their relations were not such as ought to exist between siblings. I don't know if she left him or he dropped her when he took up with the lady-innkeeper. It's a long shot, but it's always possible that affair had some connection with his death."

"Hard to trace her when we don't know her real name," Mallow observed, "and after three years, too. But there, I expect the Yard does it every day."

"Not infrequently. Unless Enderby also was using a false name, it shouldn't be too difficult. It's not as if he was a John Smith. But first we'll find out if the rumour has any basis. I don't want to trouble Mrs. Enderby with a question of that sort if we don't have to. Horrocks, how do you get on with chamber-maids?"

"Not bad, sir. If they're young, you make up to 'em, and if they're old, you let 'em mother you."

"You'll go far, Sergeant. As soon as Mrs. Enderby arrives to identify the deceased, go over to the Schooner Inn." He wouldn't have had to explain what he wanted to Tring. "Most important is to find out where she was between two and four this afternoon. Pick up any gossip about Enderby, especially the identity of the farmer's daughter and any other females he may have made the object of his affections, but don't press for it at this stage. Make sure you talk to all the staff available and get the names and addresses of any not on the premises, including the chamber-maid of three years ago if she's left since. You've got that straight?"

"Yessir!"

"Excellent. Inspector, you'll see what Anstruther and Baskin have to say about their whereabouts this afternoon."

"I thought you'd want to take them yourself, sir, seeing you know them already."

"That's precisely why I don't, at this stage. For one thing, they don't know yet that I'm a copper. It's a damned uncomfortable situation, my staying at the Anstruthers', but I don't see any alternative at present. Which reminds me, we're going to have a hard time finding somewhere for you and your men to sleep. I wonder if the Puckles have a spare room. These village police houses usually have two bedrooms."

"Mrs. Puckle's already offered it, sir. There's a bed for me and a cot for Horrocks."

"And your constables?"

Mallow frowned around the tiny room. The floor space would cramp the slumbering form of one of the large uniformed officers, let alone two. "I suppose they'd better doss in the parish hall."

"I should think the inn might have a spare cot or two to lend," Alec suggested, "or at least some blankets. See to it, will you, Horrocks?"

"Yessir!"

Alec told the inspector how to find the Anstruthers' house and sent him off. Except for advising a close examination of Baskin's walking stick, he didn't insult him with precise instructions, trusting to his intelligence, diligence and discretion. If his trust proved misplaced, he would just have to deal with the damage and reconsider calling in Tom Tring. However, he did take the precaution of sending along one of the constables for protection, just in case Peter Anstruther should take Mallow's questioning amiss.

"I'm going to see what Dr. Wedderburn has to say," he told DS Horrocks. "Wait here to show Mrs. Enderby back there when she comes, then pop off to the Schooner. Constable . . . ?"

"Smith, sir!" PC Smith saluted sharply.

"Smith, you will wait until Puckle returns. Have him leave directions to the parish hall for the rest of us. Then take whatever useful supplies he has—paper, pens, et cetera—accompany him back to the hall, and set up tables and chairs. If you're lucky, DS Horrocks will come and fetch you to carry a couple of cots from the Schooner."

"Yes, sir, thank you, sir. Uh, sir?"

"What is it?"

"Breakfast, sir?"

"Horrocks will arrange for you to get something at the inn. Great Scott, did you all miss your supper, or tea, or whatd'youcallit?"

"No, sir." Horrocks assured him. "We stopped for a bite in Abbotsford while we were waiting for the ferry."

Alec remembered why he so disliked investigations in isolated country places: One often spent as much time and effort billeting the troops as solving the case.

He knocked on the door at the back.

"Come in," called Mrs. Puckle. "Oh, you've come for your bite o' fish pie, sir. You must be famished."

"I am, Mrs. Puckle, but I haven't time right now." And after reviewing the medical evidence, he'd probably have lost his appetite. "I'm sorry about all the tramping back and forth through your sitting room."

"Not to worry, sir, I married a policeman for better or worser and there's no sense fussing when your wash'se gets used for prisoners or a body. But I do hope, sir, as they won't be cutting him up back there."

"No, the post mortem will be in Abbotsford, I imagine."

"Well, that's a load off me mind, I don't mind saying. Somehow I couldn't fancy doing me laundry where they'd cut him up. Mind the clothes-line, sir."

Alec went out into the yard, ducked under the clothes-line and, by the light from the windows of the house and the washhouse, found his way to the door of the latter. As he entered, Wedderburn was washing his hands with carbolic soap at a stone sink, next to which hung a laundry copper.

"Dr. Wedderburn says I was right!" crowed young Vernon. "About Enderby being hit on the back of the neck with a piece of wood, I mean."

"Looks like it," the doctor confirmed. Brisk and businesslike, he seemed to have recovered his sang-froid. "But I can't tell whether it was the cause of death, or very shortly before or after death."

"Will the autopsy make that clear?"

"Perhaps, but I can't guarantee it. I can tell you he didn't drown, so you can take it he fell down the cliff. Practically every major bone in his body is broken. He must have received so many blows in such a short time that which impact caused his death may be impossible to determine."

"I see."

"He died between six and ten hours ago. Rigor is just beginning in the facial muscles."

"That fits. Will you . . . can you . . . ?"

"Do I perform autopsies? Yes, Chief Inspector. By the time I've done a thorough examination, anything else I do to the poor devils seems—I suppose meaningless is the word. Irrelevant. They've already lost all their dignity, their humanity even. I'll cut him up for you tomorrow if you'll let me know when you've got him to Abbotsford. And now I'm off. I won't stay to see the widow, if you don't mind."

"Have you somewhere to stay the night?"

"I motored over and will motor home. Don't worry, I'm not inebriated. Good night."

"Good night." Alec shook his hand. "And thank you."

As Wedderburn left, Alec stepped over to the table. A neatly sides-to-middled sheet had been draped over the neatly rearranged body and turned down to reveal the upper part of the face, the lower part remaining hidden. In addition, over the right side of the lower abdomen a hole had been cut in the sheet, through which an old, jagged scar was visible.

"Probably shrapnel, he said." Vernon's voice was hushed. "Not appendectomy, anyway. He said Mrs. Enderby should be able to identify it. Sir, he said I can help him with the post mortem, with your permission."

"You have it. In return, I want to ask a favour."

"Anything, sir!"

"Wait till you hear. I'd like to put you in charge of getting the body to Abbotsford."

"Gosh. Er—how? I mean, do I need a coffin? Should I take the ferry or hire a car? I mean, I can't just squish him into my little runabout, don't you know. And where—"

"It's precisely all that detail I haven't time or manpower for. Can I trust you to find out the how and where, and to accomplish the task with decency and respect?"

"Right-oh, sir," Vernon said manfully. "Just leave it to me. I'll ask Uncle Ben."

"That sounds like a good starting point. Keep a note of any reasonable expenses and I'll see you're reimbursed. Thank you. You'd better hop it now, before Mrs. Enderby arrives."

A good lad, Alec thought. Perhaps he actually would become a second, non-fictional Dr. Thorndyke.

Alone at last, with a few minutes to think, Alec found his mind dwelling on Mrs. Puckle's fish pie. If he went asking for it now, Mrs. Enderby was sure to arrive when he had his mouth full. He should have eaten the tea provided by Mrs. Anstruther, but though he had drunk from the Thermos, it had not seemed decent to consume buttered scones and fruitcake while mounting vigil over the remains of George Enderby.

What had he done with his knapsack? He remembered taking it off as he approached the police station, entering with it dangling from his hand. He must have set it down on the floor somewhere. The camera was in it, with the photographs which might or might not prove useful. He'd have to get them developed in the morning. Was there a photographer or a developing chemist in Westcombe? If not, he'd ask Vernon to take the film to Abbotsford. Making a mental note—one among dozens—he wished he had DC Ernie Piper at his elbow with his notebook and his endless supply of freshly sharpened pencils.

Alec's reflections on the quickest way to discover the identity of the farmer's daughter were interrupted by a knock on the washhouse door. PC Smith ushered in Mrs. Enderby.

The proprietress of the Schooner Inn had not taken the time to change out of her working frock, but she had tied a dark scarf over her flamboyant hair. Though her face was calm, Alec noticed her hands were clenched together tightly enough to whiten the knuckles. Considering the errand she had come on, he didn't read anything into this sign of tension.

"I'm sorry to have to ask you to do this, Mrs. Enderby."

"For God's sake, let's get it over with." She moved towards the head of the table, but her attention was caught by the neat hole cut in the sheet. She stared down and one hand went to her mouth. "Oh, my God! It's him. I was sure he'd turn up again like a bad penny, but that's the scar he got when he copped a packet at Wipers."

"You're quite certain?"

"I'd reckernize it anywhere. He didn't like talking about it, but I used to tease him that he got hit by lightning, not the Jerries. 'Cause of the shape, see?" Two steps took her to the half-concealed head. "Georgie!"

She reached out to pull down the sheet but Alec had expected the move and caught her arm. "Don't," he said gently. "You don't want to see any more."

"Georgie!" Her voice came from a tight throat and tears glinted in her eyes. "I loved the bastard once, you know? Oh, he was a charmer, a smooth talker. And he helped me get the Schooner into shape, I'll give him that. If only . . ."

Alec handed over his handkerchief. He usually carried a spare when on a case, but this afternoon he'd set out for a peaceful walk and a picnic tea, dammit!

111

Dabbing at her eyes, Mrs. Enderby turned away with a forlorn little sniff. "You want me to sign something, Mr. Fletcher? Saying it's him?"

"If you please." He opened the door and held it as she passed, high heels clicking on the flagstones. "It might enable you to avoid giving evidence of identity at the inquest, though I can't promise. Mind the clothes-line. You'll have to attend anyway, in case the coroner wants to speak to you. I've a number of questions to put to you, but I won't trouble you tonight. What would be a good time for me to call in the morning?"

The business-woman was back in control. "Breakfast eight to nine, there's always a few lazy buggers come down at the last minute so call it ha' past. Opening's half eleven. Come round about ten, all right?"

A few minutes later Alec was at last alone in the police station. His knapsack was under the table. Taking out the camera, he hesitated over the wax paper–wrapped picnic tea. If he started to eat, Mrs. Puckle was bound to come in with the promised pie and she might be offended to find him guzzling Mrs. Anstruther's provisions. He couldn't afford to have the Puckles upset with him. The constable might not be the brightest star in the firmament but at least he was willing.

Stomach rumbling, Alec sat down at the table with a pile of blank paper and the wooden pen with the scratchy steel nib that had given Vernon such trouble. As he started to put his thoughts in order, Mrs. Puckle brought him a huge helping of slightly dried-out fish pie topped with crisped mashed potato, accompanied by a generous heap of buttered green beans, and a pint mug of tea.

"Bless you!" said Alec.

B

Daisy kissed the girls good night, turned out their light, and went back downstairs. Baskin had his two-inch Ordnance Survey map spread out again.

"I thought I'd show you where I went today, Mrs. Fletcher." He turned up a couple of lamps. "You'll see that if you let the girls go up the stream with me, I shan't take them very far. As the crow flies, it's about a mile and a quarter to the head-spring. The stream winds around a bit, of course, and as I said, it's quite a scramble in places, so we might not get so far."

Studying the map, Daisy said, "It looks to me as if I could walk that way by these lanes. And there are three bridges upstream where I could meet you to see how much farther you intend to go."

Baskin grinned. "The lanes are farm tracks and two of the bridges are water-splashes, but that sounds like a good idea."

"Where did you go today after you reached the source of the stream?"

"By farm tracks and footpaths, this way to the mouth of this river." With a propelling pencil as pointer, he indicated his route across the peninsula. "The River Avon, you see, one of many such. Did you know *Avon*, or *Afon*, is the Celtic word for river?"

113

"No, is it?"

"Sorry! The schoolmaster escapes my control now and then. I got there in time to have a pint with my lunch, at the Ferries Inn, then took the ferry across and back, just because I like ferries. Then back along the coast."

"Gosh, that's quite a walk!" Daisy didn't see how he could possibly have reached the cliff-top in time to push Enderby off before she and Alec and the girls arrived on the scene.

"Farther than it looks, actually. Not infrequently one starts along what looks like a well-trodden footpath, only to have it fade out. Or a farmer who dislikes hikers will plough over what should be a public right-of-way. As a matter of fact, I'm a member of the Commons and Footpaths Preservation Society, and I shall report to them. Then, there's a marshy bit that didn't help, down here by this stream I had to cross. I did quite a bit of backtracking."

Mrs. Anstruther brought in coffee. She leant over the table, saying, "Do you know, I've never seen a map of this district before. At school we had maps of the British Isles and of the world, with the Empire all in red, but nothing of Devon, let alone this bit of it. Would you mind if I called Peter to have a look?"

"Do," Daisy said cordially, only too pleased to have a chance to find out where Peter Anstruther had spent his afternoon.

He came in with two mugs of coffee. "I brought yours, Ceci. It's getting cold."

Taking the cup, she thanked him with a look of love and gratitude. "Have you ever seen a map like this, Peter? Look, here's Westcombe. And here's North Sands beach, so this little black square must be our house!"

"The farthest south in the town—yes, that'll be it, won't it, Mr. Baskin?"

"I imagine so," said Baskin, smiling.

"I'm accustomed to sea charts. Though navigation is not my business, the elevation—the height above sea-level, as you might say—of points on the shore often is. But I'll be damned—"

"Peter!"

"Dashed—sorry, Mrs. Fletcher—I'll be dashed if I can make this out. Too many lines! I know the area like the back of my hand, from roaming about when I was a boy, but this don't look anything like the lanes and cliffs and fields and trees I know."

"Not like the back of your hand." Baskin resumed the role of teacher. "You see the back of your hand all at once, like the map, whereas you find your way about by means of familiar landmarks viewed individually as you come upon them. But it's just a matter of learning the conventions." He explained the contour lines, the various lines for footpaths and different grades of roads, the symbols for cliffs and woods and the marshy area in which he had been bogged down that afternoon.

Anstruther was fascinated. He pored over the map, pointing out things to Cecily.

"Where is Sid's shack, Mr. Baskin?" Daisy asked.

"Just about here, in a sheltered nook on the south side of Bolberry Down."

"There used to be a shepherd's hut there," said Anstruther. "A tumbledown stone shelter. You're talking about Sid Coleman?"

"I don't know his last name," Daisy admitted. "The beachcomber. The girls met him and were rather taken with him. Do you know his history?"

"His father was a farmer. He died a couple of years ago?" He looked at his wife.

"Nearer four, I think. He was a very old man. Sid's about my age, so his parents must have been getting on when he was born."

"His mother died when he was born and his father had no use for him. He was a brute. The older son, Alfred, has the farm now, and he's no improvement on the old man. It's amazing Sid survived his childhood. He's a harmless chap. So that's where he's living, in the old shepherd's hut?"

"He's made a good, sound cabin of it," Baskin told him, "patchwork but weatherproof, with a view out to sea."

Anstruther laughed. "A view of the sea is no treat to a sailor. I haven't been up on the cliffs in years."

To Daisy, the statement had the ring of truth, and if true, it meant Anstruther had not killed Enderby. Catching Baskin's eye, she wondered if he was thinking the same. Then she wondered whether he had brought out his map with the aim of getting Anstruther to talk about the cliffs, in hopes of obtaining clues to his guilt or innocence.

Or perhaps Baskin had been practising the story he meant to tell the police. If so, he was word-perfect and very convincing.

They all sat down to finish their coffee, and the talk turned to Anstruther's travels around the world. He and Baskin discovered a mutual acquaintance, an officer on a ship that had evacuated Baskin's Army unit from Gallipoli in '16. Anstruther's ship had taken part in the early naval attacks of the Dardanelles campaign, and they were exchanging reminiscences when someone knocked on the front door.

Alec! Daisy thought, and Alec as detective chief inspector or he would not have knocked. This was going to be a nasty shock for the Anstruthers. She wouldn't blame them—well, not much—if they threw her and the girls out into the night.

Cecily started to get up. Anstruther put his hand on her shoulder and went himself to answer the door. He came back a couple of minutes later and said with resignation, "It's a police inspector."

Not Alec. Eviction postponed.

"About last night?" Cecily asked, troubled. "Is *he* pressing charges?"

"I don't know. I was going to take him into the kitchen but he wants to speak to you, too, Baskin. Do you mind coming . . . ?"

"That's all right, sir, this'll do nicely." The inspector had followed him to the sitting room. With his black suit and kindly smile, he looked disarmingly like a parson about to pronounce a blessing, Daisy thought. But behind him loomed a uniformed constable with the inevitable notebook.

Anstruther shrugged and moved aside. He seemed worried

enough for someone facing an assault charge which would do his career no good, but not for someone facing suspicion of murder. Of course, he had had plenty of time to prepare himself for questioning. His beard made it difficult to read his expression. Daisy couldn't guess whether he knew of Enderby's death or not.

She glanced at Baskin. His face was grim. He knew the inspector had not sought him out merely as a witness to last night's assault. Whether he was more concerned for himself or for Anstruther was not apparent.

"Detective Inspector Mallow, Devonshire Constabulary," the officer introduced himself genially. He looked around the room, his gaze passing over Daisy as if he didn't see her. She tried to make herself small and invisible. He went on, "I have a—"

"It's all my fault!" cried Cecily Anstruther, jumping up. "Can't you arrest me instead of my husband?"

"Balderdash." Peter went to her and made her sit down, perching himself on the arm of her chair with a hand on her shoulder. "I lost my temper and if the blackguard wants to make trouble, I'll take my medicine."

"I'm not arresting anybody just now, madam," said Mallow in a soothing voice. "Perhaps you wouldn't mind telling me what it is you want to take the blame for?"

"Why, last night, of course." Cecily's forehead wrinkled in puzzlement. "Isn't that why you're here?"

"Not exactly. I have a few questions for the gentlemen. Mr. Anstruther, would you mind telling me where you were between two o'clock and four o'clock this afternoon?"

"This afternoon!" Cecily exclaimed. She looked up at her husband. "What happened? Peter, you didn't . . . ? He was here with me," she said fiercely to the inspector.

"I'd like Mr. Anstruther to answer for himself, if you please, madam," Mallow said, his mildness unimpaired.

"No, I didn't go and give him the thrashing he deserves, Ceci. I went to see an old friend, Inspector. He lives over near South Huish."

"I'm not familiar with this part of the county, sir. I see you have a map there. Perhaps you wouldn't mind showing me where that is."

Daisy was dying to go over with the others to the table where the map still lay spread out, but she was afraid of drawing attention to herself in case Mallow asked her to leave. He hadn't asked who she was, so she assumed he guessed she was Alec's wife. The poor man must be in quite a quandary over what to do with her.

"South Huish," said Baskin, putting his finger on the map. "I walked through the village myself, this morning."

"A matter of three or four mile," the inspector observed. "More by road. You walked there, Mr. Anstruther?"

"No, I bicycled. Borrowed a bike from a pal in the village. In Westcombe, that is. You can ask him."

"We probably will. What time did you leave?"

"I don't know. After dinner. Lunch, if you prefer."

"About quarter past two," said Cecily.

"I borrowed the bicycle in the morning, though."

"Which way did you ride?"

"I didn't go back into town. I took—let me see—" He puzzled over the map for a minute, keeping his arm around Cecily's waist. "I'm not too good at reading a map, but it must have been this lane here, to Malborough. Then this lane, it's not much more'n a farm track. After that, you can see, it gets a bit muddlesome. There are several ways you can get to the village, to South Huish, but I didn't go there anyway. He doesn't live actually in the village and I can't quite make out from the map. . . ."

"I see, sir. What time did you get to your friend's house?"

"I wasn't wearing my watch, but it must have been about three."

"No doubt your friend can confirm that."

"He wasn't there," Anstruther admitted.

"Is that so? A servant?"

"He has a daily woman from the village, who wasn't there on a Sunday, of course. At least, he used to. I haven't seen him since my last leave."

"Name and address, please."

"Paul Pritchard. Sea View Cottage, South Huish. Don't go bothering him if you don't have to, Inspector. He was rather badly shot up at Jutland. What's this all about, anyway? I've told you I didn't see him today, so I can't see you need trouble him at all."

"That's not for me to say, sir. Finding your friend out, you came straight home, I take it?"

"No, as a matter of fact I went up to the old camp."

"Camp?"

"Fort, or whatever you want to call it. It's Iron Age or Bronze Age or something. We used to go up there when I was a boy, to play Ancient Britons fighting the Roman invasion."

"But you wouldn't be playing soldiers today, sir."

"Of course not. I just wanted somewhere quiet to sit and think."

"And where exactly is this old fort?"

Anstruther stared perplexedly at the map. "I couldn't rightly say."

"Here," said Baskin, pointing. "Where it says 'Camp.' I went there the other day to take a look. Nothing left but a few mounds."

"No one about to see you, I suppose, Mr. Anstruther?"

"Not a soul. That's why I went there."

"Pity." Mallow bent over the map. "Now, Mr. Baskin, I expect you can show me on this whereabouts George Enderby went over the cliff."

"What the devil?" Anstruther gasped. "Cecily!"

Pale as a ghost, Cecily Anstruther drooped against her husband's shoulder. As he supported her to the sofa, Daisy jumped to her feet.

"Brandy?" she queried.

"In the larder. Ceci, whatever he's talking about, I had nothing to do with it, I swear it."

Hurrying to the door, Daisy noted that Inspector Mallow, having dropped his bomb, was watching the Anstruthers with the same benign air with which he had arrived. The Marsh Mallow, she recalled from youthful adventures on the banks of the upper Severn, is a pretty, innocuous-appearing flower that tempts one into the bog.

119

She found the brandy and a tumbler. Shock—tea and hot-water bottles, she decided, and she paused to fill the kettle and set it on the hot plate of the big black-iron range before speeding back to the sitting room.

The inspector was peering at the map, but Daisy could practically see his ears cocked like a dog's to catch any words uttered by the Anstruthers. Peter knelt on the floor beside his wife, holding her hands. She lay back against a cushion, still horridly pale and limp. Without rising, Peter took the glass Daisy held out, with half an inch of brandy in it.

"Thanks, Mrs. Fletcher. Ceci, my dear, take a sip. There, that's better. And a little more," he urged.

A faint colour tinged Cecily's cheeks. "Peter, is he dead?" she whispered.

"That rather depends on whereabouts he fell, which Baskin seems to know."

Baskin came over. "I happened to be passing as the lifeboat was taking off the body—yes, he's dead. I stopped to watch and met Fletcher when he came up the cliff."

"Alec discovered the body," said Daisy. "I'm sorry I didn't tell you, but it was rather an awkward subject to broach after . . ."

"After last night," said Anstruther sombrely. "I don't blame you. But I didn't push him. I wasn't anywhere near the cliffs."

"It looks to me," said Inspector Mallow, appearing among them map in hand, "as if this here lane goes within a couple of hundred yards of the cliff path. And even if you was to set out on the other lane, the one you so kindly showed me, Mr. Anstruther, and went all round about this-a-way, on your bicycle, you could easily have reached the cliff-top in plenty of time to meet the deceased."

"Dammit, why should I go through all that rigmarole when I had no idea the bast—blackguard would be walking up there?"

"You might've seen him when he passed the house on his way, now, mightn't you?"

"That's quite a hill, Inspector," Baskin put in, looking at the map over the inspector's shoulder. "Here, the way you're suggesting Anstruther went round, I mean. Unless the bike he borrowed has excellent gears, he'd be pushing it up."

"No gears."

"Is that so? Well, you'd better give me the name of the chap you borrowed it from. No doubt the chief inspector will be wanting to go into all that."

"You're not in charge of the case?" asked Baskin.

"Not me. We've got a detective chief inspector from Scotland Yard right here on the spot and I can tell you, it's a proper treat seeing how he works, that's what it is." As he spoke, Mallow was looking at Daisy with a gentle, ironic smile.

At least, she now saw irony in it where before she had seen only kindliness. He wasn't leaving her much choice: If she didn't confess to Baskin and the Anstruthers now, they would have every right to be furious when they found out. "Alec's a Scotland Yard man," she revealed. "There was no reason to mention it before, and I didn't know he'd been put in charge till just now. Oh, is that the kettle whistling? I was going to make tea. It's supposed to be good for shock."

As she fled, she heard Mallow say, "Well, now, Mr. Baskin, would you be so good as to show me on this here map just where you went this afternoon?"

In the slate-shelved larder, Daisy found a canister of tea. As she turned back to the kitchen, Cecily Anstruther entered from the hall. Still pale and a bit shaky, she sat down at the table.

"I'm sorry," said Daisy, busying herself with the teapot so that she didn't have to meet Cecily's eyes. "Do you want us to leave?"

"Good heavens, no! It's not your fault we're in trouble. I'd rather have Mr. Fletcher investigating than that awful inspector." She shuddered. "Isn't there something in Shakespeare about a man who smiles all the time?"

" 'One may smile, and smile, and be a villain.' *Othello*, I think, or is it *Macbeth*? No, not *Macbeth*, no one ever smiles in *Macbeth*. Maybe *Julius Caesar*? Anyway, I know what you mean. He does rather give one the creeps, though I don't suppose he's actually a villain. Only, I bet he wouldn't have looked any further than your husband, once he heard about last night."

"Peter didn't do it. Didn't push George over. I was awfully afraid, just for a moment. But he says he didn't and I know he's telling the truth. Will . . . will Mr. Fletcher believe him?"

"I'm afraid Alec can't just go about believing people," Daisy said regretfully. "He'll have to look for clues and things. Evidence. But at least he will look very thoroughly. I doubt Mallow would be questioning Baskin, for instance, if it wasn't that I'd told Alec about all the questions he asked about Enderby. Would you like lots of sugar in your tea? I think it's good for shock."

"No, thanks." She managed a smile. "Just one teaspoon. I'm all right, really. It's just that he took me by surprise."

"The rotten beast! No, that's not fair, he has his job to do and he might have learnt something useful that way. Milk?"

"We're out, till the milkman comes in the morning. That's lovely, thank you so much. It's awfully kind of you, Mrs. Fletcher."

"I do think you might call me Daisy, if you're sure your husband doesn't want to throw us all out into the street."

"Of course not. That *would* look suspicious, as though he had something to hide, which he doesn't. I wonder why Mr. Baskin was so interested in George."

"Alec will find out." Daisy sat down at the table with her cup of tea.

"I suppose it's bound to be something to do with a woman. I can't imagine why I fell for his line, but in some ways it's a consolation to know that I wasn't the only one he fooled."

"Do you know who else was taken in?"

"Well, Nancy Pinner as was, for one. He must have told her she was the woman of his dreams, the one he'd been searching for all his life, mustn't he? Or she wouldn't have married him. I know who he moved on to after me, but I wouldn't want to tell tales on her."

"Once the police get involved, it's not telling tales, Cecily. Suppose it was . . . your successor or someone close to her who pushed

Enderby off the cliff? You may think whoever did it is a public bene-factor, but suppose it was her husband and he gets away with it, he might decide murder's easy and do her in next."

Cecily looked horrified. "Do you really think so?" she asked un-certainly.

"It happens. Besides, isn't it better if your husband is one of a host of suspects instead of the obvious scapegoat? Not so much from the point of view of the police, because Alec doesn't jump to conclu-sions, but as far as local people are concerned. If they don't catch the murderer, and can't prove for certain that your husband is innocent, there will always be people in the village who believe it was him."

"In the Navy, too, I expect. All right, I'll tell what I know. To Mr. Fletcher, not that horrible inspector."

Daisy had rather hoped that she would be the recipient of any confidences, but at least she could tell Alec she had persuaded Cecily to spill the beans. She would also tell him that she strongly disap-proved of Inspector Mallow's sneaky, underhanded tactics.

14

*A*lec crept into the house well after midnight. The light in the hall was turned down low. By its dim glow, he saw on the hall table an unlit candle and a sheet of paper headed MR. FLETCHER. He turned up the gas.

"Sandwiches in larder," the note continued in a small, neat hand. "Please lock and bolt front door and turn out gas. Cecily Anstruther. P.S. *Peter did not do it.*"

So they knew who he was. Mallow hadn't mentioned that in his oral report. Perhaps it would come out in his written report, but if not he'd have to be told that Alec expected every detail.

Of course, the Anstruthers and Baskin would inevitably have discovered his profession this morning, but Alec hoped Daisy had not been made too uncomfortable in the meantime. Probably not, he reflected. She had not been cast out into the night, and it took more than an awkward social situation to discomfort Daisy.

After Mrs. Puckle's tasty fish pie, he had no need of sandwiches. They would do for breakfast in the morning, as he had to get going before the normal breakfast hour. The door locked and bolted, he lit the candle, turned out the light, and went up to bed.

He looked in on the girls. Deva had thrown off her covers, so he pulled them up and tucked her in before turning to Belinda. As always his heart clenched with love as he gazed down on his sleeping daughter. In the months since his mother had removed herself and her Victorian strictures to Bournemouth, the last little lines of anxiety had smoothed from Bel's freckled forehead. Her mouth curved in a slight smile suggesting happy dreams. Daddy had found a body on the beach, but Mummy was not making a huge song and dance over it, as Granny would have, so why worry?

Alec kissed her cheek. She didn't stir. He went on to his and Daisy's room.

Daisy was lying on her back, the position she found most comfortable at this stage in her pregnancy. At a later stage, Alec remembered with a touch of guilt, Joan had been uncomfortable in any position. What women put up with! He was grateful that Daisy wanted to have his baby, in these days when women had a choice, almost as grateful as he was for her love and care for Belinda.

He kissed her on the nose. She stirred and murmured, "Silly nose," but didn't waken.

Grinning, he took his pyjamas and sponge-bag and headed to the bathroom. Daisy's nose wasn't at all silly. It was, in fact, a very ordinary nose, not snub, not Roman, not even the aristocratic sort of nose her birth entitled her to. It occasionally garnered a few freckles, nothing like Belinda's crop, but the summer sun had sprinkled a few that she didn't bother to cover with powder here at the seaside. He just happened to like to kiss it. What could she have been dreaming to come up with "Silly nose"?

Or had he misheard her? His grin faded as he contemplated the first substitute that sprang to mind: "Cecily knows." Whatever Mrs. Anstruther knew, he would doubtless find out. He was more concerned with the unexpected use of her christian name.

In every case Daisy had managed to get herself mixed up in, she had taken one or more of his suspects under her wing. While he didn't for a moment believe she deliberately concealed evidence tending to implicate these protégés, the fact remained that she saw them through rose-tinted spectacles. And now, unless he missed his guess, she was on christian name terms with the wife of the man he had to regard as his chief suspect.

Alec groaned.

Monday morning, waking early in spite of his late night, Alec dressed without disturbing Daisy. Then he sat down on the edge of the bed. She turned towards him. He kissed her cheek and she opened her eyes, blinking up at him.

"Good morning, love."

"Morning, darling. Morning? You're already up! What time is it?"

"Nearly seven."

"Seven! You're supposed to be on holiday . . . Oh no. Enderby."

"Enderby it is. Daisy, last night when I came in, you said, 'Cecily knows.'"

"I was asleep when you came in."

"Well, maybe you were talking in your sleep, but you still might have had a reason for those words."

"'Cecily knows'? Oh yes, Cecily knows who followed her in Enderby's affections. If affections is the right word, which I rather doubt."

"Who?"

"She didn't tell me, and she refused to tell Inspector Mallow, after the way he behaved. I must say I don't care for Mallow, darling. He looks so frightfully saintly, and then he drops a bomb and goes on looking saintly."

"A bomb?" Alec was interested in her view of the inspector.

"The Anstruthers thought he'd come about Saturday night, till he started asking about yesterday. Cecily assumed Enderby had been assaulted again and was afraid Anstruther had done it. And then Mallow mentioned quite casually, with no attempt to break it gently, that Enderby had gone over a cliff, whereupon Cecily fainted."

Alec frowned. "I can see why she wouldn't confide in him, then. But surely she must realize that widening the field of suspects can only help Anstruther."

126

"That's what I told her. She's willing to give *you* the name."

"Did you reveal my secret identity, or was it Mallow?"

"Mallow practically forced me to. At least, he deliberately put me in a position where if I hadn't, they'd have had every right to be shirty when they found out. That man has a very misleading exterior!"

"So it would seem. I'll have to keep an eye on him. Antagonizing a witness is sometimes unavoidable and occasionally useful, but the Anstruthers appeared to be cooperating—there was no call to go upsetting them unnecessarily. What about Baskin? He knew Enderby was dead, of course, but not that I'm a CID man."

"I was too concerned for Cecily to notice his reactions, but at the very least he'll be wary of the inspector after seeing the way he broke the news to the Anstruthers."

"Mallow may have had his reasons. I'll have to see if he explains himself in his written report, and if not I'll try to think up a way to ask him without giving you away as a tale-bearer."

"Beast! After I persuaded Cecily that revealing the name of her successor to the police didn't count as tale-bearing!"

Alec grinned. "Thanks, love. I'm off now." He stood up.

"Darling, is it all right if the girls go exploring the stream with Baskin this morning?"

"Do you think that's a good idea?" he asked doubtfully. Mallow had reported the hiker's staff undamaged, no sign of splintering, but that didn't let him out. "He's on my list of suspects."

"If he pushed Enderby over I'm sure he had an excellent reason, which has nothing whatsoever to do with Bel and Deva. They're frightfully keen. He's good with children. Besides, I'll walk up the lane and meet them at intervals. I shan't be far away."

"In that case, I don't see why not. Don't overtire yourself."

"I shan't. I'm going straight back to sleep now."

Downstairs, Alec found the Anstruthers and their maid already at breakfast in the kitchen. Cecily was pale and heavy-eyed as though she had not slept well, if at all. Anstruther's eyes looked more wary than tired. A sailor learns to catch his sleep when he can, whatever the circumstances, especially in wartime. He was jacketless, shirt-sleeves rolled up to the elbow exposing muscular arms with a tattoo of a twisted rope and anchor on his left wrist, a musical stave around the right. St. Cecilia was the patron saint of music, Alec remembered. Someone—Purcell?—wrote an ode to her.

"Good morning, *Chief Inspector*," Anstruther said dryly.

"Sorry about that. There was no point telling you as long as I had some hope of not being dragged in."

"Dragged in? Baskin says you found the . . . Enderby."

"Yes, but I hoped to get away with being called as a witness at the inquest. No such luck."

"That inspector of yours—"

"Peter, let Mr. Fletcher be. He didn't choose to have his holiday spoilt. Mr. Fletcher, you didn't eat your sandwiches last night."

"It was very kind of you to make them for me. Mrs. Puckle gave me something to eat, so I thought I'd save them for breakfast."

"Good gracious, no, all curled up at the edges as they are! I'll have bacon and eggs ready for you in just a moment, if you don't mind setting yourself down in here. Peter, pour Mr. Fletcher some coffee."

Whether she was motivated by hospitality or a desire to curry favour with the police, Alec didn't feel it incumbent upon him to refuse. He did say as he sat down, "I have a few questions for each of you, but most of them can wait till later."

"Long as you don't go springing any more nasty shocks on Cecily, like that Inspector Mallow did," Anstruther said truculently. "Seeing you were in the Schooner Saturday, we've nothing to hide."

"I'm glad to hear it. As I recall, you told the inspector you left here at about quarter past two yesterday afternoon. Is that correct?"

"I didn't notice the time. That's what Cecily said. It was right after dinner."

"That's about right," said Mrs. Anstruther, breaking a large brown egg into the sizzling frying-pan. "Sunday dinnertime for guests is one o'clock, same as weekday lunch, and we ate after you finished. In fact, I remember glancing at the clock when Vera took the dishes into

128

the scullery to wash up, and thinking it was time I started making your picnic tea."

Alec looked at the maid, who had continued to eat with no sign of hearing a word, lost in a world of her own. "No doubt Vera will be able to confirm the time."

The Anstruthers glanced at each other and laughed. "Not likely," Cecily said. "The only time Vera notices is what o'clock the pictures begin at the cinema in Abbotsford on her day off."

"Twenty past five, *The Thief of Bagdad*," said Vera reverently, "with Douglas Fairbanks. Last week I saw—"

"That will do, Vera. If you've finished your breakfast, go and sweep the hall, please. You see, Mr. Fletcher?"

"I do. We'll call it two fifteen. Enderby seems to have left the Schooner at roughly the same time."

"Can't have," Anstruther protested. "Sunday midday closing time is half past."

"And Nancy's busy with dinner for residents," said his wife. "She can't tend the bars too."

"Enderby left the bars untended. I gather Sunday midday is a slow time, so presumably he felt he wouldn't be missed. At least, I assume he wouldn't have walked out if customers were present. A couple came in at twenty past and found no one there. When they called for service, Mrs. Enderby discovered he was gone."

"Poor Nancy! That must have been the last straw."

"She wasn't happy," Alec confirmed, "especially as he also wasn't there to do his share of cleaning up, of course. I'm surprised you didn't see him coming this way, Mr. Anstruther."

"Even if I'd cycled into town, I might easily have missed him if I'd gone by the lane and him by the path. But I didn't go that way, as I told the inspector. I turned left outside the front door and went by the back lane to Malborough. I can show you on Baskin's map. Or, come to think of it, we could just step out of the door and I'll point it out."

"I may ask you to, later. Inspector Mallow had some difficulty explaining your route on Puckle's map of his district. Did you meet or see anyone on your way?"

"There was a motor-car passed me."

"I don't suppose you remember the number plate?"

"I had other things on my mind. Couldn't even tell you the make—I don't know much about 'em—but it was one of those little sports cars, two-seater, pale blue, I think, or grey."

"That's not much to go on, I'm afraid. Whereabouts were you when you saw it?"

He shrugged. "I don't recall exactly. Nearly to Malborough, I reckon."

"No one else who might have seen you? In Malborough, perhaps?"

"Not that I noticed. You don't get many people wandering about the streets of a small country town in the middle of a Sunday afternoon."

"No. Well, if it was a local car, we may be able to trace it." Alec paused as Mrs. Anstruther set before him a brimming plate and a toast-rack. "Ah, thank you!"

Anstruther passed the butter. "If there's nothing else, Mr. Fletcher, I'll go fill the coal-scuttle."

"Nothing else for the present. There will be more later, I'm afraid, but I want you to know you're by no means the only person we're investigating."

"Thank heaven for small mercies," Anstruther said sourly and went out with the empty scuttle.

Mrs. Anstruther sat down opposite Alec. "Did Mrs. Fletcher— Daisy—tell you?"

"She said you had some information for me."

"It doesn't seem right, talking about someone else's trouble, when I'd have given anything to keep my own secret."

"Do you know how people found out about you and Enderby?"

"I suppose someone saw him coming in here, though this is the last house in the village and he always came late at night, after closing time."

"If such precautions failed, I doubt very much that the name you're going to give me is any more secret. How did you discover it?"

"He told me," she said bitterly. "George. 'We've had a good time,' he said, 'but all good things come to an end. Rita Stebbins is a common little piece but she doesn't have your old-fashioned scruples so she's more fun.' There, now you know."

"Rita Stebbins. Tom's wife?"

"You know him?"

"He was one of the lifeboatmen who came to take off the body," Alec said noncommittally. It was true, as far as it went, but what he remembered was Tom Stebbins losing to Peter Anstruther at skittles and getting his revenge by blowing the gaff on Cecily and Enderby.

Or did Stebbins have a double purpose? Could he have hoped for revenge for his wife's unfaithfulness without risk to himself, by inciting Anstruther to attack Enderby?

Alec very much wanted a word with Thomas Stebbins.

Anstruther returned with the full coal-scuttle. Alec finished his last mouthful of breakfast, advised the couple to leave word at the parish hall if they went anywhere farther than into the village, and went out into the entrance hall. There he was waylaid by Belinda and Deva.

"Mr. Fletcher, may we explore the stream with Mr. Baskin this morning?"

"We'd much rather go with you, Daddy, but Mummy said you're going to be busy. Because of the dead man. What a pity you found him!"

Much as he deplored his daughter's casual attitude towards the violent death of a fellow human being, Alec could only be relieved that the girls were not shocked or frightened. "Yes, you may go with Mr. Baskin. I'm sorry I can't go too. They've put me in charge of the investigation."

"That's because they know you're the best detective," said Bel, "but it's not fair. You must make them give you another holiday instead."

"I will. Now, if Mr. Baskin's changed his mind, you're not to make a fuss."

"That's what Mrs. Fletcher said," sighed Deva. "Grown-ups shouldn't say they'll do something and then not do it."

"Sometimes it can't be helped. Believe me, I wouldn't be off to work now if I had any choice in the matter!"

15

*D*escending the steps to the track, Alec glanced to the south towards the mouth of the inlet. The bank of fog had dissipated, but
clouds were blowing in from the south-west. Rain would make
searching the cliff-top almost as difficult and dangerous as fog. The
sooner he sent his men out, the better. The search ought to have
been accomplished yesterday, and he could only blame his own reluctance to take charge.

He turned towards the village and quickened his stride.

Few people were about as yet. Most of those Alec saw ignored
him, but two or three eyed him curiously. If he knew anything about
small towns, it wouldn't be long before he couldn't walk through the
streets without everyone staring and whispering.

The parish hall was revealed by daylight as a shabby, weather-
boarded building in need of a coat of paint. As he approached, a figure rose from the front step and came eagerly to meet him: Andrew
Vernon.

"Good morning, sir! I've been waiting for you. They won't let
me in."

"Quite right, too."

His face fell. "Oh, I say, sir! You're not going to shut me out now,
after I made all the arrangements for a hearse to pick up the body?

It's on its way to Abbotsford now, and Dr. Wedderburn says I can attend the post mortem this afternoon."

"Thank you! Isn't that enough for you?"

"And after I battled with that pen to write a decent report for you, too! Look, my fingers are still stained with the ink the damn thing spluttered all over me. There must be something I can do to help this morning."

"Writing reports?"

"Well, if that's what you need," he said disconsolately. "At least I have my fountain pen today."

"Is that yours?" Alec indicated a small green canvas box with a shoulder-strap, in the porch of the hall.

"Yes, it's my Portable Laboratory."

"Modelled on Dr. Thorndyke's?"

"As much as I could. Freeman doesn't give all the details. Anyway, I couldn't afford a high-powered miniature microscope."

"You did a good job yesterday with your medical bag. I should think you'd better take your kit and go with Sergeant Horrocks to help to search the cliff-top."

"Really? Do you mean it?"

"If you'll follow his instructions without quibbling, and not try to teach your grandmother to suck eggs."

"I will! I won't! Gosh, thanks, sir!"

"And remember, absolutely everything you learn is confidential."

"Of course, sir. Being a policeman's sort of like being a doctor, that way, isn't it?"

They went into the hall. A couple of long trestle tables had been set up, and several of the kind of folding chairs that seem designed by someone with the most cursory knowledge of human anatomy. On one table lay two unused notebooks, a dozen sheets of official writing-paper, three envelopes, four paperclips, an eraser, half a dozen pencils, a bottle of blue-black ink, and the pen Vernon so despised. This was the total contents of Puckle's stationery drawer. He seldom filled a whole notebook in the course of a year, he had said.

On the other table was spread his map of the area. Over it pored Inspector Mallow, Sergeant Horrocks, and the two constables from Torquay. They all looked up as Alec and Vernon entered. The uniformed men came to attention and saluted.

"Good morning, sir," said Mallow, with a gentle benevolence that ought to have been followed by a sympathetic enquiry as to whether Alec had slept well. However, illumined by the natural light squeezing in through high, narrow windows, the inspector's kindly image was belied by the watchful, even sceptical look in his eyes. He didn't enquire after Alec's health but went straight to business. "Constable Puckle knocked up the local photographer early and he should be here with the prints any minute. The GPO will send someone this morning to run a telephone line extension down from the police station."

"Excellent," said Alec. He had already decided to put Mallow in charge at the parish hall to collect and collate reports, rather than letting him interview and antagonize witnesses. "Well done."

"The Abbotsford station is sending someone with supplies, an officer you can keep if you need him. He'll come on a motor-bicycle so that we can get to these places people claim to have been."

"Good thinking. When he arrives, you can send him straight to the Ferries Inn with a description of Baskin. If they recall his stopping in at lunchtime for a drink, I don't see how he could get back in time, especially if the ferryman remembers taking him across the river. And I want enquiries made for a small sports car, light blue or grey, which drove between Westcombe and Malborough yesterday afternoon. It may be well known locally, or if it's a visitor, it may have stopped for petrol somewhere."

"Number plate?" Mallow queried.

"We haven't got it. That's what we want, so as to track down the driver, who may have seen Anstruther." Alec noticed that Horrocks was looking past him, with a badly concealed grin. He swung round to see Vernon practically dancing with impatience. "You know the car?"

135

"I didn't want to interrupt, sir, but yes, I know one like it. Mr. Wallace's son has one."

"Mr. Wallace the lifeboat coxswain?"

"And solicitor. Rory has an eggshell blue Bugatti, or at least he had last summer. I haven't seen him this year."

"He lives with his parents?"

"No, he solicits too, and he's junior partner in the firm, but he and his old man don't see eye to eye. There isn't really enough business in Westcombe for two, anyway, so Rory has a separate office in Plymouth. He might have motored over to see his parents, though."

"Check it, Mallow. You can send Puckle when he gets here. As soon as we have those photos to help in identifying the right spot, Horrocks will take your two men and Mr. Vernon up on the cliffs to search. Vernon, what can you tell me about Thomas Stebbins?"

"He's a jobbing gardener. Surly type. He works at the Vicarage on Thursdays. Julia—Miss Bellamy—might know where he goes the other days."

"Am I right in thinking that you have the run of the Vicarage and could pop in now, in spite of the early hour, to ask Miss Bellamy where he lives and where he's to be found at this time?"

Vernon blushed. "Yes, sir. It's just next door. I'll be right back." He dashed off.

Turning to the sergeant, Alec said, "I hope you don't mind taking the lad along, Horrocks. He's very keen and I've impressed upon him that he's under your orders."

"Another pair of eyes can't hurt, sir. Besides which, he'll be able to show us the way, us being unfamiliar with these parts."

"Good." Alec went on to explain what they were to look for, in particular Enderby's jacket and any piece of wood which might have served as a bludgeon. As he finished, the sound of an altercation came through the open windows.

"I call it too utterly shabby of you!" exclaimed a youthful female voice indignantly.

"This isn't a game, Ju," young Vernon responded. "It's a real murder. Girls are too squeamish to be real detectives."

"Well, I like that! Lots of girls are nurses, and in the War they were right in the middle of battles. Don't tell me they didn't cope with all sorts of gruesome things! As a matter of fact, I'm thinking of going into nursing myself. I'm sure it must be more interesting than typing."

"Don't change the subject. You can't come, and that's that."

"They can't stop me walking Popsy on the cliff path."

"Bet they can."

"Bet they can't. And what's more, I bet we get there before you!"

Horrocks's dismayed glance met Alec's. Before either could speak, Constable Puckle came in with the photographs.

"These here," he announced importantly, "are what you might call extra-quick prints. Mr. Ledwick says they'll fade pretty quick. So I says to him, they'll be needed in evidence. And he says to me, d'ye want me to wash the negatives prop'ly and make another set o' prints as'll last, acos it's going to cost extra? And I says to him, yes, make 'em and you can send the bill to the County Constabluary in Exeter. So I hopes as how that's all right, sir, acos I wouldn't want 'em docked off my pay, sir, or Martha'll carry on something terrible."

"That's quite all right, Constable. Good thinking."

Swelling with pride—making his girth even more impressive than usual—Puckle spread the prints on a table. In spite of acrid fumes catching at the back of the throat, everyone crowded around to look, including Vernon, who had re-entered hard on Puckle's heels. Of the twelve photos, the close-up shots were out-of-focus, too blurred to be useful. The one of the cliff face was sharp but the details were too small to be made out plainly, even with a magnifying lens. Worth trying an enlargement, Alec decided, at the expense of the Devonshire "Constabluary."

The rest were clear and sharp. The impact of Enderby's superficial injuries was lessened by the absence of colour, but the horribly

137

unnatural positions of his limbs and head brought a gasp from one of the constables.

Alec picked out the shot he had taken after climbing to a higher spot, showing the pattern of rocks surrounding the body. "This should help you find the place where he went over, Sergeant, even if the tide is covering some of these rocks. But for heaven's sake don't risk anyone falling after him. If it seems too dangerous to look over the edge, I'm sure Mr. Vernon can give you a pretty good idea of where to look. Vernon, you got the information about Stebbins?"

"Yes, sir, he should be at the Hammetts' today."

"Thank you." Alec sent the search party on their way.

Vernon hadn't mentioned Miss Bellamy's threat. If the girl turned up, with or without her dog, Horrocks would just have to deal with her as he would any encroaching member of the public.

Puckle provided directions to the Hammett and Stebbins residences. Leaving Mallow to organize their makeshift headquarters and the evidence so far gathered, to await the arrival of supplies, and to start the search for the unknown sports-car, Alec set off to find the jobbing gardener. He had seen and heard enough of Tom Stebbins to know the interview was going to be anything but easy.

"But it looks like rain." Daisy spread marmalade lavishly on her toast.

"Oh, Mummy, what does it matter? We'll prob'ly get wet anyway."

"I asked Anstruther," said Baskin, "and he says it won't rain before afternoon. A sailor is never wrong about the weather."

"Why not?" Deva wanted to know.

Baskin explained the importance of the weather to a ship at sea, keeping Deva's interest by using the monsoons and typhoons of the Indian Ocean as an example. Daisy thought he must be an excellent teacher. His pupils would miss him if he were arrested for the murder of George Enderby. She wished she knew the reason for his interest in the philandering landlord. No doubt Alec knew by now or would find out soon. Surely she could persuade him to tell her, since he would be unaware of Baskin's possible connection with the case if she had not alerted him.

After breakfast, they all set out. The cloudy day was cool and Daisy's path was a gentle slope requiring no great exertion, little more than a rutted farm track, with grass growing down the centre. Except for occasional gates and stiles, high hedges hid the view, but the dullness was relieved by foxgloves, white campion, ragged robin and festoons of fragrant honeysuckle. Armed with Baskin's Ordnance Survey map, she managed without great difficulty to find the bridge and two fords where she was to meet them, well before they arrived.

At the final rendezvous, Bel and Deva were wet, muddy and happy. Baskin was damp, cheerful and quite willing to take them back the same way, as that was what they wanted.

"There's a fallen tree-trunk right across the stream, Mummy," Belinda explained. "Mr. Baskin wouldn't let us walk on it in case we fell in and got completely soaked, instead of just splashed, but he said we could on the way home if you say so because we can go straight home and change."

"It's such fun, Mrs. Fletcher! My ayah would never let me do anything like this."

"Nor would my gran," Bel agreed.

"Don't worry, Mrs. Fletcher, they won't come to any harm. The tree-bridge isn't high, the water isn't deep, and they'd be in the sea if they weren't in the stream."

"True. Right-oh, girls, but if you get any wetter, change and dry off as soon as you get back. I'm going to take a different way back so you may get there first." Daisy had decided to walk back by the lane Inspector Mallow had suggested Peter Anstruther could have taken, the one that allowed easy access to the cliff. At least it looked easy on the map. She wanted to see for herself.

Before seeking out Tom Stebbins, Alec paid a call on the gardener's wife. The Stebbinses lived in the end cottage of a row on the edge of the village, with nothing but fields beyond. The small front garden was a riot of roses: bushes, standards, and a glorious pink climber beside the door. Alec, who enjoyed gardening but rarely found time for it, noted and admired the luxuriant foliage and the absence of greenfly and black spot.

As he walked up the short, paved path, he saw that the garden at the side of the house was equally well cared for. Scarlet runner beans climbed to the eaves, and neat, weedless beds nourished a variety of other vegetables. A huge marrow peeked coyly through its screen of leaves. Apparently gardening was Stebbins's hobby as well as his job.

The house, what could be seen of it between the roses, was another matter, with peeling paint, cracked windowsills, and a couple of missing slates on the roof. Those were probably the landlord's responsibility, but the other cottages in the row looked to be in good condition, so Alec inferred that the Stebbinses didn't care enough to request repairs.

He knocked on the door.

The woman who opened it wasn't quite what he expected of "a common little piece." Her figure was trim, her bobbed hair naturally corn-gold, and though she had darkened her eyelashes, the bloom in her cheeks owed nothing to rouge. Her flowered frock was up-to-date in style but shoddy as to material. Bright, curious eyes studied him briefly. She sighed.

"A rozzer," she said resignedly. "Blimey, I didn't think you'd get here so quick." Her voice was pure Cockney.

"You're a long way from home, Mrs. Stebbins."

"Too true, ducks. You better come on in."

"Thank you. I'm Detective Chief Inspector Fletcher."

"Pleased to meecher, I don't think."

He followed her into a narrow, dark passage. A door on his left was probably the front parlour, but apparently rozzers didn't rate the front parlour. The doorless wall on the right was the party wall, shared with the next cottage. They passed a staircase and emerged into the brick-floored and very untidy kitchen. Breakfast dishes were stacked in dirty water in the stone sink, which had a single tap and no hot-water geyser. On top of the small coal-fired range was a frying-pan with congealing grease.

"Bloody mediæval, innit? Give me a nice gas cooker any day. Take a seat, do." They sat at the crumby, sticky table. "Got a fag?"

"Sorry, I smoke a pipe. What brought you to Devon, Mrs. Stebbins?" Alec asked with real interest.

"One port and lemon too many, that's what. Me and a couple of friends thought it'd be a giggle to enlist in the Land Army, get away from the bloody Zeppelins. Gawd, Jerry gave us 'ell in the East End! They sent me to a farm 'ereabouts, and that was anuvver kind of 'ell. No shops for miles, and the clothes we had to wear! It got so bad it made Westcombe look good, and besides, getting married got me out of the muck. And Tom brought me flowers, roses and carnations and that."

"Your husband wasn't in the services?"

"Nah, too busy turning the nobs's flower gardens over to veg, not that there's any what I'd call real nobs 'ereabouts, not like the West End. He's ten years older'n me, too, and I'm pushing thirty, I kid you not."

"You don't look a day over twenty."

"Garn!" she said, but she looked pleased. "I got to admit it's good for a girl's complexion, living out here in the middle of nowhere, but when you said that, you said it all. I did 'ope he'd go back 'ome wiv me after the Armistice, but nuffing doing. Won't leave his bloody gardens. If you want to know, that's why I took up with Georgie. The lousy bastard promised he'd take me back to the Smoke, and next fing I know he's having a bit off wiv some farmer's little girl wiv mud under her fingernails."

"Do you happen to know her name?"

"Nah. Who cares?"

"Does your husband know about your relationship with George Enderby?"

She shrugged and said again, "Who cares? He can divorce me if he wants. Only it costs money to get a divorce, dunnit? Fat chance."

"He hasn't spoken to you about it?"

"Not that I 'eard, but I don't always listen. He's always got some-fing to grouse about."

"Where were you yesterday afternoon?"

"Me? I didn't push Georgie off the cliff!" she declared indignantly.

"It's just a matter of routine, Mrs. Stebbins. We have to check everyone in any way associated with the victim."

As usual, the invaluable formula worked.

"Oh, well, if you want to know, I took the ferry to Abbotsford to see a friend."

"Her name and address, please?"

"I don't see why you need to know that." Rita Stebbins didn't blush—she probably wasn't capable of it—but she did look more than a touch self-conscious.

"A gentleman friend," Alec guessed dryly.

" 'S matter of fact, it was, then. And I don't know his address. He's a commercial I met in the village Friday. He's got a friend in London that might give me a job and he asked me to go and have a . . . a cuppa at his hotel and talk abaht it. Gawd, I'd do anyfing to get out of this dead-alive 'ole! I've had enough, I have."

Alec persuaded her to part with the commercial's name—at least the name he had given her—and the name of the hotel. In return, he agreed not to let her husband know that the friend she had spent the afternoon with was male.

"If I can possibly avoid it," he qualified. "What was he doing while you were out and about?"

"Gardening!" she snorted. " 'S all he ever does on his day off."

"Your garden, I take it?"

"*His* garden."

"His garden." That should be easy enough to check with the neighbours, a job for a constable. "Whose garden is he working in this morning?"

"Dunno. Don't care."

Alec took his leave. Portrait of a disastrous marriage, he reflected, breathing in the rich scent of roses. Ten years was no great difference, but the gulf between a stolid country gardener and a flighty East Ender seemed to be far wider and deeper than that between a middle-class copper and the daughter of a viscount.

No wonder Thomas Stebbins was a morose, deeply disgruntled man. But was that sufficient reason for him to have broken the news of Cecily Anstruther's affair to her husband? The cause was more likely an existing grudge against Peter Anstruther added to a desire to know someone else was suffering as he had suffered from his wife's unfaithfulness. Misery loves company.

From what Alec had seen of Stebbins, he was not likely to have brooded over his grievance in silence, but no doubt Rita had turned a deaf ear to his reproaches. Alec could imagine her indifference goading the man to violence. After killing Enderby, he would have had plenty of time to get back from the cliff to his cottage before the exploding maroon's flare and boom summoned the lifeboatmen.

On the other hand, could he possibly be a good enough actor to have looked so surprised when he joined his mates on the beach and saw Enderby's body?

Alec turned towards the Hammett residence. He wanted to know whether Stebbins would claim to have been in the garden all yesterday afternoon, until the maroon's summons, or would produce some other alibi. With any luck, his response to being questioned would reveal whether he had known of his wife's affair.

The Hammetts' substantial house was halfway up the hill, with a steeply terraced front garden. Climbing the stone steps, Alec saw in the flourishing flowerbeds and wall-growing plants the evidence of Stebbins's care, but the man himself was nowhere to be seen.

Alec rang the bell. Waiting, he heard a shout within. After a lengthy silence, the door was opened by a breathless house parlour-maid.

"Sorry, sir, I were doing the upstairs. The master's at work, sir, and the mistress went out."

"It's the gardener I want to see, miss. Thomas Stebbins."

"Tom Stebbins?" she asked in surprise. "He'll be out there. Didn't you see him as you came up?" Coming out onto the front step she looked around, then shook her head. "Well, sir, I dunno where he's got to, that's for sure."

"The back garden, perhaps."

"There isn't no back garden, sir. The house is right onto the street. The upstairs, 'tis. And round the one side 'tis the dustbins by the kitchen and the other side's the carriage-house. I wonder where Tom's got to?"

So did Alec. "He wouldn't be taking a cup of tea in the kitchen?"

"Mrs. Beecher, the cook-housekeeper, she's gone down to do the shopping. There's only me and the daily here, and Mrs. Watson wouldn't dare mess about in Mrs. Beecher's kitchen. I'll go look, though."

"Thank you."

The girl came back shaking her head over the mysterious disappearance of Stebbins. "I'll say this for him, he's reg'lar as clockwork and a hard worker. I can't think where he's got to!"

Alec had no more notion than she as to the gardener's whereabouts, but he could make a good guess as to the reason for his absence. It looked very much as if Thomas Stebbins had done a bunk.

16

When Alec returned to the parish hall, Puckle reported on his call upon the Wallaces. Rory Wallace had indeed driven over from Plymouth on Sunday, arriving shortly before his father was called out to the lifeboat.

"Damn!" said Alec, studying the map. "That's much too late. Anstruther said he saw him just before Malborough, but it wouldn't take young Wallace more than a few minutes to get to Westcombe. Anstruther should have reached South Huish by then if he rode straight there, or even the camp, if he didn't hang about waiting for his friend."

Inspector Mallow rubbed his hands together in a satisfied way. "So Anstruther went round by the cliff and shoved the victim over, just as I thought. It's a wonder how you cleared up the case so quick. Scotland Yard methods, eh? D'you want me to apply for a warrant, sir, or will you do it?"

"Not so fast! In the first place, we don't know that it was Wallace he saw. Secondly, Wallace may have stopped to see a friend in the village before going to his parents' house. And in the third place, Mrs. Stebbins confesses to an affair with Enderby and Tom Stebbins is not at home nor at his place of work, though I'm assured he's a regular, steady worker."

"That he is, sir," put in Puckle.

"Hopped it, has he?" Mallow frowned. "Well, that's a puzzler, for sure."

The telephone had still not been connected. Alec sent Mallow up to the police station to try to get hold of Rory Wallace; to ask the Abbotsford police to send someone to enquire at the hotel Mrs. Stebbins had named for the commercial traveller she had named; and to ring up Exeter with a request to alert all South Devon officers to keep a lookout for Stebbins. The gardener was not likely to flee far from home. In particular, because of his unhappy experiences with his wife, London surely figured in his mind as anything but a refuge.

In fact, he had probably gone to roost with some local relative or friend. Alec set Puckle to calling on Stebbins's known associates and family connections.

During Alec's absence, Mallow had brought order to the piles of rough notes of which the investigation had hitherto consisted. He had obtained a third table for Alec's exclusive use, and on it had placed the two reports he had already completed in spite of the scant supplies of stationery available. However unlikable, the man was efficient.

Alec had just sat down to read the report of DS Horrocks's enquiries at the Schooner when a hideous roar rent the peaceful morning. It grew louder, approaching, then suddenly cut off just outside the hall. A moment later, a young man in dusty overalls bounded in, goggles in one hand, a large canvas satchel in the other. This he set with a thump on the nearest table before coming to attention and saluting.

"Sergeant Tumbelow, sir, from Abbotsford. I brought the stuff you asked for, sir, and my motor-cycle. With a side-car, sir. I can take you wherever you want to go, right away!"

"Nowhere just now, thank you. But I do have a job for you," he added as Tumbelow's face fell. He introduced himself, then asked, "Are you wearing uniform under that kit?"

"Yes, sir."

146

"Good. Here, take a look at the map. You see the Ferries Inn. I want you to make enquiries about a hiker who dropped in yesterday for a drink with his picnic lunch. He claims to have then crossed over the river and immediately back again on the ferry." Alec described Donald Baskin, realizing in the process what an undistinctive young man he was—medium height, medium build, medium-brown hair, a pleasant, ordinary face. "Khaki trousers, brown boots, canvas knapsack, pipe-smoker. Oh, and a Norfolk jacket, nondescript colour. It's not much to go on. Do your best."

Tumbelow saluted and went out. A moment later, his machine roared to life and the racket receded up the street.

As quiet returned, Alec continued reading Horrocks's report. The staff of the inn confirmed that Enderby had sneaked out sometime between two and half past, and that his wife had remained on the premises, "run off her feet." No one admitted to knowing where he had gone or whom he was going to meet. An account of the quarrel between the Enderbys added nothing to what Daisy had overheard.

The chamber-maid confirmed that when Enderby first came to Westcombe, he and his "sister" had shared a bed. When he took up with Nancy, they had been heard to part discreetly and amicably, with a gift of twenty quid on one side and best wishes for good luck on the other.

Mallow came back just as Alec turned to the second report. "The word's out all over the county, Mr. Fletcher," he announced, rubbing his hands together briskly. "I don't doubt we'll have Stebbins under lock and key in no time."

"What of Rory Wallace?"

"He was out of his office, an appointment with a client. His clerk will have him telephone here when he gets in. But now Stebbins has scarpered—"

"And the commercial traveller in Abbotsford?"

"No one of that name's been staying at that hotel. I expect he gave Mrs. Stebbins a false name. But he don't matter now we know it's

Stebbins we're after . . . or do you think him and his missus was in league together, sir?"

"Not a chance," Alec said immediately, remembering the perky Cockney and the morose countryman. Then he reconsidered.

There were no flies on Rita Stebbins. Suppose she had thought up the uncheckable story about the traveller, then persuaded Enderby to meet her for one last fling on the cliffs and pushed him over. Meanwhile her husband was to provide himself with an unbreakable alibi before disappearing, temporarily. With a hue and cry out for Tom, no one would question his unfaithful wife too closely. Reappearing, Tom would produce his alibi and the couple would be written off as suspects.

It sounded like one of Daisy's wilder theories, far-fetched but possible. Alec sighed. "On second thoughts, could be. When your chaps get back, we must check door-to-door with the Stebbinses' neighbours and question the crew of the ferry to Abbotsford, as well as the hotel staff. If Rita Stebbins travelled to Abbotsford yesterday afternoon, she'd not pass unnoticed."

"Right, sir." Mallow made a note. "Still, we've narrowed it down to him with maybe her help."

"Great Scott, no! We can't by any means write off Anstruther or Baskin yet, and there's still the farmer's daughter to be found. We haven't the shadow of a clue as to who she is."

Andrew Vernon burst into the parish hall like a whirlwind, followed closely by a girl and a large black dog. Vernon skidded to a halt in front of Alec, holding up a tweed jacket.

"We found it! Oh, Julia, this is Chief Inspector Fletcher. Miss Bellamy, sir. Actually, one of the bobbies found the jacket. Then, of course, we concentrated on that area and we found a—something else. I've got it in here." He set his Portable Laboratory on the table. "I'll show you as soon as Julia leaves."

"Mean beast!" Julia Bellamy was a pretty girl not a day over eighteen, with a fair bob beneath her brown, green-banded cloche. A dark green skirt, good but well-worn, and bulky hand-knitted jumper failed to disguise a trim, athletic figure. Sturdy walking shoes emphasized long slim legs. No wonder Vernon was attracted. "I suppose," she accused him, "you're going to try and hog the credit for the earring, too!"

"Earring?"

"Julia found it. The rest of us were working back towards the cliff edge . . ."

"Actually, it was Popsy. Popsy, say 'How do you do.'" The dog sat down and raised a paw, regarding Alec with soulful brown eyes. Miss Bellamy patted her head. "Sorry, I haven't any biscuits, girl. She's awfully clever, isn't she? She was sniffing around where they found the jacket and she found an earring under a heather bush."

"And Julia picked it up so it's got her fingerprints all over it. Isn't that just like a girl?" Vernon extracted a small envelope from his case and handed it to Alec. "I put it in this, anyway."

"Most men would have done exactly the same," Alec assured Miss Bellamy as he opened the envelope and slid a dangling diamanté earring onto the table.

"Hijjous," she observed dispassionately. "Cheap and nasty."

But the sort of thing that would please a Cockney tart, or a farm-girl. He had to find out who Enderby's latest flame had been.

"It's so bright and shiny, it can't have been there long," Vernon pointed out. "I expect Enderby took it as a present for the girl he was meeting."

Mallow had come up, giving the dog a wide berth when she wrinkled her lip at him. "Where's the other one of the pair?" he wanted to know. "And where are my men?"

"Still up there, looking for it, and for the weapon—whatever he was hit with. Horrocks said we could bring you this one and the jacket."

"Thank you." Alec suspected the detective sergeant had been only too glad of an excuse to rid himself of his amateur assistants. "The sooner the better."

"Shall I dust it for fingerprints?" Vernon offered eagerly.

Alec doubted that the single earring bore useful prints on its tiny, multi-faceted surfaces, especially as Miss Bellamy had handled it. He was inclined to let the young almost-doctor have a go, but Mallow's disapproval was obvious.

"We'd better leave that to the experts," Alec said. After all, if they ever found out who the farm-girl was, she might very likely deny having met Enderby, in which case fingerprints could prove her presence. "Why don't you watch and learn? Miss Bellamy's prints will have to be taken, too, for elimination."

"Gosh, really?" The vicar's daughter was wide-eyed. "What a lark!"

"Did you touch it, too, Vernon?"

With regret, the young man admitted, "No, I took it from her with my forceps."

"Good for you. Inspector, it's all yours." As Mallow, Vernon and Miss Bellamy moved away, Alec said, "Oh, just a minute, Vernon."

"Yes?" He turned back.

In a low voice, Alec asked, "What is it you found that you couldn't mention in front of Miss Bellamy?"

With a grimace, Vernon reached into his carrying case and took out one of the stoppered phials, saying, "Rather disgusting, sir. I handled this with forceps, I can tell you. A French letter, used, recently. He was up there with a woman, all right!"

"So it would seem."

"What else could it mean, sir, with this and the earring?"

"For a start, we'll have to have Mrs. Enderby confirm that the jacket was her husband's."

"Oh yes, but then—"

"Then we can be pretty certain Enderby was up there with a woman."

"And if she didn't push him over herself, she must have seen who did."

150

"It seems likely," Alec agreed. "The only trouble is, we haven't the least idea who she is."

Waving goodbye to Belinda and Deva as they set off back down the stream, Daisy took out the map Baskin had lent her. On it, she found the lane she wanted, parallel to the cliff-tops and a few hundred yards inland. Her shortest route thither was mostly by right-of-way footpaths. She set off briskly, hoping she would not meet any of the cross-country obstacles Baskin had described.

The way tended steadily upward through farmland, mostly pasture with the odd arable field. The worst barrier she came across was a broken-down stile leading into a field infested with thistles, dock, nettles and brambles. The overgrown path seemed more a matter of disgraceful neglect than deliberate obstruction. She battled through, scratching her leg, and came out at last on the lane she was making for.

The lane continued gently uphill to her left, while on the opposite side rose a steep slope of bracken, gorse and heather interspersed with bare rock and short, wiry grass. A faint path wound upward. Daisy rather doubted anyone could actually ride a bicycle up it, especially where it appeared to plunge into a gorse thicket. It wasn't on the map.

But between her present position and Westcombe, the map showed a couple more paths and a track leading off from the lane towards the sea. Anstruther could have taken any of them.

Realizing she couldn't possibly explore them all—not, at least, without missing lunch, Daisy turned homeward.

She had nearly reached the crest and was hoping the rest of the way would be downhill when she heard a motor ascending the hill behind her with a horrid grinding of gears. Stepping aside, for the lane was scarcely one car wide, she glanced back to see a Humber touring car of pre-War vintage. The chauffeur, who wore the usual peaked cap along with a grubby brown jacket and no collar, looked disgruntled. Behind him sat a woman Daisy recognized.

As the clash of gears ceased, Mrs. Hammett poked her driver in the back and said loudly, "Stop, I say!"

The car shot forward for a few feet then jerked to a halt and stalled beside Daisy. "I'm a gardener," the chauffeur said sullenly.

"Get out and get it started, Tom Stebbins, or you won't be my gardener much longer. Mrs. Fletcher, I'll give you a lift down to the village."

Much as she would have liked to refuse what sounded more like an order than an invitation, it meant she wouldn't have to seek out the Gorgon on the off-chance that she had useful information and was willing to part with it.

"Thank you," she said, climbing in beside Mrs. Hammett, who was dressed today in a grey cardigan over a paler grey frock polka-dotted with black. The car held a faintly fishy odour—or perhaps it was just that Daisy knew Mr. Hammett dealt in fish.

While the morose gardener cranked away, Mrs. Hammett fired her opening salvo: "So, Mr. Fletcher is a London detective. It's disgraceful the local police can't manage without help, seeing what we pay in rates!"

"I dare say they could, but since my husband was already involved as a witness . . ."

"It seems mighty odd to me, a Scotland Yard man just chancing to be in Westcombe. 'Twouldn't surprise me if he were investigating George Enderby."

"We're supposed to be on holiday, Mrs. Hammett. Believe me, if we'd known a local citizen was going to be bumped off, we'd have gone somewhere else."

"There was something very fishy about that man, coming down here with his fancy woman and marrying Nancy Pinner. What became of that woman, his so-called sister? If anybody saw her leave, it's more than I've heard. What if him and Nancy did away wi' her? I reckon they guessed Mr. Fletcher was on to them and Nancy pushed him over, so's he couldn't blame her for it."

"You think his wife killed him?"

152

"Well, no, I wouldn't say that. Most think 'twas Peter Anstruther, from what I've heard, acos o' the rumpus in the Schooner. But I've got my own ideas." Her mouth set in a firm line.

Daisy would have pursued the subject, but Stebbins came round from the front of the car, crank in hand, and said grim-faced, " 'Twon't start, missus."

"What do you mean, it won't start?"

"I'm a gardener, not a shover."

"Did you pull out the choke, like the master said?"

"No," Stebbins said sulkily. "He said that's what to do when her's cold, but her bain't cold after coming up the hill from Coleman's."

"Try it!" commanded Mrs. Hammett.

A couple of cranks later, the motor started. In a clash of gears, the Humber lumbered onward.

"You were visiting the Colemans?" Daisy asked. She recalled that Sid the beachcomber was the younger brother of a farmer called Coleman, described by Anstruther as a brute.

"Edna Coleman's my cousin, and a more feckless creatur I have yet to meet. Didn't I warn her that girl of hers is a sly-boots and bound to come to no good end? And what do I find out Friday but Olive has been meeting George Enderby, and we all know what that means! And her just turned sixteen."

"Oh dear."

"So off I goes Sat'day morning to warn Edna, blood being thicker'n water, as they say. Keep her close, says I. Not a word to Alfred—that's her husband—or he'll half kill her. Free wi' his fists, is Alfred, not but what nobody could blame him for taking a strap to Olive, nor he wouldn't need to if Edna had brought her up proper. So what happens this morning first thing? I get a message from Edna by Ned Baxter that picks up the milk cans for the dairy when he's not lobstering, that Olive didn't come home last night and is she wi' me?"

"I take it she wasn't," said Daisy, unable to imagine a less likely refuge.

"That she wasn't. 'James,' says I to Mr. Hammett, 'there's trouble. I must go to my cousin Edna's this morning. You'll take the ferry to the office and let me have the motor.' Which he does, and never a complaint, I'll say that for him, though well I know he don't like that good-for-nothing driving his precious car." She jerked a fierce thumb at Stebbins's resentful back. "Aye, and Mr. Fletcher ought to take a good look at *him*, too. His wife's a giddy creatur as has been seen wi' you know who."

The car was now creeping downhill in low gear. Daisy wondered whether the "chauffeur" was nervous about hills or had wrecked the gear-box and couldn't change up. At any rate, the result was quite enough noise to shield their conversation from Stebbins.

"Is your cousin's daughter still missing?" she asked.

"Not a sign o' her. And for why? Acos Edna went and did just what I said not to. The silly goose told Alfred about Olive and George Enderby! After Sunday dinner, she said, when he were full o' beef and taties and plum pie. You'd think she'd know by now Alfred isn't one to be mellowed by a good meal. He took after Olive and she ran out wi' him after her. And he come back and she didn't."

"Gosh, you don't think he did her a mischief?"

"Her or Enderby or both."

"You must tell the police!"

"I promised Edna I wouldn't go to the police till tomorrow. Alfred'll take it out on her if they come nosing round, see, and maybe Olive'll come home today." Mrs. Hammett gave Daisy a look heavy with significance.

"I see," said Daisy.

Daisy needed time to consider how much of the woman's farrago to pass on to Alec. That rubbish about Nancy Enderby doing away with Georgie Porgie's "sister," for instance, would not be appreciated. Mrs. Hammett had not even seemed to believe it herself.

Of course, Alec must certainly be told about Olive Coleman's disappearance, but half an hour's delay couldn't make much difference. Daisy felt badly in need of inner fortification before she faced him with the information that yet another near stranger had confided in her instead of the police.

17

*B*y the time Mrs. Hammett delivered Daisy to the Anstruthers', the girls had already changed into frocks for lunch. They were sitting in the garden with Baskin, who was pointing out different kinds of seagulls as they swooped over the ruffled waters of the inlet.

"I thought they were just gulls, Mummy, but they're all different. Look, that one's a . . . a tern, isn't it, Mr. Baskin?"

"A common tern," he confirmed.

"One good tern deserves another," said Deva, sending herself and Belinda into fits of giggles.

Without mentioning that she had taken advantage of his kindness to do some sleuthing, Daisy thanked Baskin most sincerely for having kept her charges amused all morning.

"We learnt lots of stuff, too, didn't we, Bel?"

Baskin grinned. "I can't help it," he said to Daisy.

"Did you say thank you, girls?"

"Of course, Mummy. We said thank you most frightfully much. It was ripping!"

Ravenous, Daisy went on into the house for a wash and brush up. Baskin went with her. As they entered through the back door, out of hearing of the girls, he said, "Can you tell me, Mrs. Fletcher, are the police going to object if I go off hiking this afternoon? I rather gather I'm on their list of suspects. I should have made more effort to hide my interest in Enderby."

"As long as you don't leave the district, they can't object. But would you please write a note to Alec saying you'll be back, because if I tell him, he'll say I'm interfering."

"Oh, will he!" Baskin said with a laugh. "I wouldn't want to subject you to such an accusation."

"He will anyway," she sighed. "I've found out something I simply have to tell him."

"I suppose it was you who told him about the questions I'd been asking. Oh, I don't blame you! I know it looks fishy. I just wondered if it might have been Mrs. Anstruther doing her bit to divert attention from her husband."

"No, it was me."

"I."

"I beg your . . . ? Oh, grammar! I should think being married to a teacher must be even more exasperating than being married to a policeman! It was I. But don't worry, I've found another two suspects to add to the list. I don't suppose you'd like to tell me why . . . ?"

"No," he said firmly. "There's no reason now why anyone should ever know. I'll see you at lunch."

Daisy went slowly upstairs, thinking. Donald Baskin certainly didn't behave like someone who had just committed murder, nor like someone who feared arrest for a murder he didn't commit. He freely admitted that the death of Enderby had resolved a serious difficulty for him, yet refused to explain the difficulty. Innocence? Or guilt combined with overconfidence?

Approaching the parish hall after a hurried lunch, Daisy hoped Alec would be there. If she was faced with the misleadingly mellow Inspector Mallow, should she give him her information or just leave a message for Alec?

She closed her umbrella and pushed open the door. Inside was even gloomier than outside. As she peered at two indistinguishable figures seated at a table with their backs to what little light came through the high, rain-spotted windows, one of the men got up and came towards her.

Bald, lean, stooped: "Good afternoon, Mrs. Fletcher," said Mallow in his smooth, mild voice. "The chief inspector is on the telephone to London. We are rather busy." He didn't say aloud but his manner clearly conveyed, "You're interrupting important business, little woman."

"You'll be even busier," said Daisy, "when I've told Alec what I've found out." She marched past Mallow to the table.

"Hold on a minute," said Alec into the telephone and covered the mouthpiece with his hand. "Great Scott, Daisy—"

"I've important information for you, darling."

"What?"

"Two new suspects."

He sighed. "Right-oh. Half a tick." He returned to his conversation.

Sitting down, Daisy managed with difficulty not to give Mallow a smugly triumphant look. As with the shock he had given Cecily Anstruther, he was only doing his job. It was his manner she objected to, now that she had seen through the sympathetic pose.

Alec finished on the 'phone and hung up the receiver. "Who?" he asked, turning to a fresh page in his notebook.

"The first is just a possibility: Tom Stebbins."

"We know about him. He's disappeared."

"He looks like our man," put in Mallow.

"Disappeared? When?"

"He wasn't at his job when I went to talk to him this morning."

"Bolted," said Mallow.

"No he hasn't. Not this morning, anyway. He was driving Mrs. Hammett. He's the most appalling driver. I don't think their car will ever recover."

"How do you know?"

"You should have heard the gear-box! Oh, she stopped to give me a lift when I was walking home. It was lunchtime when she dropped me off, just about three quarters of an hour ago, so he hadn't skedaddled at that point. The person who's disappeared is the farmer's daughter."

"What? Wait. Mallow, see if the Hammetts are on the telephone and if so ring up and ask if Stebbins is there. And if so, cancel the alert. Say there may be another coming up. Go on, Daisy—the farmer's daughter? Who is she? What do you mean, she's disappeared?"

Daisy related the story Mrs. Hammett had told her. "And now she's afraid Coleman might have killed his daughter as well as Enderby."

"Great Scott! Why didn't she come straight to us?"

"She promised her cousin—Mrs. Coleman—she wouldn't tell the police till tomorrow. That's why she told me. They're still hoping Olive will come home of her own accord, and if your men start poking around, Coleman's liable to go for his wife, I gather. Then you might end up with three bodies."

"We may have to bring him in and hold him for questioning," Alec said grimly. "Have you a description of the daughter?"

"No. I was afraid to ask in case Mrs. Hammett had second thoughts about telling me everything and clammed up."

"Never mind, we'll get it out of the parents. With any luck, they'll have a photo. Thanks, Daisy. Don't worry, we'll do our best to protect Mrs. Coleman and we'll find Olive, alive or dead."

As Daisy left the parish hall, an umbrella with a girl's face beneath it appeared above the hedge surrounding the garden next door. "Hullo," she said.

Surprised, Daisy responded, "Hullo?"

"I suppose you've been talking to the police?"

Having just come out of police headquarters, Daisy couldn't credibly deny it, even if she had wanted to. "Yes, I have."

"Would you mind awfully if I asked you a question?" The head disappeared, then bobbed up again.

"Not at all, though I can't promise to answer."

"I say, would you mind awfully waiting just a sec while I run round by the gate? I'm standing on tiptoes, you see." Once more she vanished and reappeared. "And I can't keep it up for long."

"I'll wait." Daisy strolled down the street to meet her, reaching the gate in the hedge just in time to see the sign on it, THE VICARAGE, before the girl opened it.

"Hullo! I'm Julia Bellamy. My father's the vicar. He'd be livid if he knew I'd accosted you like that. I'm awfully sorry and all that, but you're the first person I've seen coming out who looked like someone I could talk to. I'd invite you to come and sit in the garden, only it's raining and Mother would be bound to see us and she'd start asking questions."

"Who could blame her? But as it happens, I'm quite respectable. I'm Mrs. Fletcher. My husband's in charge of the investigation."

"That divine chief inspector? He's frightfully nice, isn't he? Oh goody, you'll be able to tell me everything. Are you going somewhere? May I walk with you?"

"Certainly. I'm going up to the post office for postcards and a library book, if you want to come along. Alec doesn't tell me by any means everything, though, and I can't necessarily pass on what I know."

"There's only two things, really, though of course I'm dying of curiosity, like everyone else. Is it all right if Popsy comes too?" Miss Bellamy added as a large black dog arrived panting at her heels. "She's very friendly. Popsy, say 'How do you do?' She's awfully clever, too. She was the one who found the earring."

"The earring?" Daisy enquired as they set off towards the village centre.

"Oh, you *don't* know! That's one of the things I particularly wanted to ask you about, because it was Popsy who found it and I picked it up and I had to have my fingerprints taken, for elimination. They didn't take Andrew's—he was mad as fire. I just wondered if they'd found any other fingerprints on it. Besides mine, I mean. And whether it's an important clue. Andrew's sure it must be."

"Andrew?"

"Andrew Vernon. He's Dr. Vernon's nephew. He's been coming here every summer for ages and he's a particular friend of mine."

"Oh yes, Alec mentioned him. A medical student, isn't he?"

"That's right. Only he's frightfully interested in solving crimes, too. Medical jurisprudence, he calls it. He's gone to watch the autopsy, would you believe it? He's positively gloating over this murder and mad keen on helping Mr. Fletcher. He found the splinters in Enderby's neck that prove he was murdered, you know."

"No, I didn't know, and he really shouldn't have told you."

"Oh, he made me swear 'cross my heart and hope to die' I wouldn't breathe a word. The chief inspector's your husband, so it doesn't count. Besides, Andrew said it would come out at the inquest. If he hadn't found them, the doctor doing the autopsy would have, anyway. Andrew noticed some more splinters on the cliff path and some mysterious marks in a sandy spot, but they didn't seem to mean much, which is why he was so pleased to find something this morning."

"But it was you—your dog, at least—who found the earring which may or may not be significant. Where was it?"

"Up on the cliffs. Andrew told me he was going up there with a bunch of bobbies to search for clues. He said I couldn't go with them, so I took Popsy for a walk," Miss Bellamy revealed defiantly.

"Naturally," said Daisy with a smile of approval.

"We didn't get in their way. But I saw one of the bobbies find a jacket, which I'm sure was that snake Enderby's. It's all very well for Daddy to say, *'De mortuis nil nisi bonum,'* and not to be un-Christian, but he was a snake!"

"I know. What happened next?"

"They all hunted madly on hands and knees in the heather around where they found the jacket, and Andrew found something else, something small, but he won't tell me what it was."

"The rotter!"

"That's what I said. I hoped you might know. Anyway, they all moved away towards the cliff edge. Of course Popsy was sniffing around where they'd been crawling, but she wasn't as interested as she would have been if they'd been other dogs, not till she found a rabbit-hole right by the main stem of a big clump of heather. She started digging, and when I managed to haul her out, there was the earring caught in the ruff around her neck. Her fur is pretty shaggy there."

Daisy glanced down at Popsy, who looked pretty shaggy all over. "What sort of earring?" she asked.

"Oh, a horribly vulgar dangly diamanté thing, all sparkly."

"The height of fashion in London."

"No, is it? Mother would never in a million years let me wear anything so flashy! Oh dear, I hope you don't . . . ?"

"Not I. Did you give it to the police up there right away, or bring it down to Alec?"

"I was about to hand it over to the sergeant in charge up there when Andrew got all upset because I'd touched it and left my fingerprints on it. It's not as if I'm a burglar!" Miss Bellamy said indignantly. "Ordinary people aren't always thinking about fingerprints. Mr. Fletcher said most men would have done just the same."

"Of course they would."

"Well, Andrew took it from me with his blasted forceps—that's why they didn't take his fingerprints, which jolly well serves him right—and he tucked it away in an envelope and we brought it and the jacket down to Mr. Fletcher. And the other thing he found, as well, that he won't talk about."

"You have no idea what it is?"

"Not the foggiest. He wouldn't even give me a hint. I do think men are sometimes the pink limit, don't you?"

"Absolutely," said Daisy. Which wasn't really fair, because this time Alec had been far too grateful for the information to kick up a dust about how she had obtained it.

"Well, now," said Inspector Mallow, "it's a proper marvel what Mrs. Fletcher comes up with!"

Alec still was not sure whether Mallow was admiring or sarcastic. "If only half of what she told us is accurate, it's of vital importance," he pointed out.

"Pity she's up and vanished, this Olive Coleman, if she really was there with Enderby."

"We know he was with a woman. The earring and the condom were found in close association with the jacket identified as his by Nancy Enderby, who has half a dozen witnesses to give her an alibi. Mrs. Stebbins, who, I assure you, has only to open her mouth to stand out a mile in this part of the world, was recognized on the Abbotsford ferry and at the hotel."

"And you yourself, sir, and Mrs. Fletcher were with Mrs. Anstruther. But who's to tell how many other lady friends he had!"

"It's possible, of course, but we already knew we were looking for a farmer's daughter. Olive Coleman is our only prospect so far."

"You reckon her dad chased her up on the cliffs then waited while Enderby had his way with her before he attacked?" Now Mallow's scepticism was unmistakable.

"Highly unlikely," Alec said dryly. "Remember that we have the story of Coleman chasing the girl from the house at third hand— Mrs. Coleman told Mrs. Hammett, who told my wife, who passed it on to us. Olive may have escaped him, though, and he continued searching till he came upon them by chance. However, we haven't managed to eliminate any of the other male suspects."

The inspector ticked them off on his fingers. "Stebbins claims he was working in his vegetable garden round the side of his cottage, where it's quite credible none of the neighbours saw him. Baskin may have been at the inn and on that ferry, but it's the high season, lots of hikers and bicyclists about, and he's not distinctive enough to be remembered. And Anstruther may or may not have met young Mr. Wallace's car when and where he says: Mr. Wallace vaguely recalls several bicyclists but paid no attention being as how he was concentrating on peculiar noises coming from his carburettor, which quit

163

half a mile outside Westcombe, making him arrive at his parents' much later than intended."

"But he *was* on the road where and when Anstruther claims to have seen him, and how would Anstruther have known that if *he* wasn't there?" Alec promptly answered his own question: "He didn't specify Rory Wallace's car. We'd have had a hard time proving no grey or blue two-seater had passed that way."

"Still, they've all got reasonable explanations, sir. Let's see if Alfred Coleman does too. You want me to go and see him?"

Alec suppressed a shudder at the notion of introducing the man Daisy had described as a dropper of bombs into the already explosive situation at the Coleman farm. "No," he said, "I'll go."

18

*A*lec had only once before ridden in a motor-cycle side-car. Never again, he had vowed. The vehicle's flimsiness reminded him of his wartime spotter 'plane, a fragile construct of balsa wood, piano wire and canvas. But then he had soared through the air. The side-car was so close to the ground, every rut and pebble rattled one's bones and seemed about to shake the whole thing to pieces. Beyond the rain-streaked celluloid windows, hedges raced past in a green blur, inches from his nose, at what felt like ninety miles an hour.

He wondered at the intrepidity of regular passengers in such infernal contraptions, usually women and children!

Almost as distressing was the inferior position he found himself in vis-à-vis Tumbelow. Rampant on his bellowing machine, the sergeant was king of the road while Alec crouched at his side, utterly at his mercy. He flexed his cramped limbs, hoping to be able to extract himself with at least some remnant of dignity when they reached the Coleman farm.

He could have ridden pillion, but he suspected it was no more comfortable to the inexperienced rider. Besides, he had no overalls or dustcoat and to arrive dripping and mud-splashed was equally undignified.

At last the motor-cycle slowed. Alec breathed a sigh of relief—too soon. A moment later he was sure his teeth were being shaken loose as the side-car's single wheel lurched in and out of a series of potholes. At the same time the windows were spattered with a substance the stench of which doomed any hope that it was good, clean mud. The only mitigating factor was that it suggested they were approaching the farmyard.

With a final roar, the machine rolled to a halt. Tumbelow dismounted and came around to release Alec, who stood up, suppressing a groan as muscles and joints unkinked.

Ahead, the pot-holed lane ended in a wide, equally mucky yard delimited on two sides by gap-toothed drystone walls banked with nettles and on the third by a ramshackle open-fronted byre. The motor-cycle had stopped beside a gate in a rotting wooden fence surrounding a vegetable plot where a flock of damp chickens scratched after grubs among the dripping cabbages and Brussels sprouts. A fruit-laden plum tree badly in need of pruning sheltered a hen-coop badly in need of re-roofing.

Tumbelow opened the gate and Alec managed to step from the side-car to the crushed-shell path beyond without landing in the intervening puddle.

"Thank you, Sergeant. I want you in uniform."

Stripping off his overalls, Tumbelow bundled them into the side-car, closed its top against the steady drizzle, and joined Alec. "The back door, I should think, sir. These back of beyond farms, they often don't open the front door from one year to the next. Likely it's barred and bolted."

The stone house looked as if it had stood virtually unchanged for centuries. As they trudged along the path leading around the side, Alec noted peeling paint on the frames of the tiny windows, but to walls two feet thick, a few years, or decades, of neglect were of little account.

The back yard, surrounded by a barn and outbuildings in varying states of dilapidation, was largely given over to brambles, on which blackberries were beginning to ripen, and more stinging nettles. A

166

chained dog, staggering arthritically to its feet, barked half-heartedly at the two strangers. A man in a leather jerkin came to the open barn door, pitchfork in hand, and watched them in sullen silence.

Alec knocked on the back door.

The woman who opened the door, swathed in an apron both flowery and floury, was massive. Greying braids circled her head above a face as round and red as the setting sun, marred by the dark cloud of a bruise on one cheek. Her gaze passed indifferently over Alec, but the sight of Tumbelow's uniform brought a look of mingled fear and relief.

"Olive . . . ?"

"We haven't found your daughter, Mrs. Coleman. We're just checking that she actually is missing, and—May we come in?"

With a helpless gesture of one flour-dusted arm, she moved aside. Alec entered a large room, stone-flagged, apparently combining the functions of living and dining rooms and kitchen. The cooking facilities were primitive, an open fireplace with hooks, racks, spits and a brick oven. Around the fireplace, iron pots and pans hung on hooks. A wooden settle on one side and a rocking chair on the other provided the only seating apart from unmatched chairs at the scrubbed white-wood table, on which were pastry makings.

Everything was spotless. The farmhouse was as clean and tidy inside as it was mucky outside.

"Aye, she ran off yest'day, wi' her dad after her." Moving like an automaton, Mrs. Coleman returned to her pastry. "He come back but I ha'n't seen hide nor hair o' my girl sin'."

"Is Mr. Coleman at home?"

"Nay, he's off about the farm. And it's to be hoped he don't come home afore you're gone." She glanced apprehensively at Sergeant Tumbelow, who relaxed a bit and moved aside from the post he had taken up blocking the door. "He'll cut up rough, having the police in the house. Ellen promised not to tell you yet, not till tomorrow if Olive's still not come home."

"Ellen Hammett? It wasn't Mrs. Hammett who came to us. But

we heard your daughter hadn't been seen since yesterday afternoon, and in the circumstances we have to investigate. Oh, by the way, do you recognize this earring?"

She shook her head. "Nay, our Olive ha'n't nothing gaudy like that."

"All right. Tell us what happened yesterday."

Gentle probing brought out much the same story that Daisy had reported hearing from Mrs. Hammett. Mrs. Coleman wouldn't by any means credit that Olive had done anything worse than "walk out" with George Enderby, "which is bad enow, him being a married man. They don't seem to teach 'em right from wrong in the school, the way they did when I was a girl."

"But your husband believed . . . the worst, did he not?"

"I shouldn't 'a' tole him what Ellen said," she said wretchedly. "Ellen Hammett's a busybody as always makes bad worse, but she were right about that. He'd 'a' half killed Olive if she hadn't hopped it quick as winking."

"You said he went after her. How long was he gone?"

"He di'n't come back till after milking. I'd his tea ready for him."

"Several hours, then. Did he say where he'd been? What he'd been doing?"

"Nay, Alfred never were much of a talker, but there's allus plenty to do on the farm, Sunday or any other day."

Much of it left undone! "He must have said something when your daughter didn't come in to tea, surely?"

"I axed him where she'd went. He said he di'n't know and di'n't care, and she knowed what was coming to her if she showed her face. I'm . . . I'm afeared he done her a mischief!" Tears started rolling down the broad face. She dropped her rolling-pin, sank onto the nearest chair and blotted her eyes with her apron. "When he loses his temper, he don't know his own strength." She raised her hand to her bruised cheek, now streaked with flour.

Alec put away the handkerchief he had started to pull out. He was pretty sure Olive had been the female with Enderby. A thorough search of the area around their rendezvous had not discovered her, neither dead nor—almost worse—badly injured. "Assuming she outran him, where might she have taken refuge? With relatives? Friends?"

"She had friends at school, but I dunno their names. She never brung 'em home, as who can blame her. Then there's her aunts and uncles, my brothers and sisters, and Alfred's sister." She gave names and addresses, which Tumbelow wrote down in his notebook, using a blunt pencil seemingly in need of frequent licking. Most of her relatives resided on local farms, but one of her sisters had escaped as far as Exeter and a brother worked for James Hammett, transporting fish. "Olive wouldn't 'a' gone to him, though, acos Ellen'd've knowed about it, for sure."

"We'll check them all," Alec said reassuringly, "and find out from her teachers who are her particular friends. We'll find her."

"She won't come home, not wi' her dad angry as he is."

"He must have been very angry with Enderby, too. What did he have to say about him?"

"Nothing afore he dashed off after Olive. He were in too much hurry to get after her. When he come home to his tea, he talked very bitter."

"He made threats against him?"

"He talked wild about going over to the Schooner to have it out wi' him, but where's the use o' that, I says." She touched her bruised cheek again. "Ellen tole me about Peter Anstruther going for him Sat'day night, and much good it did him. Di'n't seem like there was much Alfred could do, wi'out as good as shouting from the rooftops as our Olive's a bad girl—though seeing summun tole Ellen, 'tis no secret. But 'tain't like it were a lad as can be made to wed her, is it?"

"I'm afraid not. When did you hear that Enderby was dead?"

"One o' the men heard it at the Green Garter in Malborough last night and tole us at milking time this morning."

"Who was that? Where can I find him?"

Mrs. Coleman gave the farm-hand's name but shrugged her

shoulders as to where he might be found. She had nothing to do with the farm management and—as she announced with a proud look around the room—her husband had nothing to say within the house. Alec asked for a photograph. The only one she had was of the whole Malborough village school. Olive was little more than a pale blur.

As Alec and Tumbelow took their leave, her mother returned to the pastry-making, saying, "You tell him it weren't me as called you in, that's all. Fit to bust, he'll be."

The sergeant was disappointed. "It don't sound like Coleman did Enderby in. He was threatening revenge after he died."

"Don't jump to conclusions. I doubt if Mrs. Coleman is capable of making that up, but until I've spoken to her husband, I can't begin to judge whether he might have deliberately deceived her. We'll see if that fellow is still in the barn. With luck he'll be able to tell us where his master is."

The man in the barn, apathetically forking hay from a waggon into the loft, turned out to be the one who had patronized the Green Garter last night. Alec asked how Coleman had received the news that George Enderby was dead.

"Eh?"

"Was he surprised? Pleased? Shocked? Angry? Upset?"

"Uh. Un just give a grunt. Mr. Coleman bain't much for talk lessn he be mad. Which he be, often as not."

"Do you know where we can find him?"

"Nay, un bain't much for talk. Mought be down Lugg's Bottom way. One o' the heifers broke through the hedge down thataway."

Alec requested directions to Lugg's Bottom. The man came out of the barn to point out the way, gesturing with his pitchfork. Since their route started out around a field of mangel-wurzels and continued across a meadow grazed by bullocks, Tumbelow was reluctantly forced to leave his motor-bike behind. Alec applauded his own forethought in having changed into boots before embarking upon this expedition, however inappropriate with his light grey tweed suit.

170

At least the rain had stopped, though dark clouds overhead threatened more to come.

Turning the corner of a hedge, they met Coleman trudging up from Lugg's Bottom, a black-and-white dog at his heels. Though he was not a large man, far less hefty than his wife if as tall, his sinewy strength was unmistakable, and on his shoulder he carried a murderous-looking billhook.

His truculent scowl on seeing Alec added to the impression of an ugly customer. When he stopped, the dog crouched at his heels, fixing Alec with an unnervingly unblinking stare. Glad he had brought the sergeant with him, Alec was about to speak when the farmer caught sight of Tumbelow.

"Bluebottles!" he snarled. "What the bloody hell d'ye think you be about, a-trespassing on my land?"

"Mr. Coleman? I'm Detective Chief Inspector Fletcher. I have a few questions to put to you."

"I got better things to do wi' my time nor gabbing wi' a pair o' blasted bluebottles. I s'pose the wife's been nattering to her cousin about our girl running off. Might as well tell all the world. Well, if so be you find Olive, you can tell the little slut from me as her dad'll leather her proper when she come home!"

"You aren't worried about her?"

"Nay, the devil takes care o' his own. Took care o' George Enderby, all right!" Coleman grinned evilly. "Di'n't need to raise a finger to the bastard, did I?"

"I s'pose you're going to claim the sight o' that ugly mug o' yours coming after him scared him into jumping!" Tumbelow exclaimed.

"That will do, Sergeant." Alec frowned him down, but he was quite glad of the outburst when it provoked an unguarded answer to the question he'd otherwise have had to pose.

"He never seen it, did he, seeing I never seen him!" said Coleman ferociously. "Mayhap the perlice ha'n't nothing better to do of a Sunday afternoon than chase around the cliffs after a wench as'll

171

come home when she's hungry. Us farmers as works for our livings ha'n't no time for such gallivanting."

"But Miss Coleman hasn't come home."

"Seemingly she bain't hungry enow yet."

"How far did you chase her?"

" 'Bout as fur as my bull chased a nosy gov'mint inspector as come poking around my dairy last year."

"Not far, then," Alec guessed with assumed indifference, hoping Tumbelow was not too obviously scanning the horizon for the bull. "What did you do after that?"

"Went to bring the cows in for milking, di'n't I, seeing my cow-man wants his Sundays off nowadays and there's no other help to be got for love nor money, thanks to the bloody gov'mint's bloody war. A fine mess they made o' the world, if you ask me. They takes your money and what do you get? A lot o' dead soldiers, and a lot o' live bluebottles buzzing around where they bain't wanted!"

At a twitch of Coleman's finger, the dog began to rise slowly from its crouch, hackles bristling, a low rumble starting in its throat. Alec hurriedly decided he had enough information to begin checking the farmer's movements the previous day.

"Thank you for your time, Mr. Coleman," he said. "I must ask you to let the police know at once if your daughter returns home, and we will inform you if we find her. I should add that it was not Mrs. Coleman's cousin who reported her absence to us, so you have no bone to pick with either lady."

He and the sergeant beat a retreat with more haste than dignity. Tumbelow nobly let Alec lead the way, in spite of which the sergeant arrived back at the farmyard with both his ankles and the seat of his trousers intact. Either the farmer or his dog had more sense than to implement the threat of violence against the police.

Whether he had been equally restrained—or unsuccessful—with regard to his daughter and her seducer was another matter.

Alec could only hope his parting words would save Mrs. Coleman from further bruising. He rather doubted it. He decided to have a word with Puckle on the subject when he got back to Westcombe, though it was no business of Scotland Yard's and police intervention was in any case unlikely to do any good. The woman would never press assault charges against her husband. If he were fined, the financial loss would be equally hers; if he were imprisoned, how was she to run the farm without him?

"Back to HQ, sir?" asked Tumbelow, following Alec around the house.

"No, to the byre, or cow shed, or whatever it is. I want a word with the cowman if he's about."

The milking shed was unoccupied, but through a door at the back they entered the dairy. Though the interior was cleaner than the dilapidated exterior of the building had led Alec to expect, he suspected it might not have satisfied the unfortunate government inspector. An elderly dairy-maid, her grey hair tucked up under a scarlet kerchief, was scrubbing out a butter-churn.

Alec introduced himself and the sergeant. "Milking time's over, is it?" he asked.

"Nay. They be just a-coming up."

"Same time every day?"

"Aye. Cows be creeturs o' habit."

"Even on a Sunday, eh?"

She looked at him with scorn. "Don't make no odds what day o' the week. You try telling a cow 'tis the Sabbath! When her udder's full, she wants milking."

"And you work every day?"

"That I do. Not like some. There's three o' the beasties won't let another pair o' hands touch 'em but mine, and what the master'll do when I'm too old for milking, I'm sure I don't know. The young girls don't stay down on the farm these days. Ifn they doesn't wed, they runs off to town for a job as gives 'em Sundays off."

"So this time yesterday, the herd came in for milking?"

"That they did, wi' the master driving 'em acos that sluggard Barney Ridd's done took into his noddle to lie abed Sundays like a townsman."

173

Alec glanced at his wrist-watch. Nearly five. He looked around the dairy. Among the milk cans, milking pails, churn, butter-moulds and other equipment less identifiable to a townsman, he saw no clock. "How do you know it was the usual time?"

The old woman's scorn redoubled. "Acos cows that's kept waiting past their time do be fair betwattled," she said, "and yest'day they wasn't. And now I hears 'em coming and I've me work to do." She took two pails from the shelf and stumped out to the milking shed.

The two policemen went after her. The yard was now full of lowing cattle, black and white, red, yellowish, every hue of the bovine spectrum. The last of the herd of a score or so were just emerging from the lane.

"My bike!" moaned Tumbelow, as a passing cow nuzzled the handlebars.

The yokel trudging in the rear gave her a whack on the rump with his stick and she ambled onward. The two dogs at his heels seemed to have little to do, the cows being eager for the relief of emptying swollen udders. As the first couple reached the shed, they headed for their accustomed places.

Hurrying out before they were boxed in, Alec and the sergeant picked their way around the side of the yard.

"Mr. Ridd," said Alec, when they were close enough to the cow-man to be heard over the mooing, "I'd like a word with you."

"Ar?"

Barney Ridd was no more curious than the dairy-maid about why the police were interested in the habits of cows. He was as convinced as she had been that his charges had been milked at the usual time the previous day, though for a different reason: If they had been early, then they would have been desperate for relief this morning, which they were not. "This dang Summer Time the dang gov'mint invented" meant that milking time was now five o'clock morning and afternoon in the summer months, the cows being unwilling to obey the clock.

"How long does it take to bring them from the pasture?"

174

Ridd shrugged. "'Pends which field they'm in and how fast they feels like walking."

"Yesterday?"

"Didn't ought to've took more nor half an hour. Less, most like. 'Sides, the master sets the dogs after 'em if they slows down."

If Coleman had been a couple of miles away at three, pushing Enderby off the cliff, he had had plenty of time to get to the meadow where the cows had been grazing and bring them up to the milking shed by five.

19

*U*ndeterred by dark clouds threatening more rain, and by the fact that their creations never survived more than a few hours, Belinda and Deva were hard at work on yet another castle. Daisy, relaxing in a deck-chair Peter Anstruther had obligingly carried down to the beach for her, tried to concentrate on a new library book.

Her mind wandered.

Anstruther was still a suspect. Though Alec hadn't been able to tell her much in that sneaky Inspector Mallow's presence, he surely would have let her know if their host was exonerated. This afternoon, Anstruther and Cecily both seemed preoccupied, not exactly worried but their thoughts elsewhere. At least they themselves were still here, unlike Donald Baskin.

Daisy had returned from the parish hall to find that Baskin had departed, his knapsack on his back. He'd told the girls he was off on an afternoon's hike with his picnic tea, as he'd mentioned to Daisy he might. But she remembered that he had arrived in Westcombe with all his possessions in the knapsack. Suppose he had quietly packed up again and scarpered?

He had come in search of George Enderby, that seemed indisputable. Foreseeing a possible opportunity to give the dastard his comeuppance, Baskin might well have used a false name, in which case the police would find it near impossible to trace him.

So, ought Daisy to go and tell them he had gone off again? She tried to weigh the pros and cons.

Baskin had originally intended to leave today, satisfied with having accomplished what he came for. He had seen most of the countryside hereabouts, he had hurried to explain. Had he stayed on just to give the girls a treat, or to watch where the police investigation was heading? If the latter, why should he decamp now? Nothing suggested they were about to single him out from the list of suspects.

Daisy tried to remember what Alec had said about Baskin's apparent reactions on hearing Enderby was dead. No, she thought, not that he was dead, but that he had fallen from the cliff. First, believing Enderby to be injured, he had seemed frustrated, or rather, as though he didn't know what to do next. Suppose he had planned to give Enderby a thrashing, why should he care that his goal was thwarted since someone else had done the job for him? But if he had planned to kill him, the injuries would complicate matters since Enderby would be under medical care. He might well be unsure as to what was now his best course of action.

On the other hand, Enderby's death meant he did not have to go through with the planned murder. Small wonder if he had been relieved!

Daisy found herself faced with the conclusion that Baskin had come to Westcombe to discover whether the landlord of the Schooner really was the man he was after, and if so to kill him. And that led her right back to the question of whether he had in fact pushed Enderby over, which could account equally well for his relief on hearing he was dead, not merely injured.

Before Daisy had time to work out whether she was indulging in circular reasoning—an error not unknown to her—or ought to tell Alec that Baskin had left, Peter Anstruther arrived.

"Not the best of weather for lounging on the beach, I'm afraid," he said. "Ceci sent me to ask if you'd like me to carry down your tea on a tray, but I expect you'd rather come back to the house."

"I don't know. The girls are having a wonderful time. I'm sure they'd rather have sand in their sandwiches than have to wash and change and brush their hair."

Looking down the beach, he laughed. "They are in the middle of an ambitious project, aren't they? When I was a boy, my mother used to have the greatest difficulty getting me to come in for meals."

"The house was your father's?" Daisy asked, then suddenly couldn't recall whether that was a scrap of information she ought not to know. That was always a risk with eavesdropping.

But for all Anstruther knew, his wife had told her. "Yes," he said, sitting down on a nearby rock. "My grandfather did well enough as a skilled craftsman with one of the local shipbuilders to build himself a cottage here. The business was booming in those days, but West-combe isn't a deep enough port to build the modern big ships. My father went into the Coast Guard. He enlarged the house when he married. I've lived here all my life."

"I envy you. It's a beautiful place."

"It's wonderful to come home to after months at sea—years during the War—but that's the trouble." He sighed. "I've been at sea the greater part of the last twenty years."

"Trouble?" Daisy said sympathetically.

"My poor Ceci! She's never complained, so I didn't realize how lonely she's been. You're too kind to condemn her for . . . for what happened, but she can't go on living here among people who know. That's what I was thinking about up at the old fort yesterday, trying to work out what to do for the best. I just needed to get away somewhere quiet where I could think! Obviously, that bast—sorry, that dastard of an inspector didn't believe me."

"Oh, Mallow didn't believe Mr. Baskin's story, either. At a guess, he never believes anything anyone says, on principle. Of course, the police have to be sceptical, but you needn't worry that Alec automatically disbelieves what he's told. Did you come to any conclusions about what to do next?"

"The first step is obvious. I'm already working at a letter applying for a shore job. Gunnery instructor, with luck, not a glorified clerk. It may mean I don't get my commission, which I was hoping for next voyage, but it can't be helped."

"Will you miss the sea?"

"There'll be plenty of short sails. You can't teach a man to shoot from a ship if he don't go to sea."

"I suppose not."

"Then, once I find out where I'm posted, I'll have to sell the house. I can't deny it'll be a wrench, but if I can't live here, there's no point hanging on to it. It's not as if I've stopped in this corner of Devon all my life. I know how to get on anywhere in the world. We'll be all right and tight."

"I'm sure you will. You seem to have had a productive session of sweet silent thought."

Anstruther looked blank. "A what?"

"Sorry! It's a bit of Shakespeare, I think. Poetry, anyway, and misquoted, and the reverse of relevant if I remember the next line correctly. I just meant you came to a lot of decisions while you were at the camp."

"Actually, I'd pretty much decided all that already. It was more a matter of thinking things through, taking a look at possible consequences, making sure I'd decided right. And, to tell the truth, I was in two minds what to do about Enderby. The temptation to give him a good hiding was nearly irresistible."

"Nearly?"

Standing up, Anstruther paced restlessly, one fist smacking into the other hand, while he explained. "It would have done more harm than good, wouldn't it? Drawn more attention to Ceci, confirmed in people's minds that what Stebbins said was true, perhaps got me thrown out of the Navy. I'd almost made up my mind the game

179

wasn't worth the candle, but the temptation was still there, I can't deny it. It's just as well for us that someone else got to him first, and more lethally than I'd ever contemplated." He stopped and looked straight at Daisy. "I didn't kill him."

"I'm quite prepared to believe you, or the girls and I would have left your house by now. But Alec needs evidence."

He smiled. "I'm cheered by the thought that the chief inspector hasn't moved out, either. What about tea?"

Daisy glanced at Bel and Deva, still absorbed in their building. "We'll have it down here, if it's really not too much trouble and if it doesn't start raining."

"Right you are. Thank you for letting me get that off my chest, Mrs. Fletcher." He sketched a salute and turned towards the house.

All very well, Daisy thought: She was indeed prepared to believe—even inclined to believe—that Anstruther hadn't killed Enderby, but that wasn't quite the same thing as actually believing. He produced lots of good reasons for not pursuing vengeance, but had he really thought better of it? On the other hand, would he be calmly making plans for his and Cecily's future if there was a possibility that he might at any moment be arrested for killing his wife's lover?

"What's done is done," he had said. "No use crying over spilt milk." Did that philosophy enable him to continue coolly with his life as though he had not committed murder?

He had means, opportunity, and a strong motive. Not that means was an important indicator in this case. If Enderby had been close enough to the edge of the cliff and taken by surprise, practically anyone could have pushed him over.

How close to the edge had the jacket and earring been found? Daisy wished she had thought to ask Miss Bellamy. As for taking the victim by surprise, Georgie Porgie would have been on the alert the instant he caught sight of Anstruther, his known enemy. Baskin would have had a much better chance of getting close to Enderby, who had no reason to suppose him an ill-wisher.

Where Donald Baskin was concerned, motive was the sticking

point. Daisy could not forget his mutter in the dark garden: "That settles it! The man's a cad and a bounder and he's got to be stopped." It sounded as if what they had overheard about Enderby and Cecily had been the last straw, making Baskin decide to act. But what were the rest of the straws burdening the proverbial camel? Impossible to believe that the mild schoolmaster was actually a maniac who went around righting other people's wrongs by murder!

Daisy sighed. She wasn't getting anywhere. Besides, for all she knew, by now Alec might have found witnesses to give both men alibis, or proof that Stebbins or Coleman was the murderer. Or he might have found Coleman's daughter and received from her an eyewitness report. She wished she had an excuse to go and ask him.

A drop of rain splotched the open page of her book. Quickly she closed it and tucked it into her bag. No tea on the beach today. She managed to lever herself out of the deck-chair. As she straightened, she looked towards Bel and Deva and saw that Sid had arrived upon the scene.

He looked very much more respectable since his night in the washhouse gaol. Though his feet were still bare, the trousers of dark brown duck had no visible holes. His shirt, a green and brown check, was collarless, but he wore a red handkerchief around his neck. It clashed abominably with the pink and purple band of the Panama Belinda had given him. Beneath its brim, the stubbled chin and shy, innocent eyes were the same. His hair was short and neat, though. Mrs. Puckle must have trimmed his mane. He didn't have his cart with him, but he had brought something to give the children.

Sid the beachcomber was Sid Coleman, the farmer's brother and thus uncle to the vanished Olive. Might Olive have taken refuge in his shack? Surely Alec wouldn't mind if she asked.

Daisy walked down the beach. The rain was spitting down now, and it was time to go in to tea. The girls skipped towards her, each adorned with a necklace of shells and feathers strung on fishing line.

"Look, Mummy! Sid made these for us. Isn't he clever? It'll be perfect with my Red Indian costume you brought me from America."

Behind them, Sid beamed and nodded, took out his mouth-organ and played a snatch of "Widdecombe Fair."

Deva pulled a face. "My ayah," she said softly, "would say only an Untouchable would wear such rubbish."

At least she spoke softly. Some of Belinda's care for other people's feelings had rubbed off on her. "How nice of Sid," said Daisy. "I hope you both thanked him."

"Of course, Mummy."

"Good. Then collect your things and go on up to the house for tea, before you get any wetter. If that's possible. I'll be with you in a moment. I just want to ask Sid a question."

Sid cocked his head with an enquiring look. Then his gaze moved beyond Daisy. His face convulsed with fright and he took to his heels.

"Sid!"

He scuttled on, heading for his cart, which he'd left on the track a short way up the hill, Daisy saw.

Turning, she found Peter Anstruther approaching. He was in civvies but had on his RN cap, presumably the first thing that came to hand to keep his hair dry. He stared after Sid. "What's up with him? He's never been afraid of me before."

"Perhaps it's your headgear. He's probably afraid of any uniform since Constable Puckle hauled him off to the clink for the night."

"Puckle arrested Sid? What on earth for?"

As they followed the girls back up the beach, Daisy told him about Sid's brush with Mrs. Hammett and the law.

"Meddlesome old bi—witch," he said with the easy tolerance of one rarely present to be meddled with. He stopped to fold the deck-chair. "This is what I came down for, to help you with the chair. Ceci was sure you'd not want tea on the beach in this rain, not that it's what we'd call rain at sea." Deck-chair in one hand, his other under her elbow to help her through the rocks, he went on, "Fred Puckle's not a bad chap, a bit slow, but when Ellen Hammett gets on her high horse, it's easier to knuckle under."

"She does rather steamroller one," Daisy agreed.

While he put the deck-chair away in the shed, she went into the house and upstairs to make sure Bel and Deva scrubbed the sand from their fingernails. Belinda wanted to wear Sid's necklace to tea. Deva didn't. Daisy failed to see a problem, but they assured her they both had to do the same. Bel won, by pointing out that as they weren't at a huge, grand hotel such as Deva had occasionally stayed at with her parents, no one would see them anyway.

When they went down, Daisy was surprised to find that Donald Baskin had already returned. He made the rain his excuse, though it was still only spitting, enough to deter a picnic but not a seasoned hiker. To Daisy, he seemed to be on edge. Of course, being suspected of murder was enough to unsettle anyone.

Over tea, his schoolmaster aspect came to the fore. Challenging the girls to a memory game, he told them what all their shells and feathers were and proposed that after tea they should each write a list to see how many they remembered.

When they were thus occupied, he said to Daisy, "As I think you guessed, it wasn't the rain that drove me back. To tell the truth, I started wondering whether your husband had found anyone to confirm my movements yesterday, or if he might be looking for me to ask more questions."

"As far as I know, he hasn't been looking for you. It might mean that your alibi's been confirmed, or just that he's too busy with other threads of the investigation."

"At least that suggests that I'm not the chief suspect! I assume the people at the Ferries Inn and on the ferry at least haven't denied the possibility of my having been there at lunchtime. There's something else: I didn't get a chance last night to mention to the inspector that I exchanged greetings with two or three yokels as I walked. Not that I could pinpoint where. I can't see how the police would find them and it seems unlikely they'd know what time I passed, anyway. But do you think I ought to go and tell them?"

"It can't hurt. You'd be amazed at what they can find out when they put their minds to it. As a matter of fact, I have something to tell Alec. I was thinking of popping over to the parish hall if Mrs. Anstruther doesn't mind keeping an eye on the girls. Why don't you go with me?" With any luck at all, Daisy thought, as they walked along together he would confide the reason for his interest in George Enderby.

She went to the kitchen. At one end of the table Cecily was rolling pastry. At the other end, Anstruther was chewing on a pencil, in the throes of drafting a letter. Several balls of crumpled paper testified to his difficulties. From the scullery came a splashing and the chink of china as Vera washed up the tea things.

Daisy asked if Cecily would mind taking charge of Belinda and Deva for a while.

"Not at all. Do you think they'd like to help me make jam tarts?"

"I expect so." Bel certainly would, and she could probably persuade Deva it would be fun. "But don't feel you have to entertain them. Mr. Baskin and I are both going over to the parish hall. I don't suppose we'll be long."

"I'll come with you," said Anstruther, throwing down his pencil. "I want to know what's going on. And the inspector said we'd have to make formal statements. Might as well get it over with."

Daisy suppressed a sigh. With Anstruther along, she had to abandon all hope of confidences from Baskin.

20

Do you feel, Mrs. Fletcher," said Baskin as the men dropped back to let her enter the parish hall first, "as if you're leading a pair of lambs to the slaughter?"

"Not at all," Daisy said crossly. "Assuming you're both innocent as lambs, you have nothing to fear. And if . . . Oh!" She came to a halt, face to face with a horde of policemen making for the door, Mallow in the lead. "Good evening, Inspector. Are you off to arrest someone?"

"Good evening, Mrs. Fletcher. No, alas, we're not about to make an arrest. Unless you've brought these two gentleman to confess?" he added with the smile that failed to reach his hard eyes.

"What, both of them?"

"Conspiracy is always a possibility."

"I can't help feeling that if Mr. Anstruther and Mr. Baskin had conspired to bump off Enderby, they'd have provided decent alibis for each other."

"You told us you needed us to make formal statements," Anstruther said impatiently, regarding the inspector with venomous dislike. "Since no one has come to us, we've come to you."

"That's very good of you, sir." Mallow's voice was smooth and bland, but Daisy, disillusioned, was sure he was being sarcastic. "Do come in." With a jerk of his head he sent the uniformed crowd on their way. "I expect you realize that you are not obliged to tell us anything, but anything you choose to say will be taken down and may be used in evidence. And you have a right to the presence of a lawyer."

Baskin and Anstruther both shook their heads.

Alec and a second plainclothes man sat at one table, Constable Puckle at another, near the door. As Mallow led the three newcomers forward into the Stygian gloom of the hall, Daisy hung back behind the men, so that Alec's eye would fall on her last, when his mind was already occupied with the voluntary arrival of two of his suspects.

"These gentlemen are here to make statements, sir," said Mallow, his tone congratulatory. "I've given them the warning. I'll stay and lend a hand."

"No, thanks, Inspector. Horrocks and I will manage. You go and eat with the others now so that I can leave you in charge later. Puckle, you'd better light a few lamps, please. It's getting dark in here already."

"There'll be a downpour before nightfall," Anstruther prophesied. "Thunder, too, I shouldn't be surprised."

"And close the windows," Alec added to the local bobby.

"Since you still want statements, Chief Inspector," Anstruther continued, "I take it you haven't found anyone to confirm our whereabouts?"

"In your case, Mr. Anstruther—Sit down, won't you, both of you?" Alec motioned them to chairs in front of his table.

Daisy slipped away to find herself a seat out of his direct line of sight but within hearing. He glanced at her with a frown. She could practically read his mind:

He was wondering whether she had information to give him or had tagged along with Anstruther and Baskin in hope of finding out what was going on; he might consider the possibility that she had persuaded them to come, either to be helpful or because she wanted to hear what they had to say. One way or another, he was dying to deal with her first and send her on her way—Daisy held her breath—

but he was afraid the delay might be enough to make the men change their minds about offering voluntary statements.

She let out her breath on a long, silent sigh of relief as his attention returned to Peter Anstruther.

"In your case, we've found a motor-car matching your description of the one you passed. The driver was in the lane you say you took, at about the right time. Unfortunately, he passed several bicyclists on his way from Plymouth and can't specify when or where, let alone describe them. If you—"

"Mr. Fletcher!" A young man bounded in, waving a sheaf of papers. "I've brought the autopsy report, sir. Dr. Wedderburn said to tell you he's sorry it took so long but there were so many injuries . . . I can tell you, it was perfectly ripping watching the dissection. I think maybe I'll be a police surgeon."

"I'm glad you enjoyed it," Alec said dryly. "You can leave the report with me, but it looks as if it'll take as long to read as it did to produce. Could you come back in a while to give me a précis of the highlights?"

"Right-oh. Sorry, I shouldn't have barged in like that when you're in the middle of something. I'll go and put the hood up on the old bus or she'll be nothing but a tub of water in no time. It's going to be coming down cats and dogs any minute. Cheerio!"

Daisy was glad she had brought her umbrella. The young man, she assumed, must be Andrew Vernon, the medical student. He certainly sounded quite as bloodthirsty as Julia Bellamy had given her to understand. She rather thought she'd leave before he gave Alec his report on the post mortem.

Alec turned back to Anstruther. "Your description of the car you saw was pretty vague. Try and think back to it, see if you can come up with more detail. You were cycling up the lane, thinking about . . ."

"Thinking about how much I'd tell Pritchard. I wanted his advice, you see, about asking for a shore job, but I didn't need to go into details about my reasons. The car came down the hill towards me, making quite a racket. I'm pretty sure it was blue, light blue, not grey. But I didn't look at the number plate, and I couldn't tell you the make to save my life."

"We'll hope it doesn't come to that."

"Give me the silhouette of a ship and I'll tell you her class, tonnage—give or take—and likely her nationality. Maybe even her name, not to mention her armament. But motor-cars . . ." He shrugged.

"Making quite a racket, was it?"

"Not so much loud, though those little machines tend to be noisy. More like sort of a cough and hiccups combined. I wouldn't want to put to sea with an engine sounding like that, not unless the whole German Army was shooting at me from the shore."

"Did the driver look worried?"

"Can't say I noticed him at all—or her. I was busy keeping out of his way without going into the hedge."

He sounded convincing to Daisy. Of course, he might have heard about the car's colour and engine trouble from someone in the village, but then he'd know the make and that the driver was male. Was the straightforward sailor subtle enough to realize that uncertainty on those points could serve him better than the facts?

In any case, his telling the truth about the car didn't invalidate Mallow's theory that he had cut across to the cliffs.

"You don't recall seeing anyone else all afternoon?" Alec asked. "Even in Malborough?"

"I wasn't in a mood to notice. You haven't found anyone who saw me, then?"

"Not yet. It's a matter of time and man-power. But I did have an officer go to Sea View Cottage, and Mr. Pritchard confirms he was out all yesterday afternoon." Alec stood up. "Come over to the map, will you, and show me your route. Horrocks, Puckle, come and witness this, please."

They went over to the table on the far side of the room from

188

Daisy. After a moment's indecision, Baskin followed, but Daisy didn't quite dare.

What she heard sounded much the same as what Anstruther had told Mallow. Then, also, she had been unable to see the map. Nor had her attempted exploration been successful—except that it had led her to Mrs. Hammett and thus to Olive Coleman's disappearance. The shortage of man-power for investigating Anstruther's movements could be because all the available officers had been searching for Olive.

If they had found her, then Daisy's snippet of information about Sid being her uncle would fall flat. Or PC Puckle or Mrs. Coleman might already have told Alec. Still, he couldn't blame her for bringing stale news.

Baskin was going over his route on the map now. She couldn't be sure it was exactly the same as what he had said before, but she thought so. The fact that Alec was bothering with it must mean no witnesses to his movements had been found, either. Both Baskin and Anstruther were still suspects.

The men all moved back to the other table, except Puckle, who resumed his seat by the door. Prompted by Alec, Anstruther began in a low voice to tell his story, starting with the fracas in the Schooner bar. Daisy caught only snatches of what he said, because the cats and dogs had arrived and were drumming frenziedly on the roof. Water streamed down the high windows. Puckle lighted a couple more lamps.

The door opened and the bloodthirsty young man dashed in, dripping. He took off his hat and shook it, showering the floor, then looked around and came over to Daisy.

"Simply bucketing down!" he announced unnecessarily, setting a green canvas case on the table. "I say, d'you mind if I introduce myself? I'm Andrew Vernon. I'm helping the chief inspector with this case, don't you know." Trying to appear nonchalant, he succeeded only in sounding very youthful and proud of himself. "Are you waiting to see him?"

"Yes. I'm—"

"Don't tell me! Let me deduce." He regarded her with sparkling eyes. "You're Mrs. Fletcher."

"How did you guess?"

"Not a guess, a deduction. Actually, I saw you in the Anstruthers' garden when we came down from the cliffs yesterday. But if I hadn't, I would have worked it out anyway. If you were an ordinary witness, Mr. Fletcher would have spoken to you first, because you might know something that would clear Mr. Baskin or Mr. Anstruther, so he wouldn't have to interview them. Or if you were a suspect, again he'd see you first. You might incriminate yourself and he could let them go."

"But since I'm merely his wife, I may await his convenience."

Vernon grinned. "You said it, not I."

"I gather you attended the autopsy. I don't want to hear the details, but would you say it produced anything interesting? I don't mean interesting to you, because Miss Bellamy told me about your taste for the grisly and gruesome, but anything helpful to the investigation."

"Not really. Dr. Wedderburn says all the injuries were produced in such a short period, just a few seconds, that he can't tell which killed him, or distinguish between ante and post mortem. There's one odd thing, though."

"What's that?"

"I expect Mr. Fletcher told you about the splinters in Enderby's neck? He probably didn't mention that I found them," Vernon said modestly.

Actually, it was Julia Bellamy who had told Daisy about the splinters, but she saw no reason to disillusion Vernon as to how much—or how little—Alec confided in her. "What about them?" she said.

"Dr. Wedderburn says they weren't the result of a straight blow. He found abrasion—grazing—and the splinters entered the skin at an angle. It must have been more of a glancing impact. If you were going to hit someone with a cudgel, wouldn't you strike straight at them?"

"I expect so, though I can't say I've ever considered the matter. But suppose Enderby saw the blow coming and ducked—"

"Oh yes, that must be it," said Vernon with heartfelt relief. He must have been afraid of being cheated of the glory of having been the one who found the evidence of murder. "Wedderburn refused to speculate, said that was the job of the police. If Enderby was near enough to the edge of the cliff, even a glancing blow would have sent him over."

"It's funny," Daisy mused, "I always pictured a cudgel as being sort of smooth and polished. But I suppose there's no reason why it shouldn't be splintery. Or not a proper cudgel, if you know what I mean, just a splintery piece of wood that came to hand. Alec had better check the hands of his suspects for splinters."

"That's a knacky notion!"

Hearing the envy in his voice, Daisy said generously, "I'll let you suggest it to him."

"That's jolly decent of you, Mrs. Fletcher. But I'll give you credit, of course."

"No, don't do that!" The last thing she wanted was for Alec to know the idea came from her, though she supposed he was bound to guess she'd been talking to Vernon about the autopsy. "You'd have thought of it sooner or later, I'm sure."

"Perhaps. It's quite difficult, this detection business, isn't it? Dr. Thorndyke makes it all seem so obvious and easy."

"You're not doing so badly, considering you aren't even qualified as a doctor yet, let alone a lawyer, and you have no training as a detective. As well as the splinters, you found another clue up on the cliffs, according to Miss Bellamy."

Vernon crimsoned. "I shouldn't have told her. And she swore she wouldn't talk about any of it to anyone," he added with indignation.

"I'm sure she only told me because I'm the chief inspector's wife," Daisy said soothingly, leaving him without a leg to stand on since he, presumably, was confiding in her for the same reason. "Besides, she didn't tell me what it was you found."

"Because I wouldn't say, and I'm sorry but I'm not telling you that bit either, even if you are the chief inspector's wife." He was still very pink in the face, and went on with obvious relief, "Ah, Mr. Fletcher seems to have finished with those two. Your turn, ma'am."

"Hadn't you better suggest looking for splinters in their hands before they leave?"

"Oh, right-oh!"

He went over to Alec and Horrocks. Anstruther and Baskin exchanged a few words, then joined Daisy.

"Well, at least neither of us is under arrest yet," said Anstruther. "We'll wait and escort you back to the house."

"In the hope that the rain may have let up a bit by then." Baskin smiled. "Though our sailor claims it's going to get worse before it blows itself out."

"Westcombe is sheltered from the high winds but you can bet it's pretty rough out at sea. Listen!"

Above the drumming of rain on the roof, Daisy heard the rumble of thunder. A flash of lightning suddenly illuminated the hall. She jumped to her feet. "Oh dear! Belinda's not afraid of thunderstorms but I don't know about Deva. Perhaps I'd better run back."

"Not to worry, Mrs. Fletcher, Cecily will take care of them. You don't want to go out in this unless you have to."

Another and much brighter flash was followed after a few seconds by a crack of thunder.

"Coming closer," said Baskin. "Hello, Vernon, having fun?"

"Mr. Fletcher's asked me to help him again," the young man said importantly. "If you gentlemen wouldn't mind stepping over closer to this lamp . . . Oh, and Mrs. Fletcher, he'd like a word with you now."

As she moved away, Daisy read nothing but curiosity on the faces of the two suspects—no trace of alarm. Glancing back, she saw Vernon abstracting a pair of tweezers and a magnifying glass from his case. Aha, a splinter hunt!

Horrocks was joining them, notebook in hand, Daisy was glad to see. She sat down on his chair, firmly on Alec's side of the table.

"I take it this splinter in the hand idea is yours," he said, resigned.

"Why should you think that, darling?"

"Because he had just been talking to you and he looked back at you twice." He grinned at her. "And his manner was definitely sheepish. Of course, a lack of splinters won't eliminate them, but if either has splinters matching what was found in Enderby's skin, he'd better have a jolly good explanation. Was that what you came here for?"

"No, I only just thought of it. Don't forget to check Stebbins—or is he out of it?"

"No, no one saw him working in his garden. But a gardener probably has such tough hands no splinters would penetrate. Same goes for a farmer."

"You haven't found Olive Coleman yet?"

"Not yet. I've had people out checking all her relatives, not a single one of whom is on the telephone. No luck so far. We've also been trying to find out if she had any particular friends in Malborough, where she went to school. She left a couple of years ago, at fourteen, like most of these farm-girls, but she might have kept in touch."

"Did you know that Sid the beachcomber is her uncle?"

"No! Great Scott, Daisy, how did you find out? Are you sure? Mrs. Coleman never mentioned him."

"Yes! Chance. Quite sure. She might not have thought of him. He's Coleman's brother, not hers, and I expect he keeps well away from the farm. He's been pretty badly treated, I gather. They're probably ashamed of him, too. But it's just possible Olive might have taken refuge in his shack, isn't it?"

"We'll certainly have to check." Alec looked up at the streaming windows as thunder followed lightning. "But not this evening. I can't send the men out searching the cliffs for his shack in this weather."

"Mr. Baskin knows where it is. That is, he's seen it, though I don't know if he could pinpoint the spot on the map. And it started out as some sort of shepherd's hut that Mr. Anstruther knew when he was a boy. But I doubt either of them would happily lead you there in near darkness in the middle of a thunderstorm."

"It'll have to wait till tomorrow. If Olive's there, she won't be going out either. I'll send someone up in the morning. Thanks, love. Anything else you know that I don't?"

" 'Fraid not. Not that I know of. Will you be home for dinner?"

"I'm not sure. Don't wait. By the time I've heard Vernon's report on the post mortem, I rather doubt I'll have any appetite anyway!"

21

*B*y morning the storm had blown over, leaving streamers of cloud racing north-eastward before a blustery wind. Long swells surged up the inlet in spite of its sheltered position.

"Don't let the children play on the beach today," Anstruther advised, sticking his head into the dining room at breakfast time. "The tide's low now but as it comes in there'll likely be freak waves, bigger and more powerful than the general run. We wouldn't want the girls washed out to sea."

"Thanks for the warning." Alec could only hope he wasn't going to have to arrest the man, who seemed in so many ways a decent chap. If it came to that point, he'd leave the job to Mallow, under guise of letting the locals reap the credit.

The girls were round-eyed. "You mean we could drown?" Deva asked breathlessly.

"Not if you stay off the beach," Daisy pointed out. "We'll go for a walk. It's fun on a windy day like this."

"I'll go with you, if I may, Mrs. Fletcher," said Baskin. "If that's all right with you, old chap?"

Daisy accepted the schoolmaster's escort, and Alec gave his permission, not sure if he was playing the rôle of husband or policeman. Both, he supposed.

On his way to the parish hall, he reflected that arresting Baskin would be almost as difficult as arresting Anstruther. He wouldn't much mind putting Stebbins behind bars, though he was sorry for him with that flighty wife of his, and as for Coleman, it would be a positive pleasure.

Olive Coleman must be found. She was almost certainly the only person other than the murderer who had seen what happened up on the cliffs.

As he stepped across the threshold into the hall, his breath caught in his throat. After the fresh, brine-scented wind gusting in from the sea, the fug inside seemed almost thick enough to be cut with a knife. Several large, damp, hardworking policemen had slept and smoked therein. Sweat, wet wool, tobacco and stale beer mingled in a noxious miasma. Alec's one thought was to find an excuse to escape.

Mallow had already sent most of the men out to continue with enquiries begun yesterday. After an unctuous greeting, he immediately made Alec feel guilty by continuing, "A telephone call came last night, sir, after you left. I didn't disturb you as there wasn't much to be done about it till this morning, in my opinion. I hope you'll agree."

"Who was it?" Alec tried to hide his irritation. "And what about?"

"Leigh, the local constable at Malborough, found someone who saw a bicyclist riding along the main street just about when Mr. Anstruther claims to have been there. She couldn't recognize him from the photograph—says he looks just like a thousand other naval officers in his uniform with all that face fungus. But she claims she might recognize him if she saw him again dressed as he was then."

"Was the bicyclist she saw bearded?"

"She wouldn't swear to it. Saw him at an angle from the side and rear."

"Damn! It doesn't sound very hopeful. We'll have to give it a try, but if there's one possible witness, there may be more to come. We can't start sending Mr. Anstruther all over the countryside to see people who may or may not recognize him."

"No, sir. I was going to send Sergeant Tumbelow to fetch her, but I thought I'd better check with you first."

Alec recalled his frightful ride with the sergeant. "Is she an elderly lady?"

"I didn't ask her age, sir," Mallow said reproachfully.

"Well, ring up Leigh and find out if she's willing to travel in a motor-cycle side-car. If so, say we'll fetch her." As the inspector crossed to the telephone, Puckle approached and came to a sort of attention in front of Alec. "What is it, Constable?"

"I bin thinking, sir."

Sternly repressing an urge to congratulate the man, Alec gave him an encouraging "Yes?"

"What I thought is, seeing summun's got to go and see him any-ways, acos o' the girl, it might be just as well to ask Sid Coleman did he notice anyone up on the cliffs Sunday arternoon. Acos he's a wandering sort of chap and he mought as well have bin there as anywheres else. That's what I thought."

"Good thinking, Puckle! I'll go and talk to him myself." Though the foul air was slowly dispersing through open windows and doors, Alec now wanted to escape his conscientious, efficient, unsettling inspector. Indisputably, Mallow was not the right person to question the timid beachcomber. "I know he can't speak, but I gather he understands quite well?"

"Aye, sir. Dessay he knows all the suspects by name, but anyhow, was you to show him their photygraphs, he could nod or shake his head."

"Hmm, it'll be more difficult if he saw someone other than those four. But we'll cross that bridge when we come to it. Constable Leigh knows where his cabin is. He's going up this morning to look for the girl. I'll go with him."

Alec found himself once again bumping and rattling along in the lowly side-car, wishing fervently for his Baby Austin. As he clambered out in front of the Malborough police house, he said severely to Tumbelow, "Take it easy on the way back. We don't want a willing witness too shaken up to see straight."

Tumbelow started a grin then swallowed it. "Yessir!"

PC Leigh was a sturdy countryman of about thirty. He introduced his witness, Miss Flick, a thin woman with a sharp, twitchy nose, who had been walking her corgis on Sunday afternoon. Her nose twitched even more when she heard that Alec was a detective chief inspector from Scotland Yard.

She started to explain that she had been in a side lane, approaching the main street, when a man on a bicycle had crossed in front of her. "He was almost past when I noticed him, so—"

"We very much appreciate your willingness to help," Alec said. "If you recognize the man in question, you can describe the circumstances to Inspector Mallow in Westcombe and he'll ask you to sign a statement. Sergeant Tumbelow here is ready to take you over there now."

"Me too!" piped up a youthful voice. A tow-headed lad of nine or ten, eyes bright with excitement, dashed into the room. "Me mum *would* scrub me face afore she'd let me come. I'm a witness too, been't I, Mr. Leigh?"

"That you be, lad. This here's Jackie Diggory, sir, and we won't be asking what he was doing atop Mr. Benson's orchard wall of a Sunday afternoon." Leigh frowned darkly on the miscreant. "You see, sir, he didn't notice the man on the bike but he'd swear to the bike, being as how he's saving up his pennies to buy one for hisself and looking around him, like, to see what kind he fancies. This gentleman's Detective Chief Inspector Fletcher of Scotland Yard, Jackie."

"No kidding? Cor!" Jackie exclaimed ecstatically. "And a ride on a motor-bike? I don't care if I does get a dusting for scrumping owld Benson's apples!"

"Not on *my* pillion," Tumbelow asserted. "In the side-car you'll go, with Miss Flick."

Miss Flick wasn't at all sure she wanted Jackie as her fellow passenger.

Already chagrined at not being allowed on the bike itself, Jackie naturally took exception to this. "No more does I want to ride wi' such a fusspot," he declared.

It took all Scotland Yard's authority to reconcile them to travelling together, but at last they were sent off. Alec rang up Mallow to warn him that the boy was coming. "Make sure you get a description of the bicycle from him before he sees it. And get Anstruther to put on the clothes he was wearing that day. Miss Flick's evidence won't be worth much at the best, but Jackie's might if you do it right, Inspector."

"Always supposing it's the right bike." Mallow still hankered to arrest Anstruther, who had looked so obvious a choice at first.

"Let's hope," said Alec. "I'd be happy to eliminate a suspect."

"Oh, Stebbins is out, sir. A young fellow just came in, was walking with his girl in the fields near those cottages and saw him in the garden at the end of the row. He knows it was round about three because the girl wasn't supposed to be with him and she was afraid she'd get caught if she wasn't home by half past, so they kept an eye on the time. Constable Puckle says there's no reason he'd lie for Stebbins."

Perversely, Alec was disappointed. If Anstruther's borrowed bicycle was identified, he'd be left with only Baskin and Coleman on his list.

Where Baskin was concerned, so far the only reason to suspect him at all was a few odd questions and reactions. No motive had yet come to light, though someone was supposed to be working on it at the Yard—someone no doubt engaged with a dozen other cases whose chief investigators were at hand to chivvy him.

Coleman seemed far more likely as a murderer, but the case against him was equally in need of an eyewitness. His daughter was the most probable person to have seen what happened. If he hadn't killed her in his anger at her shameful behaviour, might he have done so to silence her? Either way, dead or alive, Olive Coleman must be found.

Should she not turn up alive by tomorrow morning, Alec decided, he'd have to start a thorough search of the area between the Coleman farm and the murder site. That would mean mustering all the police he could persuade the CC to send him, and calling for volunteers.

"How likely is it that the girl might have taken refuge with her uncle?" he asked Constable Leigh as they crossed Malborough's main street and turned down a muddy lane between high hedges.

"Not very, sir," Leigh said apologetically, glancing from the mud to Alec's suit and obviously wondering why so senior an officer should choose to tramp through the mire on a wild goose chase.

"Why?"

"Well, sir, she's bin brung up to think him a disgrace to the family, and as for him, he keeps well away from them, being afeard o' his brother. Rightly so, from what I've heard. He don't come into Malborough for fear o' meeting him."

"So you don't know him personally?"

"I bin out to his hut a few times, seeing it's in my district, but you can't hardly get to know a chap that can't talk. A harmless, docile sort of chap he do be. I niver had no complaints about him."

"Not likely, then, to have taken a swing at Enderby to avenge the honour of the family," said Alec with a smile. He hadn't seriously considered Sid as a suspect, only as a possible witness.

"Oh no, sir, not at all. I misdoubt he'd understand the notion—the honour o' the family, I mean—and he's no reason to care what becomes o' her."

The beachcomber had no motive. Someone else besides Coleman might, however. "Did you ever hear of a local lad, one of Coleman's farm-hands perhaps, being sweet on Olive? I assume she's reasonably attractive, or Enderby wouldn't have been interested. You've seen the only photograph we have. Even blown up it's not much use."

"Aye, she's pretty enough if you don't mind a sullen look. Some men like a pout, but I niver knew a girl that pouted as didn't turn into a bad-tempered woman."

"Very true, but Enderby wouldn't concern himself with what kind of woman she'd grow to be."

Leigh shook his head with a frown. "Didn't concern hisself wi' aught but his own pleasure, seemingly. Far as I know, none o' the village lads has a fancy to Olive Coleman. Her parents work her hard and she's hardly ever seen in Malborough."

"The farm-hands?"

"Now, they're another matter. For all I know, they could all be mad after her, specially as she's the only child and'll come into the farm some day. Or would've afore she brought shame on the family. But they're none o' them young men. The youngsters all went off to War and not a one came back. Them as survived found greener pastures. We'll take the left fork here, sir."

After another stretch of muddy bottom, the lane started rising. Then the hedges became banks, and soon unfenced, heather-clad slopes spread to either side. Leigh turned off on a nearly invisible path winding through purple-belled heather, bracken and occasional clumps of bright yellow gorse. At least the footing was much drier here, in spite of last night's downpour. The blustery wind was invigorating.

They climbed over the brow of a hill. Another, higher, rose before them but Leigh skirted its foot. As they rounded the shoulder, the next valley came into view and Alec saw a clear, shallow brook. What he at first took for a heap of dead bushes resolved into a brushwood fence surrounding a patch of cleared ground where vegetables, gooseberries and currants struggled in the poor, thin soil.

On the opposite slope, explaining the need for the fence, sheep stopped grazing the wiry grass to stare at the intruders. The only sounds were their intermittent bleating, the babble of the brook, and the cry of a solitary seagull circling overhead.

The original stone shepherd's hut must have blended perfectly into the background of the rocky crag standing sentinel at the head of the valley. Sid Coleman's repairs and additions were nearly as well camouflaged, built mostly of wood weathered to a silvery grey by sea and sun. The roof was patched with sheets of corrugated iron, rusting to the hue the bracken would take on as autumn approached.

201

Pausing, Leigh surveyed the scene. The coconutty fragrance of gorse filled Alec's nostrils. Attuned now to the hush, his ears picked up the constant hum of bees among the heather blossoms.

It was almost possible to envy Sid.

Leigh broke the peace. "No smoke. He may not be—" He stopped as several short, sharp sounds rang out: hammer on nail, at a guess. "No, he's here all right."

"We don't want to alarm him. You go ahead. He knows you."

The constable trudged ahead. "Sid!" he called. "Hulloa there!"

The beachcomber appeared, hammer in hand, from a lean-to shed to one side of his cabin. Alec had no time to take in his appearance before, with a wordless cry, he bolted.

Leigh was already in motion when Alec shouted, "Go after him! I'll look around." If the girl was there, they didn't want her taking to her heels too.

Disappearing around the cabin, Sid had a twenty-yard lead over Leigh. By the time Alec reached the far corner, the fugitive was nearing the top of the crag.

Police boots were no match for bare feet that clung to the rock like a monkey's. Leigh slithered down the short distance he had managed to climb and made for the steep, scrubby slope to one side. As he scrabbled upward, Sid appeared momentarily in silhouette against the sky, then vanished over the top.

A thud within the cabin made Alec whirl.

He found himself facing a small, glassless window. Above it hung a piece of heavy tarpaulin, hooked up out of the way with a bent wire, a sort of outside curtain or shutter against foul weather. A small part of Alec's mind admired its ingenuity, while the rest concentrated on peering through the narrow opening.

No one was visible, but his field of view was limited. Straining ears heard no movement inside.

Leigh was making a fair racket as he toiled up the slope. Small stones rattled down behind him and he swore as a clump of grass came loose in his hand. Under cover of the noise, Alec slipped around the hut, noting how chinks in the wood and stone walls were stopped up with tarred slivers of cork. Sid Coleman might be dumb but he was no idiot.

Alec came back to the west side, facing down the valley, without seeing a soul. The door stood open. He stepped into the doorway and stopped, scanning the room.

A sleek grey and black–striped cat was lapping water from a tin bowl on the floor. It gave him a supercilious look, leapt up with a thud onto a battered old door which served as a table, and thence sprang to a shelf where an ancient knit garment made a comfortable bed. Obviously regarding Alec as unimportant, it started to wash with an air of deliberately ignoring him.

The cat was the only occupant. Alec searched the room, a matter of a few minutes, without finding any trace of the presence of a female. The bed was heaped heather spread with sailcloth and a holey blanket. The sole chair had been rush-bottomed once; its deficiencies were compensated for by the lid of a cask and a cushion so salt-stained and faded that its original colour was unguessable. A sea-chest with a broken lock held tattered oddments of clothing and another blanket. All were as clean as soapless washing in the stream could make them.

The Panama hat Belinda had given Sid hung from a nail, several feathers stuck in its pink and purple band. Alec was sorry his daughter had befriended the beachcomber. He was used to the awkwardness of Daisy taking one or more suspects under her wing, but how was he to explain to Bel if he had to arrest her protégé?

Because why should Sid run for it if he was simply an innocent witness?

22

Bosh!" said Daisy. "Of course he ran away! He's absolutely terrified of the police, ever since Constable Puckle locked him up for the night. If you'd gone alone, without the bobby in uniform, he wouldn't have taken to his heels."

To put it mildly, Alec had not been pleased to find Daisy waiting for him in the parish hall when he returned from his fruitless errand to Sid's shack. But he had let her listen while he told Inspector Mallow and Sergeant Horrocks that the beachcomber, having fled, was to be considered a suspect.

Now exasperated, dark brows lowering, he ran his fingers through his crisp, dark hair, leaving it unruffled. "Why the dickens didn't you tell me before, Daisy? It's entirely on account of your telling us he's Olive Coleman's uncle that we went up there in the first place. Why didn't Puckle say something?"

"He may not realize how much he frightened him. Mr. Baskin was talking to him at his cabin and he managed to convey that he no longer comes down to Westcombe as he used to, because he's afraid of being locked up. He does come as far as our beach, though."

"You've seen him? When?"

"Yesterday. He gave the girls necklaces of shells and feathers—I suppose they haven't shown you as you're out all the time. I was going to ask him if he'd seen Olive, but then Peter Anstruther came down to the beach to fetch my deck-chair. Sid took one look at him and scuttled off as if the hounds of hell were on his heels. Anstruther said he'd never been afraid of him before, but he was wearing his naval cap, and I'm sure that's what scared him. I don't suppose he can distinguish between uniforms."

"Possibly not," Alec admitted grudgingly. "I'll have a word with Anstruther."

"Darling, isn't it marvellous? Inspector Mallow says Mr. Anstruther is in the clear. A boy recognized his bike in Malborough and he knows the time because the church clock struck three shortly after he saw it."

"That's right, sir," Mallow admitted even more grudgingly. "I don't see how it can be got round. He couldn't've done it."

"Nor could Sid," Daisy insisted. "He's constitutionally incapable of violence."

"Ah," said Mallow, "but you never know what the peacefullest chap'll do if he's threatened."

"I know just what he does. I told you, Alec. He turns his back and bends down and looks backwards through his legs."

"That certainly doesn't sound very aggressive."

"On the contrary. But it's very disconcerting."

"That's as may be," said Alec. "We'll still have to find him. There was no sign that the girl had been at his cabin, but he might have seen something on Sunday. We've put a watch on the cabin."

"He'll just run again if he sees a uniform."

"The man's been told to keep out of sight. He's probably asleep in the heather! Did you drop in just to see what's going on, Daisy, or have you found out something new?"

"Not exactly found out. Well, sort of."

"Great Scott, Daisy!"

"I mean," she said hastily, "something someone said made me think of something."

Donald Baskin had taken Daisy and the girls to see a ruined castle. Very little of it remained, mostly grassy mounds with a few fragments of walls still standing. But Baskin kept Bel and Deva amused with tales of mediæval chivalry, the sun shone and the wind blew, and it was altogether a pleasant outing.

However, they returned to Westcombe with Daisy none the wiser as to the reasons for his interest in Enderby.

As they walked through the town, Daisy was waylaid by Mrs. Hammett. She waved to the others to go on, which they did, hastily and without demur.

"Does your husband know you've been out walking wi' that young man?" Mrs. Hammett demanded.

"It's useless to try to hide anything from Alec," Daisy said mournfully. "He's a detective, remember."

"Young Olive don't seem to have much trouble hiding from him! I've just been to the parish hall to ask did they find her yet, and they ha'n't seen nor hide nor hair."

"Were you able to help them with the names of any friends she might have gone to?"

"Nay, Olive didn't have no time for friends. Even when she was still at school, she had her chores to do at home after. There's allus something to be done on a farm, as none should know better than I, that was bred on a farm, and not ashamed of it."

"No, why should you be?"

"There's them as is jealous because I've raised myself," Mrs. Hammett said darkly. "But I don't pay 'em no heed. And they needn't think the wife of a man in a good way o' business don't have enough to do to keep her busy, neither. But it's not like on a farm, where you don't get a minute to sit down from dawn to dusk."

"So after she left school, Olive pretty much only saw people on her father's farm?" Daisy wasn't surprised Olive had gone astray, if she was never allowed to have fun with other young people. "I wonder how she met George Enderby."

"I reckon it must ha' bin one time when Edna sent her to me on an errand. Mr. Hammett's very good about sending my relations a present o' fresh fish now and then, being in the fish wholesaling business. And they'll do likewise, wi' a leg o' lamb or a piece o' pork when they slaughter, or the like. Even Edna, though she dasn't let Alfred know. 'Twere just a few weeks past Olive brought me a nice cheese."

"I don't suppose she hurried home afterwards. I expect you're right, that must be when she met him."

"Aye. And after that, she wouldn't find it too hard to slip away for an hour now and then, Edna thinking her one place and Alfred another. Sly, that's the word wi' no bark on it. It's to be hoped she ha'n't got herself into more trouble than she can be got out of."

"I hope not." Feeling she was not learning anything of use, Daisy politely extricated herself and went after Baskin and the girls.

The trouble Mrs. Hammett referred to must be the possibility that Olive was pregnant, Daisy assumed. Suppose she was, she would have demanded Enderby's assistance. A thoroughly selfish man, he would probably have refused, perhaps laughed at her or just up and walked away from her. What more likely than that she should lose her temper, run after him, and hit out at him with whatever came to hand? She might not even have meant to knock him over the cliff and kill him.

Daisy wondered whether Alec was considering Olive as a suspect or only as a witness.

At this point in her musing, she found that her feet had carried her to the parish hall, so she went in. Inspector Mallow gave her a suave welcome, but she could see that her arrival annoyed him.

"No doubt you have something to report, Mrs. Fletcher?"

"Not exactly." She wasn't about to discuss Olive's possible pregnancy with Mallow. "But I think I'll wait and have a word with Alec, if you're expecting him reasonably soon?"

"The chief inspector didn't know just how long he'd be."

Daisy glanced at her wrist-watch. She had half an hour to spare before lunch. "Right-oh, I'll wait for a bit."

"As you wish, madam. I'll ask you to sit over here, if you don't mind, out of the way of my men as they report in."

"Of course. By the way, have any of the suspects been cleared yet?"

That was when the inspector had told her about Peter Anstruther's bicycle, reluctantly but, she suspected, unwilling to risk offending his superior officer. Delighted, she nearly rushed off to congratulate Anstruther and Cecilia. She really wanted to speak to Alec, though, to find out if he'd considered the possibility that Olive might have killed Enderby.

Sitting near the door on the extremely uncomfortable folding chair typical of parish halls, Daisy had had plenty of time to think before Alec turned up. She decided Olive Coleman was unlikely to have deliberately murdered Enderby. To do so would be to abandon all hope of his helping her. It didn't sound as if she could expect much help or sympathy at home. No wonder the poor girl's head had been turned by George Enderby's charming manner. She led a miserable life, rarely seeing anyone other than the farm-hands.

Of course, Mrs. Hammett's cheese suggested a dairy on the farm, and where there was a dairy, milkmaids and dairy-maids were to be found. Olive herself was surely expected to work in the dairy, so she might have friends amongst the maids.

"So you see, darling, it all depends on whether the dairy-maids live in or out. If they have homes to go to, Olive could have gone to one of them."

Alec was frowning again, but thoughtfully, not irritably. "You have a point," he admitted. "Though it's not quite that straightforward, alas. I met an elderly dairy-maid at Coleman's who said the girls don't stay down on the farm these days. They either marry or soon go off to look for jobs in town."

"Then they're not necessarily local. They could be absolutely anywhere," said Daisy, disappointed.

"Yes, but that doesn't mean she didn't make friends amongst them and keep in touch somehow with one or more, in which case she might have managed to make her way to one of them. It's a good idea, love, and will have to be followed up. I can only hope Mrs. Coleman has the names of departed dairy-maids, if not their addresses."

"Blast! It's going to take forever, isn't it? I was hoping you'd arrest Coleman quickly and manage a few days of holiday before we leave."

"You shouldn't come up with good ideas, then," he said with a grin. "I was going to send someone to the farm anyway, to try to find out whether any of the labourers was keen on Olive to the point of murdering her seducer. Horrocks and Tumbelow can go. A couple of hefty sergeants, one in uniform, one plainclothes, ought to be able to cope with the Colemans. In fact, I think I'll have them bring Coleman in for further questioning." He started to get up, turning away from Daisy.

"Just one more thing, darling. Is Olive Coleman on your list?"

"Certainly. If she asked him for help in escaping her father—"

"Or because she was pregnant."

"I hadn't considered that. It's possible, of course. In either case, if he refused to help, she might have struck out at him. Until we find her and hear her story, there's nothing to be done about it. Right-oh, thanks for your help. You'd better go and join the girls for lunch. Tell Mrs. Anstruther I'll try to get back for dinner."

"Right-oh. Bel's getting a bit fed up with never setting eyes on you."

"She's used to being a policeman's daughter, but I admit it's a bit thick when we're supposed to be on holiday. Tell her I'm sorry. Oh, and tell Baskin I'd like to see him here this afternoon, will you? We've found out he's telling the truth about teaching at that school, and that he's not married, but the rest will take some digging. It's time he came clean about his interest in Enderby."

"Darling, too utterly mortifying to be bearer of a message like that when we've just had such a nice walk together and he's so kind keeping the girls entertained. Don't you think you ought to send a policeman?"

"Can't spare a man at the moment. It's entirely your own fault for meddling."

Entering the Anstruthers' house, Daisy heard Cecily singing in the kitchen. She stopped to listen.

> We'll rant and we'll roar like true British sailors.
> We'll rant and we'll roar across the salt seas,
> Until we strike soundings in the Channel of old England.
> From Ushant to Scilly is thirty-five leagues.

Daisy stuck her head in. "I'm so very happy for you," she said.

"You've heard?" Cecily turned a joyful face from the range. "It's all thanks to you and your husband! I know the local police would have arrested Peter at once."

"If it had been left up to Detective Inspector Mallow," Daisy agreed. "Where is he? I must congratulate him."

Cecily laughed. "He's borrowed the bicycle again and ridden over to show his friend Mr. Pritchard his letter to the powers-that-be in Devonport. With any luck, he'll be sticking close to Scilly in future."

"I hope so."

"Lunch in five minutes, unless you need longer?"

"No, I'll be ready. I'm ravenous."

Daisy saved Alec's summons for Baskin until after lunch. She passed it on over coffee, the girls having gone off to change their library books.

"Righty-oh. I'll go, but I haven't anything new to tell them. I wish they'd find someone who saw me."

"I think they're concentrating on finding"—she realized she wasn't sure whether Baskin knew about Olive Coleman, or even that Enderby had had a girl with him shortly before meeting his death—"on finding someone else," she concluded.

"Well, it's good to know I'm not the chief suspect, now that Anstruther's out of it."

Daisy hoped she wasn't misleading him. But no, Coleman must be top of the list because of his obvious motive and his violent character. No doubt Alec had put Sid on the list now, but right at the bottom, she hoped, after what she had said about his meekness. He was far more the sort to be a victim than a villain.

A horrid thought struck Daisy: What if the murderer heard that the police were hunting for Sid as a possible witness? The beachcomber might be in deadly danger—and she simply couldn't think of anything useful to do about it.

Baskin departed for the parish hall. Daisy fetched her book and went out to the garden. Though the wind had strengthened, it had cleared the last clouds from the sky, and she found a sunny, sheltered spot to set up a deck-chair. She opened the book, but the latest Edgar Wallace could not hold her attention. Worrying about Sid, she watched the swells roll up the inlet. Their rhythm proved hypnotic. Her eyelids drooped and she fell asleep.

13

*A*lec was simultaneously reading reports and eating sandwiches brought in from the Schooner when Baskin arrived at police headquarters.

"Tell him I'll be with him in five minutes," he said to Mallow.

The inspector went to meet Baskin, ushered him to a seat at the map table, and returned to announce, "He says not to hurry. He's told us all he can remember about his movements and he hasn't got anything to add."

"We'll see about that."

"D'you want me to have a go at him, sir?"

"No, leave him to me. I want you to see if you can get anything out of Coleman when they bring him in." Alec looked at his watch. "Which should be any minute. You can hardly have less success than I did."

"Belligerent, wasn't he?" said Mallow uneasily.

"He won't have his dog or his bull with him. Smith can leave off his typewriting and stand by to give you a hand if he gets obstreperous, and Puckle's due back from his lunch. Horrocks and Tumbelow are to get on with following up any leads they've obtained as to the girl's possible whereabouts."

"Right, sir."

Maybe he was making a mistake in letting Mallow tackle the farmer, but the inspector's sneaky ways just might be more effective than Alec's own more straightforward approach. He finished a last bite of beef with rather more horse-radish than he cared for, washed it down with the Schooner's first-rate ale, and joined Baskin.

"Thank you for coming along."

"I was rather under the impression that it was the sort of invitation one cannot refuse."

"Not at all, though a refusal would certainly give the wrong impression. You can always send for a lawyer, if you wish."

"No need. I haven't anything to say."

Alec regarded the young man with exasperation. "We'll find out what your interest in Enderby was, whether you tell us or not. I've had a man at Scotland Yard put on to ferreting."

"Good luck to him. He's not likely to find anything before the inquest. It's later this afternoon, isn't it? If I tell you now, my business is bound to come out at the inquest, and then the press will get hold of it. So far, the London papers haven't been interested, but as soon as word gets out of a verdict of murder . . ."

"At least you're not denying an association with the deceased."

"I can scarcely expect get away with that," Baskin conceded with a touch of sarcasm, "after having turned for information about him to the chief investigator's wife."

"Daisy had to tell me," Alec defended her.

"Oh, I don't hold it against Mrs. Fletcher, I assure you. A charming lady, but not one in whom one might choose to confide if one had the slightest expectation of getting mixed up in a murder case."

"We can be discreet, you know, if it's nothing to do with the case."

"It's nothing to do with the case in the sense that I didn't kill Enderby, therefore it's irrelevant."

"But it gave you a motive for doing away with him."

"I'm sorry to be disobliging," the schoolmaster said politely, "but I think on the whole it's time—in the vernacular—to button my lip."

Was it worth pressing him? He had more or less admitted to a motive. Exactly what that motive was ought to be revealed by the Yard's digging, and in any case did not have to be proved, though convincing a jury without one was difficult.

Means and opportunity were another matter. Baskin's walking stick had been thoroughly examined and was definitely not the weapon. Someone might yet turn up to give him an alibi. The forces at Alec's disposal had not yet looked for any of the yokels with whom he claimed to have exchanged greetings, in indeterminate places. The police were too busy hunting first for Olive Coleman and now for her uncle Sid. When found, one or the other or both should be able to identify the murderer, whether Baskin, Alfred Coleman, or some as yet unguessed third party.

Alec was very conscious that he hadn't yet delved into the history of George Enderby's philanderings in the district. That Mrs. Anstruther had been his first mistress here seemed unlikely. Nancy Enderby might be able to provide more names, or the abominable Mrs. Hammett, or any of the gossipy villagers.

It was one more thing to be gone into, if Olive failed to turn up and provide a name. Where were Tumbelow and Horrocks?

"May I go, Mr. Fletcher?" Baskin asked.

"What?" Alec jerked out of his brown study. "Oh, no, not yet."

"I really am not going to say anything else."

"Let's just go one more time over your route on Sunday afternoon."

Baskin sighed heavily and turned to the map. "Even if I'd made it up, which I didn't, I've described it so many times already I could do it in my sleep."

"One more time, and this time try harder to think of anyone you spoke to. The bar at the Ferries Inn was crowded. Surely you exchanged a word or two with a customer or two. Who did you sit next to on the ferry? You're not the sort of chap to sit in silence."

"I suppose Mrs. Fletcher's told you how I butted in on the ferry here," Baskin said with a grin. "Yes, I did speak to two or three chaps, but we didn't exchange names. They were ordinary sort of chaps, fellow hikers, nothing distinctive about them, and all going off in different directions. I couldn't give you a useful description of them to save my life, any more than Anstruther could tell you the make of motor-car he saw."

"Did you by any chance mention that you're staying in West-combe?"

"Yes, we all talked about where we were staying and where we were going. As a matter of fact, I wrote down the Anstruthers' address for one of them."

"For pity's sake, why didn't you say so? If we have to, we can probably track him down. What can you remember of where they all said they were staying? Come on, put your mind to it!"

Baskin was busy putting his mind to it when Tumbelow's leonine roar approached. Outside the hall it throttled down to a snarl. A backfire rang out like a gunshot, and the beast fell silent.

Mallow and Puckle moved towards the door. Constable Smith stopped pounding on the typewriter keys and sat up straighter, alert. The general air of expectation diverted Baskin from his quest for an alibi. He and Alec both turned to watch.

"What's up?"

"My two sergeants are supposed to be bringing in Alfred Cole-man. He may or may not be a murderer, but he's unquestionably a brute with an explosive temper. Altogether a nasty piece of work."

A couple of minutes passed in tense anticipation. Then voices were raised outside. Puckle went out, drawing his truncheon.

Puckle returned, walking backwards. After him came Coleman, handcuffed, a mutter of mingled profanity and barnyard obscenity issuing from his lips. Tumbelow followed, also with drawn truncheon, and then Horrocks. Horrocks's hand was tied up in a blood-stained handkerchief.

"Set his dog on me," he explained, his voice slightly shaky. "If Tumbelow hadn't taken along his truncheon—"

"I gave the beast a little tap on the head. Not to worry, sir, it'll live to wake up with a headache. No signs of hydrophobia, just trained to be nasty, but his hand could do with a couple of stitches."

"Smith, ring up Dr. Vernon," said Alec. "See if he or his nephew can drop by. If they're both out, try the Vicarage. For heaven's sake, sit down, man."

"I'm all right, sir."

"Good, because as soon as you're stitched up, I have work for you. Go and wash the bite thoroughly for a start. Tumbelow, you did get the information I sent you for?"

"Yes, sir. No trouble there."

"Excellent." Alec contemplated Coleman. The farmer stood in sullen silence, having either run out of curses or bored himself with repetition. "Inspector, he's all yours. Right-oh, Baskin, where were we?"

With half an ear he heard Mallow suavely expounding to Coleman the penalty for assault upon a police officer in the execution of his duty. Baskin also seemed to have one ear cocked in that direction. Nonetheless, he managed to provide enough information about the hikers he had met to make it worth looking for them.

Alec let him go, with the usual warning not to stray too far from Westcombe nor change his lodgings without notifying the police.

"I don't suppose you'd let me stay and watch?" Baskin said persuasively. "My boys are going to be thrilled to death that I've had a chance to see Scotland Yard in action, and they'll think it a very poor show if I just walk out when you're making an arrest."

"Unfortunately, we're not, at least not for murder."

"Assaulting a policeman will do. Better, in fact, as an object lesson. It's the sort of thing any high-spirited lad might contemplate, whereas murder is, I trust, rather beyond their purview."

"I hope so!" Alec was about to refuse his request when Andrew Vernon arrived, black bag in hand.

The young would-be Thorndyke was panting and his step had lost some of its accustomed bounce. "I ran all the way to my uncle's and back to get my bag," he announced breathlessly, giving Baskin a curious look and a nod of greeting before turning back to Alec. "Didn't think I'd need it for the inquest. I say, sir, jolly clever of you to guess I was at the Vicarage."

Alec smiled. "Not at all."

Vernon's cheeks turned pink. "Yes, well . . . A dog bite, is it? Not rabid, I hope! Those shots of Pasteur's vaccine are a pretty painful business, and he'd have to go to Plymouth or Exeter to get 'em. Where is he—my patient?"

"There's a sort of scullery at the back."

"Oh yes, home of the dreaded urn tea. You've no idea what one suffers, being devoted to a vicar's daughter!" He dashed off, bag swinging.

Alec sent Baskin off, ironically aware that he would in all probability go straight back to the boarding-house where he'd spend the rest of the afternoon with Daisy and Belinda. Still, he never had fancied the schoolmaster as a murderer, and the possible alibi witnesses he'd come up with sounded pretty convincing.

Setting Smith to telephone a bulletin to the police in the districts where those witnesses might be found, Alec glanced over at Mallow and Coleman. The farmer had sat down but he appeared to be stubbornly silent. The inspector's voice, soft and insidious, continued its undermining efforts. Alec left him to it and went on into the scullery.

The men stood by the sink. Vernon was examining the wounds, a set of tooth-marks and a nasty, ragged tear across the ball of the thumb.

"It's a bit of a mess all right. Hold on while I dissolve some permanganate." He found a thick white china cup in a cupboard and ran some tapwater into it. With a glass rod he stirred in purple crystals from a phial in his bag. "Right-oh, hold your hand over the sink while I slosh it on, then we'll stitch it up and paint it with iodine. You'll need to get it re-dressed daily till the stitches come out, by someone who knows what to look for in the way of infection."

Sergeant Horrocks looked rather green about the gills. Tumbelow came in with a couple of the folding chairs and set them up. Patient and doctor sat, and Vernon delved into his bag for his needle and sutures. Alec and Tumbelow met each other's eyes and quietly left the room.

"Pop along to the Schooner and fetch him a tot of brandy," said Alec, taking out his wallet. "Leave me your notebook with the names and addresses you got from Mrs. Coleman."

The elderly dairy-maid had spoken nothing less than the truth: in the past two years no fewer than five girls had come and gone from the Coleman farm. Mrs. Coleman had provided their names and the names of the farms or villages where their families lived, all in the Malborough area. What had become of them after they left her service she was unable or unwilling to say.

PC Leigh of Malborough was sure to know some of the answers. Where he didn't, Tumbelow could run out on his bike and ask the families. By this evening they should have found out where all the girls had ended up, and at latest tomorrow morning they'd know whether Olive Coleman had taken refuge with any of them.

And if she hadn't? Alec didn't want to think about that possibility. It might mean she had somehow managed to run away to London, where finding her would be next thing to impossible, or it might mean she was lying dead or injured on the cliffs, or in the sea below.

Tumbelow came back with brandy. Alec set him and a neatly bandaged Horrocks to follow up the leads on Olive. He and Vernon and Puckle in their turn set out for the Schooner, where the inquest was to be held. There they met Dr. Wedderburn, the police surgeon, and Mr. Wallace in his capacity as coxswain of the lifeboat.

The coroner was a solicitor, and a friend of Wallace. Without fuss, he took a minimum of necessary evidence from the men, followed by Nancy Enderby's identification of the body as her husband's. His direction to the jury was a masterpiece of brevity. It brought an inevitable verdict of murder by person or persons unknown.

24

Then I asked for the usual," said Alec, "an adjournment for the police to pursue their enquiries. The coroner immediately granted it. I don't know when I've had such an obliging coroner." He had managed to get away for dinner—an especially lavish meal to celebrate Peter Anstruther's vindication—and, over coffee in the sitting room afterwards, he was satisfying Daisy's and Baskin's curiosity about the inquest.

Daisy had been obliged to attend and even testify at a number of inquests. She frankly disliked them, but that didn't mean she didn't want to know exactly what had happened. "Nothing was said about whom you suspected? No mention of any of the Colemans?"

"Or me," Baskin put in.

"No, we're playing the cards close to our collective chest, the few we possess. There was no need for evidence from any of the available suspects, and so no need to draw them to the attention of the press."

"Thank you!" said Baskin in heartfelt tones. "I'm already dreading what my headmaster is going to say about my getting involved in this business."

"You'd better hope the chap at the Yard finds out whatever it is you're hiding," Alec said grimly, "before we have to ask the papers to advertise for anyone who knows you to step forward."

Baskin's good-natured face paled a little. "I hope you'll let me know if it comes to that, so that I can consider what to do for the best."

"Why don't you just go ahead and spill the beans?"

"No. I'm sure one of the fellows I spoke to on Sunday will turn up and give me an alibi."

"Wishful thinking! It's a long shot. You said yourself, none of them had fixed plans to stay in this area."

Daisy decided it was time to intervene. "Don't be beastly, darling. What about Coleman? You had him in for questioning?"

"And arrested him for setting his dog onto DS Horrocks."

"Oh no, is the sergeant hurt?"

"Not seriously. A rather nasty bite on one hand."

"Did you shut Coleman up in Mrs. Puckle's washhouse?"

"No, he's in the lock-up in Abbotsford. I'll be surprised if the magistrate doesn't bind him over to assizes. Assaulting a police officer is a serious offence."

"I'm sorry for poor Mr. Horrocks," Daisy mused, "but in a way, it's a good thing. Olive is more likely to cooperate if her father's well out of the way, isn't she?"

"That's a good point. I'll make sure whoever brings her back tells her."

"You've found her?"

"We think so. We're pretty sure. One of the milkmaids from the farm now lives in Newton Abbot. She married a traveller in farm machinery, chap named Dabb. The local police sent someone round. No one was at home, so he spoke to a nosy neighbour, who says a young girl arrived Sunday evening, without luggage, and is staying. The husband's gone off on his route. The visitor and Mrs. Dabb went to the pictures this evening. She's calling herself by another name but I'd be astonished if it's not Olive Coleman."

"In that case," said Baskin, "she'll tell you I wasn't there and you can stop—"

Vera drifted in, holding a telegram in one limp hand. Her vacant gaze was fixed, as usual, on some inner vision.

220

"Who is the telegram for, Vera?" Daisy enquired.

"Douglas Fairbanks, m'm," murmured the maid.

"No, really!"

"Oh, I mean Donald Crisp, madam."

"Donald Baskin?" Baskin took it from her unresisting fingers and looked at the front. "Yes, it's for me. Excuse me a moment."

As he opened the envelope, Vera drifted out again. He read the message, a brief one, and started to laugh. To Daisy's ears, his laughter had a tinge of hysteria.

"Good news?" she asked, with the unladylike " 'satiable curtiosity" that so often got her into trouble. "Bad news?"

Baskin dropped the telegram into her lap and flung himself into his chair. "Read it. Go on. Here I am practically getting myself arrested for obstructing the police, and all for nothing."

Daisy read aloud, "Consulted solicitor must have death certificate all my love Bethie." She handed the form back.

"Bethie," said Baskin, "is Elizabeth Enderby. Otherwise, Mrs. George Enderby."

Daisy and Alec stared at him.

"I don't understand. What—?" Daisy began.

"Great Scott!" Alec interrupted. "You don't mean . . . bigamy?"

"That's just what I do mean. Let me tell you the story. It starts in the last year of the War."

To the military hospital where Elizabeth was training as a VAD nurse came Sergeant-Major George Enderby, with a nasty abdominal wound. Good-looking, smooth-spoken, charming, he swept her off her feet long before he was able to leave his bed, and married her the day he was discharged. Combining convalescence and honeymoon, they spent a month in Wiltshire with her family before he had to return to the Army and she to her hospital.

"Bethie had two letters from France, and then another from Germany, after the Armistice. After that, nix. She never saw him or heard from him again. Well, you'll say there's nothing really surprising in that."

"No," Alec agreed, "soldiers still died after the Armistice, of mines, accidents, and so on."

"Of course. So when she hadn't heard for several months, neither from Enderby nor from the Army, her father made enquiries. He's a nice old boy, Justice of the Peace, trying to uphold the old standards when they can really only just make ends meet. To cut a long story short, George Enderby had been demobbed, leaving only an accommodation address. Apparently he had never listed Bethie as next-of-kin."

"Who was his next-of-kin?" Daisy asked. "Couldn't they enquire of his relatives?"

"According to what he'd told Bethie, his only living relative was an ancient cousin in a nursing home somewhere in the Midlands. He'd listed Emma Bovary as next-of-kin, believe it or not."

"Good heavens!" Daisy couldn't help laughing at the man's cheek. "No one questioned it?"

Baskin grinned. "I don't suppose many military clerks read Flaubert. As a matter of fact, Bethie's father didn't catch the reference and was all for trying to track down Madame Bovary. Bethie and her mother persuaded him it was more to the point to ring up every Enderby in the London telephone book—it's not so common a name—but no one admitted to a George in the family. They couldn't afford a private 'tec. I think, too, by then Bethie wasn't at all sure she wanted to find him if he didn't want to be found."

"What did she do?"

"She went on living at home and got a job in Swindon to help out the family coffers."

"And where do you come into this appalling story?" Alec demanded, glancing at his wrist-watch.

"Darling, that's obvious. Mr. Baskin went on a walking tour of Wiltshire and met Miss Elizabeth—Mrs. Enderby. What does she call herself?"

"Mrs. Enderby. All the village people know she married him and assume he was killed in the War. Yes, I met her last summer. They changed the divorce law last year, did you know? A woman can now divorce her husband on the same grounds on which he can divorce her. That means she no longer has to prove desertion as well as adultery—sorry, Mrs. Fletcher, but that's the legal lingo—she only has to prove his adultery. Which, as you can imagine," Baskin added with understandable bitterness, "is difficult if you have no idea where to find him."

"The two of you wanted to get married but couldn't see how she'd ever be able to get a divorce."

"Got it in one! Desertion alone is insufficient cause."

"How did you discover his whereabouts?" Alec asked impatiently.

"Pure coincidence. A friend of the family who had met him during their month of wedded bliss happened to stay here at the Anstruthers' last month. She and her husband went to the Schooner for a drink. She had only met George briefly, once or twice, six years ago, and not unnaturally couldn't believe it was the same man, now married to another woman. But she told Bethie, bless her, and I came down to reconnoitre."

"You concluded it was the same man? You had a photograph?"

"Yes and no. Bethie only had a couple of snaps and she'd got rid of them. But she'd described him in detail—"

"Including the scar," Daisy said severely.

"Yes." He flushed. "I suppose it was obvious I wanted to know where it was on his body, not where he got it."

"I had a feeling that was the case, but I don't think Cecily noticed."

"I hope not. I had no idea then that Mrs. Anstruther was one of his victims or, believe me, I'd never have asked. In any case, she said he was wounded at Ypres, which matched. And she said he'd turned up out of the blue three years ago, no one knew where from, and he never talked about his past. I was as certain as I could be."

"Then you had him cold, didn't you?" said Alec, obviously sceptical. "Proof of adultery no one could argue with. No motive for murder. At least, I presume you consider the scandal of divorce somewhat less daunting than the scandal of being arrested for murder?"

"You bet! As my pupils would say."

"So why hang about, asking more questions and awakening suspicions instead of rushing back to Wiltshire and starting divorce proceedings?"

"Bethie was worried about the present Mrs. Enderby," Baskin explained. "If George had settled down and was making another woman happy, even if it was a bigamous marriage, she'd have felt terrible about ruining things if there was the slightest possibility of avoiding it."

"Hence your questions about whether Nancy was happy with Georgie Porgie!" said Daisy.

He nodded. "I didn't find a chance to ask you until Friday. Well, on Friday, Bethie went to see the family solicitor to ask if a divorce could be managed without George and Nancy's knowledge. He's never handled a divorce case and wanted to ask an expert for advice, and his expert was away for a long weekend. He didn't get hold of him till late yesterday afternoon."

"By which time the question had changed."

"Yes, but I simply couldn't think how to tell her by phone or telegram that the man was no longer a thorn in our flesh. That we could marry, I mean, while leaving Nancy Enderby in happy ignorance. I mean, if I'd rung up, or wired something like 'Enderby dead name the date,' some meddlesome operator somewhere might have thought it was mighty fishy and reported to the police. I wrote a letter to the same effect, and she got it by the midday post today. This," he waved the telegram, "is the result."

"Can't you get a death certificate, a copy, without Nancy knowing?"

"I've no idea, but simply going about finding out will probably give the game away. To the police, at the very least, hence my confession."

Alec stood up. "Well," he said, "you've wasted a lot of our time, Baskin. We'll have to check your story, of course, but if it's all right, I may be able to do something about the death certificate. I'm making no promises, mind. I doubt Dr. Wedderburn will object, so it'll depend on the coroner, I imagine. We'll hope for the second Mrs.

Enderby's sake that he's sympathetic. And right now, you'd better come down to the parish hall and give us the address of the first Mrs. Enderby and the family friend, and a few other details."

"Right now, darling," said Daisy, "you go and kiss Bel good night before you disappear again. You promised." She turned to Baskin as Alec obediently departed. "Your Elizabeth sounds like a sweetheart. I can't see many women in her situation being concerned about Nancy's humiliation if her fake marriage became known."

"She's one in a million," Baskin said fervently.

"I wish you both very happy. I'd like to meet her sometime, if she wouldn't be embarrassed by my knowing the story. And now, if you'll excuse me, I'm going up. I'm utterly exhausted!"

Alec walked back to the parish hall with Baskin. They talked on the way, and Alec came to the conclusion he'd have to cross another suspect off his list.

Coleman still refused to utter anything but obscenity and blasphemy, not a word about either the assault charge or his movements on Sunday afternoon. In the morning he would be provided with a lawyer, who might or might not get something out of him. But meanwhile, his daughter had been found. The Newton Abbot police were going to pick Olive up, when the Alexandra Cinema let out at eleven, and bring her to Westcombe.

All Alec's hopes were banked on Olive Coleman being able to tell him whom she had seen on the cliff-top. Suppose she had seen no one? What would he do next? He needed a contingency plan in place, so as not to waste time.

He fell into an abstracted silence and, when they reached the hall, turned Baskin over to DS Horrocks.

Little though he wished to, Alec had to consult Mallow, or the man would be justifiably miffed. As it was, he was obsequiously flattering about Alec's forethought, but he did provide one or two ideas which might prove useful in the event that the plan was needed.

———

Half past ten. Baskin was long gone. The Schooner's bars closed and the hall filled with weary officers looking longingly at their stacked bedding. Alec tried to imagine interrogating a young and probably frightened girl in these surroundings, and failed.

"You fellows can turn in," he said. "I'll see Miss Coleman up at the police station."

He, Mallow, Horrocks and Puckle walked up the hill together. As they entered the station house, Puckle yawned enormously. Alec sent him to bed, then caught Inspector Mallow trying to suppress a yawn. "You'd better go too."

"I'm not tired, sir. Yawns are catching."

"Undeniable, but it's been a long day and I want you fresh in the morning. Off you go."

He was glad of an excuse to get rid of the man. There was no knowing what effect one of Mallow's "bombs" might have on Olive. They didn't want to be accused of bullying a sixteen-year-old female witness. In fact, he ought to have arranged for a woman to be present. The thought of bringing her mother over from the farm had occurred earlier, only to be dismissed, and then he had forgotten in the press of other business.

Mrs. Hammett? Heaven forbid! Daisy? If she had not been expecting a baby, Alec would have been tempted, but she needed her rest. Maybe the Newton Abbot people would think of sending a woman with her, perhaps even the friend she was staying with. If not, Mrs. Puckle would have to be roused.

Eleven o'clock. "The picture-palace will be closing now," said Horrocks. "Mr. Mallow arranged that they'd ring up when they picked her up, before setting out."

Quarter past eleven. No telephone call. "I hope to heaven they haven't missed her," said Alec, "or discovered we're after the wrong girl."

"They'd've rung up for sure, sir, if it turned out not to be Olive Coleman."

Half past eleven. "Do you think she ran for it, sir?" asked Horrocks.

"I hope not, Sergeant. I hope not."

Quarter to twelve. "I suppose they forgot to telephone. They should be here soon."

The call came at five minutes before midnight. Horrocks picked up the receiver, handling it awkwardly with his bandaged hand. "Westcombe Police Station—DS Horrocks here." Horrocks fell silent. All Alec could hear was a sort of quacking noise coming over the wire. Then the sergeant said, "Oh lor'! You'd better speak to the DCI."

"No, no!" came through clearly. "You tell him. We'll be in touch in the morning."

"He's rung off." Horrocks hung up and turned to Alec. "Well, we could've gone to bed an hour ago, sir. They've botched it good and proper. When they tapped the girl on the shoulder, she fell into a fit of hysterics and they had to call in a doctor. She's under sedation and won't be fit to question till tomorrow."

"Damn!" said Alec. "Did they at least find out whether it's Olive?"

"Yes, sir, from the friend, Mrs. Dabb. It's her, right enough."

"That's something. But damn, I'd hoped we could get this business sorted out tonight and wound up first thing in the morning. I'll be very surprised if they get her to us before noon, and in the meantime we'll have to go on digging elsewhere, just in case she hasn't got the answer . . . No, I'll tell you what, Horrocks, we'll leave the digging to Mr. Mallow and you and I will go to Newton Abbot to talk to her at her friend's house. Surely she's less likely to throw a fit there than at a police station!"

" 'Spect so. Unless . . . Sir, d'you think she went all to pieces because she done it?"

"It's possible. Or because she thought her father had caught up with her."

"Or the murderer, if so be it weren't her pa."

"We can't rule anything out. Did they put a watch on the house?"

227

"Dunno, sir. He didn't mention it."

"Then ring back and tell them I want a man on the front door and another on the back. Whatever Olive Coleman's running from, we can't afford to let her run any farther."

25

A steady wind still blew up the inlet when Alec stepped out into the early morning sun. Walking into the village, he noted that the great swells rolling up the inlet had not subsided overnight, as he had hoped. He would without fail be thoroughly seasick if he took the ferry to Abbotsford. It was out of the question.

That meant Sergeant Tumbelow would have to give him and DS Horrocks a lift to the station. Though unattractive, the discomfort of the motor-bicycle was immeasurably to be preferred to the agonies of *mal de mer.*

But when he saw Horrocks's pale face and the gingerly way he used his injured hand, Alec decided taking him along was out of the question.

Young Vernon, haled out of bed long before his usual hour, put on a fresh dressing and prescribed aspirin and a sling. "I don't *think* it's infected," he said cautiously, "but perhaps you'd better go along to my uncle's surgery at ten. After all, I'm not actually qualified yet, don't you know, and animal bites can turn nasty."

"I'm quite all right to go to Newton Abbot wi' you, Chief Inspector, sir!"

"Not on your life. I'm sure Inspector Mallow can make use of you here. Vernon, would I be taking my life in my hands if I asked you to drive me into Abbotsford to catch a train? You did say you own a car?"

"She's just a little Gwynne, but she'll get you to Newton Abbot faster than the train. Even if I obey the speed limit," Vernon added with a grin, "having a copper on board. Or does being on police business give me licence to speed? Anyway, I'll take you all the way, sir."

He was as good as his word. By ten o'clock, Alec had called in at the Newton Abbot police station and was knocking on the door of the hideous, jerry-built, modern bungalow where Olive Coleman's dairy-maid friend resided.

Daisy slept like a log. When at last she awoke, the pillow beside her was dented, so Alec must have been there. She hadn't the faintest recollection of his arrival or departure.

The clock on the mantelpiece opposite the bed said nearly ten o'clock. Twelve hours' sleep! No wonder she felt bright and full of energy. She also felt ravenous. She gave her abdomen an apologetic pat. "Sorry, you must be starving, baby. Breakfast's long over, but I expect Cecily will give us some bread and butter to keep us going till lunchtime."

Alec had left a note on the dressing-table. He had to go to Newton Abbot to interview Olive Coleman, but hoped to wrap up the case this morning and, with any luck, be back for lunch.

What were the girls up to in Daisy's absence? She washed and dressed quickly and went downstairs.

Cecily looked round from the flowers she was arranging on the hall table. "Good morning, sleepyhead," she said with a smile. "Bacon and eggs in five minutes?"

"Really? Yes, please! I'll come and eat in the kitchen if it's more convenient. It's too noble of you—I was hoping to beg a crust of dry bread."

Leading the way to the kitchen, Cecily laughed. "When the others finished breakfast with no sign of your appearance, Belinda begged me to leave out something cold for you. She said you'd be dying of hunger. What a dear that child is!"

"Isn't she? Where are the girls?"

"On the beach."

"Alone?" Daisy asked anxiously. "Have the waves gone down?"

"They're about the same, but the tide is an hour later. Peter said they're safe for a while yet, but he and Mr. Baskin went with them anyway. I popped down to see what was going on, and you've never seen two grown men have such fun messing about in the sand!"

How Cecily had changed in a few short days, Daisy thought, as sizzling bacon filled the kitchen with its heavenly smell. Her sins were forgiven, her husband safe from arrest, and her aloof diffidence metamorphosed into cheerful sociability. If Alec had not been on hand, Peter Anstruther might now be languishing in a gaol cell, while his wife tried frantically to find a good lawyer to defend him.

It was worth the loss of half their holiday—not that Daisy didn't intend to make sure Superintendent Crane gave Alec another holiday to make up.

As she was finishing her breakfast, the beach party came in, covered with sand. Daisy sent the girls to wash and change into clothes suitable to walk into the village. She needed yet more postcards, Belinda ought to write again to her grandparents, and Deva must write to her mother. Baskin decided to go with them to drop into the parish hall and find out what was going on.

"I hope your husband has made an arrest by now," he said privately to Daisy as the girls raced ahead along the track, "so that he won't have to trouble Elizabeth."

"I hope so too, so that he can have a few days to enjoy this beautiful place before we go back to town!"

Having bought their postcards and stamps and exchanged their library books, Daisy and the girls headed down the busy street towards the quay. They were halfway down the hill when an earsplitting *crrrack* startled them to a halt. Everyone in the street looked up as a

231

series of bangs rang out and a burst of fiery multi-coloured stars sparkled high in the blue sky.

"A rocket!" Deva exclaimed.

All the local people were suddenly in motion, most of them running down the cobbles to the waterside. Daisy couldn't move.

"For the lifeboat," said Belinda. "You remember, Mummy, like when Daddy found the body and they fired a rocket—they called it a maroon—so the lifeboatmen would come to man the boat."

"To go and fetch the body, Mrs. Fletcher, 'member?"

Daisy remembered all too clearly. Not another body at the bottom of a cliff. It couldn't—mustn't—be another murder!

"Come on, Mummy. Let's go and watch them launch the boat. Everyone's going."

She let the girls shepherd her down to the quay. Everyone was talking at once, the broad, slow Devonshire accent confusing her ears.

The lifeboat house at the end of the quay was bedecked with fading bunting in celebration of the centenary of the RNLI. Its doors stood open. Half the population of the village seemed to be helping to drag the white, blue and red lifeboat out on its wheeled carriage and easing it down the slipway.

Mrs. Hammett emerged from the crowd. "It's the idiot, that Sid Coleman," she told Daisy. "A couple of fishermen saw him climbing into a cave. They say it's quite safe in the ordinary way, but today's the spring tide and wi' the waves kicked up by the storm and a strong onshore wind, the cave'll fill wi' water and drownd him."

"Why didn't they go and stop him?" Daisy was horrified. It was her fault Sid had been driven from his humble home and gone into hiding, all because she had told Alec he was Olive's uncle. If he drowned, she'd never forgive herself.

"They shouted and waved, is what I heard, but he just went faster. Their boat not being built for inshore work, they came back in a hurry to call out the lifeboat. Though why a dozen able-bodied men should risk their lives for an idiot is more than I can tell!"

"They've volunteered to help anyone in danger, haven't they? Not to pick and choose. And they have life-jackets."

The boat was floating now, and several men were in it, shrugging into the bulky life-jackets. Two of them looked familiar to Daisy, but she couldn't place them. A couple more came running. Timing their jumps to the rise of the boat on a swell, they dropped down.

"Mummy!" Belinda pulled urgently on Daisy's sleeve. "Mummy, it's the men who were so horrid to Sid! The ones who were going to steal his cart. They'll frighten him. He'll never go to them if they call to him. He'll go farther into the cave and get drowned, for sure."

Daisy moved without thinking. Afterwards, she was quite unable to explain or even recall exactly what she did. She would remember her own voice, in her mother's best *grande dame* manner, saying, "Help me aboard, please, I must go with them."

The next thing she was fully aware of was an educated voice shouting irritably, "No, we can't stop to put her ashore. Wind and tide are against us. Lean to those oars."

She was seated on a locker. One of the men she recognized—Ned Baxter?—was guiding her hand through the armhole of a life-jacket. The boat was already several yards from the quay.

"Let's get the other arm through this here hole, missus," said Ned Baxter patiently, "and I s'll lace un for 'ee. I dunno what you've gone and took into your head, to come along o' we, like, but if so be you was to fall overboard we don't want you a-drownding of afore we can pull you in."

"Gosh, no!"

Daisy saw Belinda and Deva up on the quay, staring after her in horror. Baskin was beside them. He would look after them. They'd tell Alec where she had gone.

Alec was going to be absolutely, enormously and justifiably furious. She must have run mad!

"I been't going back. You can't make me!" Olive Coleman's pudding-face was not improved by a sullen pout, but she had the voluptuous

233

figure of an Edwardian chorus girl, and Enderby's taste in women was already proven to be catholic. It might have appealed to other men, too. Alec hoped he wasn't going to have to investigate all Coleman's farm-hands.

In Alec's eyes, the girl's true beauty was her hair, spun gold, braided and pinned up in an old-fashioned coronet about her head. No doubt that would not last, judging by her friend's crimped bob.

"I'm not trying to take you home, Miss Coleman," he said. "At present I just want to ask you some questions."

"Don't know nothing."

"In that case, you won't be able to give me answers, will you? But I must ask the questions all the same, and you might prefer that your friend not hear them."

"I'll stick by you, Olive." Mrs. Dabb's face was avid with curiosity. "Is it about this murder, then, that's in the papers? The landlord at the Schooner, as fell off of the cliff? 'Tweren't that far from the farm, was it?"

Olive looked mistrustfully from her friend to Alec and back. "I don't know nothing. I din't do nothing."

"I'm not here to charge you with any crime, Miss Coleman, but you may request a lawyer if you wish. Or your friend may stay, or I can call in a constable, or—"

"No," she said sulkily. "I don't want nobody. You don't need to stay, Mavis."

"You sure, dear? Well, then, I'll be right next door in the kitchen if you was to want me. Just call out." Mrs. Dabb whisked out, not quite closing the door behind her.

Alec remedied the omission and turned to face the room. Olive stood by the gas-fireplace, fidgeting with a garish china clown holding a concertina with *A Present from Paignton* written on it.

" 'Tis a music box," she said. "Listen." In tinny tones, "Oh, I do Like to Be Beside the Seaside" started up. "I never seen one afore."

Alec let her listen. Whatever she had done with Enderby, she was still in some ways a child, he thought. He wished Daisy was with him, to reassure her, to win her confidence.

The tune ended. Before the mechanism started a repeat, Alec said, "Do sit down, Miss Coleman."

Clutching the tinkling clown, she subsided into the nearest arm-chair, one of a suite upholstered in shoddy tangerine plush. Her healthy colour had faded, and she moistened dry lips with the tip of her tongue. "What is it, then? What d'you want to know?"

Alec sat down on a matching chair, and discovered that it was as uncomfortable as it was hideous. "Think back to Sunday," he said. "Just four days ago. Tell me about it."

She took him literally, beginning with getting up at dawn to help milk the cows. The recital of the morning's chores in dairy and house seemed to calm her, so he didn't interrupt.

"And then we had dinner, roast beef wi' apple pie after." She paused. "No, I tell a lie, it were plum pie. And then me dad got his-self into a fine taking, so I cut and run. When me dad flies off the handle, you don't hang around if you don't want a thick ear—or worser."

"He followed you."

"He come out roaring for blood."

"So it was you he was angry with, not your mother. What did you do to upset him?"

" 'Tweren't nothing I done," she whined. "Mum tole him some gossip Aunt Ellen tole her. She'm a terrible tattler, Aunt Ellen."

"She told him you had been seen meeting George Enderby."

"Well, if so be you knows, why ask?"

"I want to hear your version, Miss Coleman."

"All right," she said uneasily, "so I met Mr. Enderby a couple o' times, when I were out walking. Bain't nowt wrong in talking to a fella that I knows on."

Enderby was not available to be charged with causing the deli-quency of a minor, Alec reflected, so, for the moment at least, what exactly had occurred between them was not material. The way she called her lover "Mr." was rather pathetic. "How far did your father chase you?"

" 'Tweren't no distance. I hid, and he stamps about a bit, shouting. Then he yells out, 'Just wait till you get home, you'll get what's coming to you.' And off he goes down the lane."

"Then you come out of hiding and set off across the cliffs, and he turns around and follows you."

"That he did not! I went ever so careful. I'd stop and watch to see were he coming after, and he weren't. He were certain sure I'd have to go home soon or late and he'd get me then."

Lips compressed, Alec swore silently. If anything was "certain sure," it was that Olive had no desire to protect her father. It looked as if Coleman was out of the running.

"And he can wait forever," Olive continued. "I bain't going home and you can't make me!"

"How did you get to Newton Abbot?"

"Mr. Enderby give me money for the bus fare. He give me earrings, too, but I lost one o' they," she said sadly. "He were nice to me and I be sorry he's dead."

"How did you come to lose the earring?"

Olive scowled. "He were a-watching of us! Disgusting, I calls it. I seen him peeping and tole Mr. Enderby and up he jumps, and I pulls down me frock and I were in that much hurry to get away I must've dropped the earring wi'out noticing."

So much for meeting the man to talk! But who was the observer? "Your father caught up with you and watched . . . what you were doing?"

"Dad? Nay, I tole you I lost him," the girl said scornfully. " 'Twere me simple uncle, Sid."

26

With ten men at the oars, the lifeboat and its towed dinghy scurried down the inlet, rising and falling as the swells passed beneath the wooden hull. Daisy was glad she was not subject to seasickness. In a comparatively small craft, close to the water, the gentle pitching felt quite similar to the effect of a North Atlantic storm on an ocean liner.

"You been't dressed for this, missus!" Someone thrust a yellow oilskin and sou'wester at her as they approached the mouth of the inlet. She took off her hat and struggled into them, turning up the brim of the sou'wester so that she could see out.

Beyond the shelter of the hillsides, the wind grew boisterous, and waves broke over the sandbar in clouds of spray. Huddled in a corner out of the way of the crew, Daisy closed her eyes as the boat dived head first through a breaker and emerged into the open sea. Water trickled down her oilskins, soaking her feet and ankles. She regarded with envy the seamen's boots and trousers. If she ever again went to sea in a small boat . . .

"Mrs. Fletcher?" The middle-aged man shouting to make himself heard over the clash of wind and wave, the creak of oars, looked distinctly peeved. She had seen him steering; he had handed the tiller over to someone else. His oilskin had COXSWAIN emblazoned across front and back. "You *are* Mrs. Fletcher?" His voice was educated—and outraged.

"Yes. I'm sorry . . ."

"What the deuce do you think you're doing here? This is a rescue mission, not a sightseeing tour!"

"I know!" Daisy yelled back. "That's why I came. It's no good trying to rescue someone who's scared to death of his rescuers. He'll just try to get away and make things worse for himself, and probably endanger your crew. I know Sid, and I think I can persuade him to come to me."

"Do you realize we're going to have to send the dinghy into the cave to get him out? With the waves washing in and the tide rising? It's already dangerous as Hades. You're out of your mind if you imagine for a moment I'll let you go in!"

He turned away to return to the tiller. The coxswain: Mr. Wallace, the solicitor, she thought. Solicitors were notorious for their excessive caution.

The lifeboat added roll to pitch as she crawled diagonally up a dark blue slope, over the emerald green crest fringed with blown spume, and down the other side of the wave. Daisy remembered, on that trans-Atlantic voyage, watching the ship's lifeboats in heavy seas. From the upper decks, they had looked like beetles climbing mountains.

She was rather glad she couldn't see herself from above.

Whenever they reached the top of a roller, Wallace gazed landward, presumably to judge their progress along the coast. It seemed to Daisy that they were moving not parallel to but away from the cliffs at an angle. Keeping well away from the rocks, she supposed. Every now and then she caught a glimpse of a white line of breakers at the base of the cliffs. In a couple of spots, huge fountains of spray burst over headlands.

Chilled and cramped, she started to stand up to change her position. A heavy hand on her shoulder pushed her down, as Wallace shouted another order and the sailors sprang into motion.

Bill Watson, the ferryman, gave her a gap-toothed grin. "Us don't want to have to stop to pull 'ee out," he admonished her. "If you goes over the side, the life-jacket'll keep you afloat, but for all 'tis August, the water's colder nor you might think. Stay out o' the way, missus."

Daisy scrunched down lower against the gunwale and gripped the nearest projection. "What are they doing? Oh, changing places?"

"Aye. Bain't no mite o' use raising sail lessn the wind's abaft, so us be taking turn and turn about, giving a rest to they as has been rowing. 'Twill be heavy work enough for all, belike, when us gets close in."

It dawned on Daisy that to reach the cave they were going to have to brave the breakers. "Is it very dangerous?" she asked nervously.

"Nay, missus. She'm pretty near unsinkable, self-righting they calls it, watertight deck, and packed full o' airtight compartments, and cork on the sides to ward off the rocks."

"Good." As she had suspected, Mr. Wallace had grossly exaggerated the danger. "Come to think of it, a lifeboat that's liable to sink would be rather pointless."

"Aye, that it would. 'Tis the chaps going into the cave in the dinghy as'll be facing trouble. Our strongest oarsmen Cox is sending." Watson grinned again. "And seeing as how rowing's me livelihood, one o' they chaps'll be I."

Daisy was dismayed. She hadn't properly grasped the lawyer's mention of the dinghy. "You mean you're going to take that little rowboat, the one tied on behind, right into the cave?"

"Bain't no other way to get the poor chap out, not as I knows on."

"I suppose not." She had been crazy to come, and she would be crazier to go into the cave. Perhaps she wouldn't have to. Perhaps Sid wasn't afraid of the ferryman. "Who's going with you?" she asked.

"Ned Baxter. A lobsterman he be, allus rowing around his string o' pots. 'Twixt the two on us, us'll manage it."

Ned Baxter: he was the man who had wheeled Sid's cart down to the Anstruthers', under Bel's watchful eye. Nancy Enderby had told Daisy the girls would come to no harm with him, that he and the others just liked to tease poor Sid. But Sid had obviously believed they were going to steal or wreck his precious cart. Whatever he felt about Bill Watson, he'd never trust Ned Baxter.

What should she do? If she went along, would her presence just make the endeavour more dangerous for everyone concerned?

She had practically decided she had better stay aboard the lifeboat, when the crewmen who had been resting moved to double-man the oars. An ominous roar she had been distantly aware of grew louder. The cliff towered over them now, with headlands on either side. From the crest of the next swell she saw waves breaking in thunder on the rocks.

There was the mouth of the cave, a black hole shaped like a crooked horn, wide at the base, narrowing to a point at the top. Daisy caught a glimpse of a swell surging into it unbroken, half-filling the opening.

Watson appeared beside her again. "Hold tight, missus!" he bellowed in her ear.

Daisy hung on. The sudden jerk would have thrown her overboard had she been standing. "Have we hit a rock?"

"Nay, Cox set the anchor. A right-down clever seaman, he be. They're paying out the chain and she's drifting down gentle-like t'ards the cave, atween the rocks, so's they'll just have to fend off. If 'ee'll move forrard a bit, missus, us'll pull up the dinghy alongside."

The point of the bow had stopped just a few yards short of the cave mouth when Baxter and Watson swung over the side into the dinghy. A third man, carrying an acetylene lantern, moved to join them. Daisy recognized him as the other joker who had threatened to "take care" of Sid's cart after his fracas with Mrs. Hammett.

Her memory filled with a vision of Sid's distraught face. She pictured him scrambling away in terror as they called to him, hiding beyond their reach, drowning—because she had set Alec onto him.

Before she quite realized she had made up her mind, she was scrambling over the gunwale. One foot found purchase on a loop of rope, the other waved around until the men in the dinghy caught hold of her. Above, shouting faces looked down, inaudible amidst the crash of waves breaking over nearby rocks.

The coxswain appeared, looking furious. However, he waved at the dinghy's crew to go ahead. His lips appeared to form the words, "No time to be lost!"

Daisy crouched in the bows, as far out of the men's way as possible. Baxter knelt in the stern with a boathook at the ready. Watson was seated on one of the rowing benches, his oars in the rowlocks but resting inboard. The third man pulled the dinghy forward by the rope looped along the side of the lifeboat. A cable linked bow to bow, Daisy noticed. A couple of men on the lifeboat winched up the slack as the boats drew level. The dinghy slowly swung around to present her stern to the shore, Baxter alert to fend her off if she came too close to the rocks.

The men above paid out the cable and the dinghy slid backwards into the shadow of the cave mouth. A swell exploded into froth against the rock face on either side but the unbroken centre lifted them into the cave. The sound of breakers diminished. For a moment the mass of water blocked most of the light, then it rolled on.

Their umbilical cord to the lifeboat was no longer taut, Daisy noticed, as the men outside, unable to see what was happening, gave the dinghy some slack. Watson had his oars out, sculling just enough to hold their place. The third man fiddled with the lantern.

Ahead of them the wave reached the end of the cave and flung back a shower of spray with a boom felt as much as heard.

"See him, Jimmy?"

"Nay!"

Daisy had assumed the cave would open out into a lofty chamber once they passed the entrance. Before the murky daylight dimmed again, she saw that though wider, it was no higher inside. In fact, the ceiling widened from the crack at the mouth but then sloped unevenly downward to meet the receding water, which swirled about their bobbing cockleshell.

Jimmy got the lantern lit just as the next swell arrived. For a moment the air seemed to thicken and press upon them. The brilliant white light flashed wildly about, then, in the slack water between waves, it steadied and started to quarter the cavern.

Boom! and a shower of spray. The light jigged about on the rocky, inward-sloping walls. Again that curious compression as another swell arrived.

"There he is!" Eyes straining, Daisy had caught a glimpse of a white face as the light passed. "Back a bit. Down. There!"

Sid crouched on a rock shelf, clinging to a crack in the wall. The passing swell had drenched him. Water streamed from his clothes and hair. His face was turned towards the dinghy, his eyes closed against the blinding light.

"Throw un a belt and us'll haul un in."

The dinghy was bobbing in the backflow again, but Baxter's throw was perfectly timed and placed. The white life-belt landed right beside Sid.

He flinched and backed away.

"Sid!" Daisy called, as the dinghy rose on the next swell. Her ears felt funny from the air pressure and her voice sounded strange.

The swell moved on and the beam of acetylene light steadied again on the floundering figure of the beachcomber. Somehow he was holding on. Scattered light showed the cork ring floating nearby, unreachable.

Swearing, Baxter pulled in the line. "Reckon us'll have to go in after un?"

"Jimmy, turn the light on me for a moment. Sid! This is the lady on the beach, the one with the two little girls." *Boom!* and a shower of spray. "We've come to help you. He's throwing the belt again. You must catch it and put it over your head, put your arms through it. Hurry!"

The boat rose. Sid disappeared as the wave caught him. The light reflected off the dark water. Then his head reappeared, gasping.

"Keep that light out o' his eyen, Jim!"

The light slid to one side, reflecting off the water, and once more Baxter flung the belt.

"Catch it, Sid! Put it on!"

Sid grabbed at the belt. Daisy thought it was slipping from his fingers, but he hung on. He crouched there holding it, uncertain.

Daisy yelled, "Sid, put it—" *Boom!* Jimmy flashed the light on her again, then back to Sid. "Put it over your head and under your arms. That's right! And the other arm."

"Best he come when the water's high," said Watson as another swell darkened the entrance. "Less like to knock on the rocks."

As the dinghy rose, as the swell reached for Sid, Daisy shouted: "Jump! Now, Sid. *Jump!*"

At the same moment, Baxter yanked on the line. Whether deliberately or not, Sid was floundering in deep water, moving towards the boat, his instinctive dog-paddle aided by Baxter's steady pull.

"Missus, over to this side, now. Careful!" Jimmy set down the lantern and crossed to join Baxter as Daisy scrambled the other way. Watson, his oars never still as he kept the boat in place, shifted along his bench towards Daisy.

Boom! and a shower of spray. The choppy backwash arrived just as Sid reached the dinghy. He caught hold of the gunwale. The boat tilted, and Daisy automatically leant back over the water to balance it, gripping tight with fingers beginning to feel like icicles. Baxter and Jimmy reached down to haul Sid aboard. Daisy leant further back, very glad she was wearing a life-jacket.

Sid flopped onto the bottom boards and lay there coughing and shivering convulsively. The next swell arrived as Baxter sat down on the second rowing bench and lifted his oars into the rowlocks. Daisy thankfully—and carefully—moved to the stern, while Jimmy took the boathook to the bows. He gave three tugs on their umbilical cord to the lifeboat. It tautened.

Oars beating time, the dinghy slid down the back of the swell and out into daylight.

———

"Baxter *and* Watson *and* Jimmy whatever-his-name-is all told Mr. Wallace they'd have had to go into the water after Sid if I hadn't been there," Daisy defended herself before Alec had a chance to open his mouth. She was sitting up in bed, well wrapped in her dressing-gown and a shawl of Cecily's, and well supplied with hot-water bottles.

Alec stood over her, glowering. "Great Scott, Daisy!"

"Daddy," Belinda said anxiously, "Mummy's a heroine. I heard people saying so, on the quay when the lifeboat came in, didn't we, Deva?"

Deva nodded. "Everyone in the village came to see. It was a great occasion, like a festival in India. You were there, Mr. Fletcher, you must have heard them say Mrs. Fletcher was very brave."

"Bat-witted!"

"Off you go, girls," Daisy said hurriedly. "You can come back later. Darling, *please* don't rag me. Try to imagine how I'd be feeling if Sid had drowned because I'd funked it. It was . . . it was pretty terrifying in the cave, though I was too busy to worry about it at the time." In spite of all the aids to warmth, she shivered.

Sitting down on the bed beside her, Alec took her into his arms. "You're a bat-witted little idiot," he said, nuzzling her hair, "but I love you anyway. I was terrified too, you know, for you and the baby."

"If I'd thought it might harm the baby, I might not have . . . But after all the walking I've been doing, not to mention rushing up cliffs to report bodies, I've been feeling so well, it never crossed my mind. I'm perfectly all right now, and Dr. Vernon says there's no harm done. But what about poor Sid?"

"Sid's as tough as boot leather from tramping the hills in all weathers. But Dr. Vernon has him under observation."

"He must be so frightened!"

"He's not keen on the doctor but he seems to trust Andrew Vernon, oddly enough. Apparently he's once or twice presented young Vernon with tennis balls he found on the beach. Soggy and quite useless, of course, but Vernon paid him a few pennies for them."

"Where is he?"

"At the doctor's house. With a constable at the door. Daisy, Sid was seen right where and when Enderby went over."

"By whom?" Daisy demanded.

"By Olive Coleman."

"Did she say she saw Sid push Georgie Porgie over? She probably did it herself!"

"It's possible, but I think she's telling the truth. She says she ran away. She doesn't claim to have seen Sid attack Enderby, which she might have done if she had wanted to shift the blame from herself."

"Well, I'm sure he didn't."

"In that case, he probably saw whoever did, and the constable is there to protect him. Though if that's the case, I don't see how he'll ever manage to tell us whom he saw."

"Darling, let me talk to him. If you try to question him, he'll just be too scared to attempt to explain what happened. Besides, you'd be limited to yes or no questions. You couldn't count it as evidence if he did try to show you with gestures and actions, could you?"

"It's debatable, certainly. That's why I've asked Baskin to give me a hand."

"Is he in the clear?"

"Yes, the hiker he gave the Anstruthers' address to actually turned up on the doorstep this afternoon asking for a bed."

"Good. I can't help liking him, and he's been so good to the girls."

"Yes, I was happy to cross him off my list. He's sent a wire to his friend in London, the one who's an expert in teaching the deaf and dumb. The man's coming down tomorrow to help us question Sid, but I want to get a preliminary interview this evening."

Daisy threw back the bedclothes. "It'll be much better if Mr. Baskin and I do that, honestly."

"Baskin, yes. He seems to have established some rapport with Sid. He was very helpful in getting him from the lifeboat to the doctor's, and he's offered to give us a hand."

"Only he and I. You're a stranger and a policeman. You won't get anything out of poor Sid. Just your being there would be enough to stop him trying to communicate. Baskin can ask the questions and I'll take notes in shorthand, on what he says and what Sid does."

"Since neither of you is a police officer, that won't do me much good."

"But, darling, once he's told us, he may not be nearly so shy of telling you. And at least you'll *know* what happened, even if it doesn't count as evidence."

It took all her persuasive talents, and a good deal of time, but in the end she talked Alec round. If Baskin agreed, if she was good and stayed in bed till dinnertime, if Dr. Vernon said Sid was well enough, after dinner she and Baskin could tackle him.

27

Uncle Ben is not at all pleased to have his house turned into a cross between a nursing home and a prison," Andrew Vernon said cheerfully, "but he even lent Sid one of the old-fashioned night-shirts he insists on wearing. Your husband can be very persuasive, Mrs. Fletcher. Sid's up here."

He led Daisy and Baskin up a narrow staircase to the second floor. Servants' garrets, thought Daisy, from the days when a country GP's income ran to more than a housekeeper and a house parlour-maid.

At the end of the corridor, a large policeman in uniform was sitting on a hard chair by a door. Seeing them, he stood up.

"This is Constable Smith," said Vernon. "Smith, I've brought Mrs. Fletcher and Mr. Baskin. Chief Inspector Fletcher warned you they'd be coming."

"That's right, sir." The constable knocked, listened, shrugged. "There's not been a sound from him . . . well, not that you'd zackly expect much." He opened the door, peered in, then stood aside.

Daisy followed Vernon into a small, white room with a partly sloping ceiling and a dormer window, dimly lit by an oil-lamp. It was simply furnished with coir matting, a deal wardrobe, a washstand, a single wooden chair, and an iron bedstead against the far wall. On the bed, squeezed into the corner of the walls, Sid lay curled with his back to the door, wrapped in a blanket, a ball of silent misery.

Vernon turned up the lamp. "Come along, old chap," he said, with a gentleness remarkable in so jaunty a youth. "Here are friends come to see you, Mrs. Fletcher and Mr. Baskin. Turn yourself around, there's a good fellow."

With a sound like the mew of a cat, in one convulsive movement Sid rolled over, sat up, and reached out both hands to Daisy. She took them in hers, conscious of relief that he didn't blame her for luring him from the cave to his present predicament. How little kindness he must have met in his life if her small civilities had touched him so deeply!

"I'm glad to see you looking so much better, Sid," she said. "I can see Dr. Vernon and Mr. Vernon have taken good care of you."

He flinched at the doctor's name but gave the young man an uncertain nod and his shy smile. Vernon, lounging against the washstand, smiled and nodded back.

Daisy continued, "Mr. Baskin wants to ask you a few questions."

"About the day I met you at your cabin," said Baskin. "You remember? You showed me the shed you were building and we . . . talked for a while."

Sid nodded eagerly, and with gestures he painted a picture of raising a beam and banging in nails. Daisy sat down on the corner of his bed and from her bag took notebook and pencil to try to paint a word-picture of his actions in her idiosyncratic version of Pitman's shorthand.

Baskin turned the chair and sat with his arms folded on its back. "I want you to remember what happened earlier that same afternoon, when you were walking on the cliffs."

With a frightened look, Sid shook his head violently.

"It was something bad, wasn't it? Something dreadful. We need to know exactly what happened, and you're the only person who can tell us. You're very important, you see. You saw a man there, and a girl. Did you recognize him?"

A half nod.

"He was Mr. Enderby, from the Schooner."

Sid nodded.

"And the girl? She was Olive Coleman, your brother's daughter."

Sid glanced nervously around the crowded room as if he half expected his terrible brother to materialize. Reassured, he nodded again. As Daisy had seen with many witnesses and suspects in her various unauthorized experiences of murder investigations, he was quickly becoming accustomed to the rapid fire of questions.

"Was anyone else there?"

Sid placed his hand on his own chest.

"You were, yes. You saw no one else?"

The negative shake of his head dismayed Daisy. She had hoped he would at least claim to have seen someone else, someone to divert suspicion from his own head. Was he simply too naïve to realize where Baskin's questions were leading?

"What happened?" Baskin asked. "What did you see? Uh, Mrs. Fletcher, perhaps you'd better close your eyes or turn your back or something. Vernon can witness this part."

Momentarily indignant, Daisy recalled Alec's warning that part of Sid's testimony was likely to put her to the blush. She duly blushed and, before she shut her eyes, noted that both Baskin and Vernon were decidedly pink-faced. Enderby and Olive had met for one purpose. Curious as she was as to how Sid would go about describing what he had seen, his performance wasn't something a lady—even a married lady—could decently watch.

Hand gestures must have sufficed, since Daisy didn't feel the bed bouncing.

"Uh, thank you, Sid, that'll do for the moment," Baskin said after a couple of minutes. "Vernon, you'd agree that what he showed us was a man and woman . . . uh . . . engaged in . . . in intimate relations?"

"Absolutely."

"Uh, Mrs. Fletcher, would you mind noting down our joint conclusion?"

"With my eyes shut?"

"No, no, it's all right to open them now."

Baskin's face was now bright red, whereas Vernon appeared to be suppressing a grin. The difference between a schoolmaster and a medical student, Daisy supposed, scribbling down the syllabic symbols for the euphemistic statement of Enderby and Olive's mutual misbehaviour.

"What happened next, Sid?"

The beachcomber's rough brown hands moved delicately to shape a woman's body, then went to his eyes like binoculars. He pointed to himself. Olive had seen him.

His mouth opened and closed. She had told Enderby.

Sid jumped up from the bed, shook his fist, fumbled at his borrowed night-shirt where his flies would have been had he been wearing trousers, doing up Enderby's buttons. Sitting down on the bed, he hastily fastened Olive's bodice over her generous bosom, smoothed the night-shirt over Olive's knees, jumped up again, and ran the two paces possible in the tiny room. Two fingers continued running, along his arm, as Olive fled.

"Sorry, Mrs. Fletcher," said Baskin, redder than ever. "It was a bit early to let you open your eyes."

"Never mind. Isn't he clever? You're doing a very good job of explaining, Sid."

He flashed her his shy smile, then turned back to Baskin, who said, "Miss Coleman ran away? And Mr. Enderby was angry?"

Daisy remembered her first encounter with the beachcomber and the innkeeper as Sid shook his fist again, with a frightful scowl. He opened his mouth and a sort of roaring noise emerged.

"He shouted at you. What did you do?"

Daisy held her breath. It was safe to assume that Sid had had his cart with him, with its collection of odds and ends. Had he taken a piece of wood from it and whacked Enderby on the back of the neck? Surely not! Not only was it not in character but Enderby, threatening, must have been facing him. Or had Enderby, in disgust and frustration, stalked away as he had that day on the beach when Sid . . .

Sid turned his back, bent down, and looked backwards through his legs.

"That's what he does when he's frightened!" Daisy exclaimed. "That's exactly what he would have done."

Sid straightened, turned, became Enderby again, shaking his fist and producing that painful, wordless shout. He ran a couple of steps, then raised his foot to kick.

And Sid was himself again, flinging himself sideways to dodge the kick, one leg bent under him, the other stretched out.

Enderby kicked, missed, tripped over the outstretched leg, staggered a few steps, tumbled.

Fingers circling his eyes, Sid stared down an imaginary cliff at the falling body.

"Accident, by George!" Vernon exclaimed.

"Darling, I'm quite sure that's exactly how it really happened," said Daisy. "It's a repeat of what happened on the beach a week ago, only that time Enderby didn't carry through with the kick. I believe every word . . . that is, I believe Sid's story absolutely."

She and Baskin and Vernon had joined Alec, Mallow and DS Horrocks in the parish hall. As she read through her notes, Baskin and Vernon had added their comments. Horrocks had taken it all down in shorthand which was surely more orthodox than Daisy's.

"It all hangs together, sir," young Vernon seconded her enthusiastically. "The next bit explains the splinters and the marks I saw on the path—"

"You did find marks on the path, did you?" said Alec. "You didn't tell me about them."

"They didn't seem to have anything to do with anything. I told Julia—Miss Bellamy—though, so you can ask her what I said. I'm not making it up now to fit in. It looked as if something had been dragged up the path. Mostly it was too rocky or smudged with footprints, but in one place . . . I sketched it. I can show you."

"Later. Go on, Daisy."

Sid had left his cart at the top and gone down the path. From some distance above, he could tell that Enderby was beyond help. He was turning back when he noticed a sturdy plank, rough-sawn, tossed by the waves up the cliffside some distance above the body.

"I suppose the theory is that Enderby hit the plank on his way down?" Alec interjected. "Possible, I suppose, but where did it disappear to?"

"It was just what he needed to complete the shed he was building," Baskin explained.

Clambering across the rocks, Sid had retrieved the plank. He could show them where it had been and how he had reached it. Then he had dragged it up the path and wheeled it home on his cart. When Baskin happened upon his shack he was knocking in the last nail.

"Calmly building his shed?" Alec demanded incredulously. "And it never dawned upon him to notify anyone of Enderby's death?"

"I doubt it," said Baskin. "He's far from stupid, but he's completely—I don't know what you'd call it—unsophisticated, ingenuous, untutored in the ways of the world. Any ten-year-old boy in my form, or Belinda or Deva, understands better how the world works."

"Even if he thought of it, darling, as I keep telling you, he's scared to death of the police since Puckle locked him up. And now you have him locked up again—"

"He'll have to stay where he is tonight," said Alec. He sighed. "In the morning, I'll take him home. Baskin, Vernon, you'll come with us. He can show us where he found the damn' plank. Baskin can identify it, and you, Vernon, will take a sample to be compared with the splinters. But I must say, the whole thing sounds to me far too unlikely not to be true."

"You mean you actually believe the simpleton's story, sir?" Mallow bleated. "You're not even going to question him yourself?"

"I can't see the point, frankly, Inspector. We have three good witnesses. It strikes me as an utter waste of time to make him repeat his . . . rigmarole, if that's the word I want. Of course, if you're not satisfied, I shouldn't dream of preventing your interviewing him. Mr. Baskin's friend will have a go at him, too. But in the end, it's for the coroner and his jury to decide."

EPILOGUE

Verdict: accidental death," Daisy sighed with satisfaction, sinking into the deck-chair Alec had just set up for her on the beach—Friday had turned out to be a gloriously sunny day, already hot by noon. "Thanks to your brilliant explanation to the coroner, darling."

"And to his direction to the jury. Thank heaven! If he or they had kicked up a dust and insisted on questioning witnesses . . ." He disentangled his own chair and set it up beside her. "Well, the thought of producing Sid Coleman in court, even just a coroner's court, boggles the mind."

"It does rather. I hope he'll decide to go with Mr. Baskin's friend and learn to read and write."

"He seems quite taken with him." Alec started to sit, then straightened as a large, shaggy black dog bounded towards them.

"Popsy?" said Daisy a trifle nervously.

Popsy it was, her tail wagging in delight as she recognized her name. She laid her heavy head in Daisy's lap and gazed up at her adoringly.

"Down, Popsy!" Miss Bellamy was not far behind her dog, Andrew Vernon at her heels. "I'm so sorry, Mrs. Fletcher. Popsy, heel!"

Popsy obeyed to the extent of transferring her affections to Alec.

Vernon seized her collar. "You really must teach the brute some manners, Ju."

"Her manners are perfectly good!" Julia said indignantly. "She *likes* the Fletchers. Mr. Fletcher—or should I call you chief inspector?—the verdict means poor Sid is absolutely exonerated, doesn't it? He didn't do anything wrong?"

"That's right," Alec assured her.

"Good. We've been talking to him and to the chap from London, Mr. Baskin's friend, you know, the teacher? The trouble is, Sid wants to learn to read and write, but he doesn't want to go to London. So I offered to teach him, but Mummy wouldn't let me if there was any suspicion still attached to him."

"All the same, Ju, I don't think you ought to go over to his cabin alone."

"I shan't, silly. He can come to the Vicarage."

"Do you have any idea how to go about teaching him?" Daisy asked.

"Not much, but that's the best thing—Mummy says I can go up to London and learn how."

"Baskin's friend's offered to give her some tips, Mrs. Fletcher." Vernon grinned. "But if you ask me, she just wants an excuse to spend a week in town."

"Beast!"

"Not that I'm complaining. I have to go back this weekend."

"I shall be far too busy to see you," said Julia loftily. "Except perhaps just once or twice. Briefly."

"That's all right, I'm going to be busy, too. Back to cutting up bodies," Vernon said with relish. "Oops, sorry, Mrs. Fletcher."

"I think," Julia announced, "I shan't be a nurse after all. I think I'll be a teacher. Look, Andy, there's Sid now, with those girls. Let's go and tell him it's all settled and leave Mr. and Mrs. Fletcher in peace. Isn't that your daughter and her friend over there, playing in the sand, Mrs. Fletcher? I used to spend hours building towers and digging tunnels when I was a child."

"You still are a child, Ju. Come on, if you're coming." They said their goodbyes and went off down the beach.

Alec sank into his deck-chair at last, with a groan. "Those two do make me feel old."

"Nonsense, darling, they're juvenile and you're in your prime. Well, that's Sid settled. What about Olive Coleman?"

"Her father will probably get six months or a sizable fine for assaulting a police officer."

"Neither of which is going to do the farm or the family any good."

"I'm afraid there's nothing I can do about the family situation, and not much the local chaps can do, unless Mrs. Coleman is willing to bring a charge. They seldom do. No one is going to force the girl to return home, though."

"I suppose that's something. I'm glad her affair with Enderby didn't have to come out at the inquest."

"Yes. The jury was so flabbergasted by the rest of the rigmarole, no one questioned just why Enderby was so angry with Sid. Is there anyone else you're worried about, before I give myself up to doing absolutely nothing for the remaining day and a half of my holiday?"

"Of course, darling! There's Mr. Baskin's fiancée. Or rather, Nancy Enderby, but his Elizabeth will be upset too if Georgie Porgie's bigamy becomes public knowledge."

"No doubt Baskin will let us know what the coroner says." Alec closed his eyes and turned his face up to the sun.

"Here comes Sid."

Alec groaned and said softly, "I'm asleep."

"All right. Hullo, Sid."

The beachcomber was spruced up in case he'd had to appear in court, shaved and combed, and with a collar and tie in place of his red neckerchief. His shy smile had been replaced with a broad grin and there was a reminder of Popsy's bounce in his walk as he dragged his cart across the sand. He looked at Alec, whose eyes remained determinedly shut, and put his finger to his lips, turning to Daisy.

Then he joined his hands like an open book and wagged his head back and forth as if he was reading. One hand became a sheet of paper, the other held an invisible pencil which wrote busily on his palm. He pointed at his chest: Me! and produced a strange sound that Daisy interpreted as a laugh of delight.

"You're going to learn to read and write," she congratulated him. "That's marvellous."

Sid nodded, beaming. He took out his mouth-organ, looked at Alec, and put it away again in favour of playing an invisible instrument while he danced his clumsy little dance.

Daisy clapped silently. With a bow and a wave, Sid went on his way, the cart trundling behind him.

Gazing after him, Daisy wiped away an unexpected tear.

Alec's eyes were still closed. She suspected he might have actually fallen asleep, so she picked up her book. As she opened it, she glanced towards Belinda and Deva. Julia Bellamy was kneeling beside the girls, enthusiastically digging in the sand. Young Vernon stood hands on hips looking down at her, his stance eloquently expressive of scorn and disgust. But just at that moment, with a resigned shrug, he took off his shoes, rolled up his flannels, and joined the construction party.

Daisy laughed. Alec opened his eyes. "Wha . . . ?"

"Never mind, darling. Go back to your forty winks or you'll only fit in thirty before lunch."

She had read only a few pages when Alec was jerked awake again by a hail from behind them. Donald Baskin came striding down from the house, his knapsack on his back.

"I've come to say goodbye," he announced. "The coroner's given me a letter for Dr. Wedderburn, giving permission for him to issue a second death certificate, so I'm off to Abbotsford. I'll be going straight back to Wiltshire to give Bethie the good news."

"I'm so glad," said Daisy, "for you and both Mrs. Enderbys."

"That could have been better phrased," Alec grunted, "but I second your sentiments. Glad I didn't have to arrest you, Baskin."

"Not half as glad as I am, believe me! Well, so long. Perhaps we'll meet again some day. It's been a delight knowing your girls—I must go and say goodbye to them."

"I'll walk over with you." Alec heaved himself out of his deck-chair with another grunt. "I suppose it's my paternal duty to admire their works. I haven't had time so far on this singularly exhausting holiday."

The two men went off together and Daisy returned to her book. When she looked up a few minutes later, Alec was on his knees in the sand, building a castle.